D0645245

NOTHING LIKE THE SUN

ANTHONY BURGESS

Nothing like the Sun

A Story of Shakespeare's Love-life

W · W · NORTON & COMPANY

New York · London

First published as a Norton paperback 1975; reissued 1996
Copyright © 1964 by Anthony Burgess

Printed in the United States of America

ISBN 0-393-31507-x

W. W. Norton & Company, Inc., 500 Fifth Avenue, New York, N.Y. 10110
www.wwnorton.com

W. W. Norton & Company Ltd., Castle House, 75/76 Wells Street, London W1T 3QT

7 8 9 0

My mistress' eyes are nothing like the sun,
Coral is far more red than her lips' red,
If snow be white, why then her breasts are dun,
If hairs be wires, black wires grow on her head . . .

MR BURGESS'S
farewell lecture to his
special students (Misses Alabaster,
Ang Poh Gaik, Bacchus, Brochocki, Ishak,
Kinipple, Shackles, Spottiswoode and Messrs
Ahmad bin Harun, Anguish, Balwant Singh, Lillington,
Lympe, Raja Mokhtar, Prindable, Rosario, Spittal, White-
legge etc) who complained that Shakespeare had nothing to
give to the East. (Thanks for the farewell gift of three bottles
of *samsu*. I will take a swig now. Delicious.) The text being
the acrostical significance of the following lines: '. . . My
love is as a fever –
Feeding on that which doth preserve the
ill,
The uncertain sickly appetite to please.
My reason, the physician to my love,
Angry that his prescriptions are not kept,
Hath left me . . .'

157?—1587

I

IT WAS ALL A MATTER OF A GODDESS – dark, hidden, deadly, horribly desirable. When did her image first dawn?

A Good Friday, sure. '77? '78? '79? WS, stripling, in worn tight doublet, patched cloak, but gloves very new. Beardless, the down on his cheek gold in the sun, the hair auburn, the eyes a spaniel's eyes. He kicked in youth's peevishness at the turves of the Avon's left bank, marking with storing-up spaniel's eye the spurgeoning of the back-eddy under the Clopton Bridge. (Clopton, the New Place hero, who had run away to get rich. Would he, WS, die as great a Stratford's son?) He smarted to be treated as a child still, he and the family idiot Gilbert charged to take young Anne and younger Richard on a glove-delivering walk in the healthful air. Air blue and sweet over the greenery where the hares darted, away from Henley Street's dunghills, the butchers sharpening their knives and sorting their pricks and making ready for Easter-Eve market. Young beasts dying maaaaaaa for fine appetites. Jack of Lent ready to be turned out of doors and belaboured. Sweet hopeful air, sad, with a mild south-westerly whisper of afternoon rain. Spring and, battering and belabouring his ears, the moans of another sort of dying, another sort of beast – all white, all clawing fingers, froglegs swimming on the bed, sepulchrally white. He had seen, that Maundy Thursday afternoon, dupping their chamber door in all maaaaaaa innocence. He should not have seen nor heard. All that busy whiteness. They could not have known he saw.

'Do not that, Dickon,' he said yet again to Richard, who this time poked his snotty finger at his sister's eye. And then, 'Go not too near the water, neither. Water hath a trick of

3

drowning and, at best, is a wetter.' And then the jingle ruled him, already a word-boy. 'Water wetter water wetter water wetter.' Sly Anne, with the trolling eye that her father, before his nail-gnawing troubles, had used to net wenches withal, said:

'Poor Will is mad Will. Will he nill he. Chuck Will's widow.'

'Wetter water.'

Gilbert, the family idiot, gaped up at the spring sky, on whose washed blue clouds were gently and seriously propelled, a snouty lad with lips of slack red meat. 'Is heaven up there?' he asked heaven. 'Is God and His saints up there?'

'Debtor daughter. Ducats suckets. What was that,' asked WS, 'about Will's widow?'

'A goatsucker,' answered Anne. Richard, whose left leg was shorter than his right by an inch and a half, limped a pace, thought, then whipped out his little thing to piss on the grass, a brief-lived golden arc in the spring sun. He gathered spittle on his lips and was thinning it to a bubble, a popping membrana. 'And that tree yonder is a goat willow,' said Anne. Richard wore a little velvet cap and his cloak, now back from his shoulders, had a frayed tassel.

Goat. Willow. Widow. Tarquin, superb sun-black southern king, all awry, twisted snakewise, had goatlike gone to it. So *tragos*, a tragedy. Razor and whetstone. But that was the other Tarquin. WS saw great-bellied slack whiteness in the spring of a southern country, a Lucy lawn peacock ghost-aglimmer, Arden, patrician, screaming. No willow she. But a willow was right for death. He watched the strange back-eddy under the arch. Back to the strait that sent him on so fast. As great a Stratford's son as Clopton ever was? He seemed to himself to be dreaming of dreaming of straining after some dark image just beyond the tail of his spaniel eye.

'Tha didst go all a shudder then,' said Gilbert. 'Shudder shudder shudder.'

WS made a wry pinched face, flushing. A nipping English spring, he shrugged to say. He pulled his worn cloak closer

4

about him, as King Stephen in the song. A worthy peer. Indeed. But now Richard had finished and was tucking it away. He made little bellowing noises, his hands still there, and ran, with limper's agility, after pale-lashed no-eye-browed Anne. Pallor, the endless winter's pale, sunless England, white ghosts coupling in watery light. Anne feigned to be frightened and ran, gleefully screaming, towards the bushes. She looked back at her little pursuer, crying, 'Boar, boar, bristly boar!' Then she raced full tilt smack into the bulky figure that emerged from behind the thick and warty oakbole. They all knew him. A palliard, some said on Henley Street, a wild rogue. Jack Hoby his name was. Filthy shirt, old hat with broken crown. A true canvas-climber or a freshwater mariner? He was far enough inland, sure. WS believed he had known the sea. He was, as ever, cup-shotten.

'So,' says Hoby to Anne, whom he held by the shoulders an instant in unwashed hairy paws. 'I have thee, nops, sucket, little ringocandy. Queen of Fortunato and Eractelenty, so shalt be. I will take thee to where geese dance trenchmore and apes play at tickatack.' Anne broke away, unaffrighted. Richard laughed. Hoby's face was too much the painted devil's to summon a child's fear in daylight – an eye shut forever, cheek-scores that dust loved, black teeth showing their waists, a party beard full of crumbs. He grinned, a pirate. He stank of Banbury cheese. He belched forth the soul of an alehouse. 'Master glover,' he grinned at WS. 'A holy day is on us, all free from tranks and fourshits.'

'Fourchettes.' WS made a cold correction. And then he felt shame at seeming too ready to correct, as out of a craftsman's pride. It was not his craft, though his father had taken him away from school to practise it, pleading poverty. A trade at his son's finger-tips. *Ad unguem.* A dunghill. He reddened; he reddened to know he reddened. Oh, the ancient glories of the Ardens, long before the Conqueror came. The Arden lands, the Arden hauteur. The pigeon-house at Wilmcote, with its coocoocooing of more than six hundred pair. ('And and and,'

5

cried his mother, all Arden, 'they passed through Stratford, mine own cousins, and they would not call, not for a glass of wine, no, nor to give a word of family news. Oh, the shame, the shame. I have married beneath me. I was taken unawares by a rogue's eye. I was ruined.') Tears came to the eyes of WS. It was, he feigned, the spring wind freshening. They had best get home to their dinner, greasy Joan and the great lady their mother and their anxious smiling father.

'Put to sea while time is,' jeered Hoby. 'See the wide world. The isle of Ruc in the Can's land. Madagastat in Scorea, where the kings be Mahometans and black as devils. And their queens be queans, for they will take any man to lie withal.'

Was it at that moment? England grew all heat, Avon glowed like Nilus and bobbed with watersnakes. WS saw it: a golden face in the East, a queen on a gold coin, galleons sailing towards her. He gulped, swallowed the vision. He counter-jeered: 'You will say that you filled galleons with gold and ambergris and musk and unicorn's horns and then sailed by the adamant stones and lost all and that now the black ox treadeth upon your foot.'

'A dog shall have his day,' said Hoby, no whit abashed at hearing his words so well remembered. 'I have gained, I have spent, no niggard ever. I have seen Leviathan on the waters and fishes that did climb trees like boys for apples. I have eat of camel's flesh and been to lands where men do eat men and have eyes set in their breasts.' Richard was picking at the cold-sore round his nether lip, gaping up at Hoby; Anne smacked his hand away. 'Wilt thou ever see the world in such manner, with waves like great toothed hounds howling all about and slime on their backs, and the sun that would melt a man's eyes like butter did he not wink?'

'Tha couldst not see naught then.' So Gilbert said with idiot's acuteness.

'Too much of thou-and-thee.' It was that prim boy, WS, the gentleman. 'We will have a proper distance.'

'So,' says Hoby, sweeping off, all astagger, his bad hat and disclosing rotten unraked hair, pied of grey and dirty brown, knotted and conjoined locks which shut in the merry leaping life that would be wild and roving else, 'we must bow to their worships the gentry. His Worthiness Sir Skite going hum hum hum through the clean and holy holes of his long nose. Mercy, your grace and favour. Grant me the honour of licking your dirty shoe.' And he bowed so deep that, drunken as he was, he near toppled, and Anne and Richard laughed.

And then the great gentleman took pity on this poor mendacious wretch whose breath smelt so rotten, bethought him of the lone small wren of a coin in his purse, given to him by Mistress Mistress (her name was gone) to whom he had delivered a pair of fine calfskin gloves that Wednesday past, blushing again to see himself treated thus, with a there's-for-thy-pains-boy, and he took it out and said, 'Here.' His brothers and sister stared; Hoby stared too but took the proffer wordlessly, wondering. Yet he could not forbear to cry after those he called the Chaxpers or Jackspaws as they moved homeward:

'Get to sea, lad! There is no world here, God help us. Aping gentry, it is no life. Out out out, before it be all too late!' And he seemed to stagger back to the bushes where belike drunken sleep, his constant mistress, awaited him. WS let Anne straight-run and Richard limp-run ahead, renewing their chasing sport. Gilbert walked in a pattern of zeds, still full of the sky's blue milk. His slack mouth was raised agape, as thirsty for God. WS brooded. His spaniel's eye saw and did not see the cowslip, burnet, green clover nor did his ear take in the lark's soaring cantilena.

Was that, then, where it had to lie, the restoring of fortune and honour, the redemption of a name Snitterfield had pride in ere ever Wilmcote drank glory of Arden blood? (Such work of restoration he had vowed.) Was it, he wondered then, to be the way of the adventurer, mythical raker of carbuncles and diamonds from beneath the spicetrees, but first and last the hold's stink and the foul water after the weeviled biscuit, men rent and filthy and reechy like their shirts of the hogo of earwax, the hap of wrack and piracy or, at best, spewing among rude and rough rascals made roaring lustful with salt beef and, a mere week at sea, cursing and raging in their fights over the ravaging of the soft white body of a boy, a boy refined and gentled with snippets of Ovid and maxims out of Seneca. A dark excitement came that guilt at once pounced on in a rearing wave to wash away. Yet the names fired: America, Muscovy, Selenetide, Zanzibar, Terra Florida, Canaria, Palme Ferro . . .

His father was his betrayer. Yes yes, that gentle-voiced man, so patient under the Xantippe railings and Arden scorn, had sunk and sunk to one of little account. John Shakespeare, once Bailiff (of all magisterial glories the most high) paid no more his levies for the poor's relief, was alderman still but of low rate for the musters, dared not appear at the Corporation's meetings. He had sold the greater part of his most meagre properties. He had sold his eldest son into kidskin slavery. Tears pricked at the thought of a life spent so, in oh a fair trade, a cleanly trade, but till the end of his days, the end, the end of his days. The cutting of the trank, the slitting of the slim fourchettes, the bitty gussets, the thumb, the slit binding, the patient glover's stitch. A pair of mirror-twin poems. Then the deliveries by a well-spoken boy who, at the doors of the greater houses, must meekly wait on the pleasure of servants, sniffed at by little dogs. And then . . .

That vision! He knocked, he waited. Then the servant said that the steward said that the great lady asked that he might be sent in to her, alone at table in a fair room full of tapestries (Susanna and the lustful elders; the Ark and the dove and a son of Noah looking for landfall; Judith raising her sword to Holofernes). He saw so clearly, he smelt the great fire of spitting pearwood. Dinner was done, the trenchers and silver castle of salt cleared, the steward with his tasselled staff had bowed out backward. Little dogs (his spaniel's eyes encountered many) leaped and fawned about her, their sharp neat teeth clogging in the soft candy they chumbled from her gloved hand. She was veiled, a widow, nothing of her to be seen save the richness of her brocade. She rustled, the fire cracked, the scent of burning pear ravished, overpowered; she set down by her the silver cup of sweet wine (he knew it was sweet, he could taste its sweetness; the cup was embossed of writhing cherubim, the feet of the cup were silver lions' feet) and took from it the rosemary sprig for stirring in the spices. WS could not breathe. She beckoned him with a waving of this sprig, then rose, looking to him to follow. The doors opened as by sorcery. He padded after her through rooms and galleries of rich wood and carving, pictures of heroes on the silken walls. And then came a bedchamber, a bed all gold and damask, smelling of all the Indies, and there were screens all about blazoned with the wanton loves of the gods. He could hear the little dogs, that had followed, scratching and whining to be admitted. He was to turn away, he was to wink a space. Her voice was soft, low, made all his senses shudder. He heard above the beating of his blood the rustling of linen, a gentle panting at the restraining fingers of tapes and laces that yielded all too slowly. WS kept his eyes tight closed. Soon she said:

'Turn, O my beloved. Oh, turn now.'

He turned, ready to swoon, unwinking, at the vision. She was naked, gold, glowing, burnished, burning, the sun, all desire of him.

'I am altogether thine. Do thou take what is thine.'

Oh, his young heart. Oh, the giddiness, the mad beating. He fell before her, fell at her golden feet. She raised him with strong arms of gold. They fell into swansdown, behind curtains of silver silk. And there was the promise that when the moment came, and soon, too soon, it must come, he would be possessed of all time's secrets and his very mouth grow golden and utter speech for which the very gods waited and would be silent to hear.

And then the gold had all departed. It was Stratford, Good Friday noon with the wind fresher than before. That boy was at his father's house, the doorway wide, the others already within, shouting their hunger. He must needs pause to still the great fluttering of doves in his breast. He looked up and down the tumbled toppling street, black and white timber awry, cobbles, cats fighting squawwwwwwwwk for the fish-heads the Quiney girl next door had thrown out. From his father's house marched on muffled feet the smell of stockfish baked with cloves and cinnamon. Bread, ale, applejohns. The Geneva Bible on his father's lap. Remember that this day did Christ die for thee.

No! The blistering sun and the watersnakes, the Queen of Sheba all bare on a silken bed. He desired the whole wide world to hug in his arms. Trembling with desire, he stripped off his gloves before entering. He cupped his right hand and the south-west wind blew wetly in. What made a frail fistful on Henley Street was elsewhere bellying the sails of ships home-ward bound from the Americas, outward bound for isles of gold and spice. The world, the wide world crying and calling like a cat to be let in, scratching like spaniels.

'Will!'

'Poor Will! Mad Will!'

He was bound fast there, the fingers that would caress the world's mystery, probe the world's secrets, muffled home in a mean craft. The voices called him in to dinner.

II

He thought he might get away then, that time of Alice Studley's father and mother coming, terrible in righteousness, to tell John Shakespeare that it was his son, aye, Will, that had filled their daughter with kicking feet and must now, aye, marry her, go to, he is forward for his years, he but a lad scarce breeched, but now must he play the man and do right.

He had thought that was one way toward the goddess; he had thought he saw golden feet on the dying sun, that former apparition of Good Friday returned on Easter Sunday evening. The spring a warm one. It had been in a ryefield.

'Nay, never!'

'There! Aaaaaaah!'

It was this one ready wench – black-eyed, the flue on her body black, her hair black and shining as blackbirds that fed on thrown-out bacon fat – but it might too have been Bess, Joan, Meg, Susan, Kate. What else, he saw already, offered in the lightening evenings of Stratford? Or of Barford, Temple Grafton, Upper Quinton, Ettington (in Ettington, at that ramshackle house of the disbarred muttering lawyer, a ready wench to end all ready wenches), Shottery? WS was growing into a proper young man, ripely pout-mouthed and with a good leg, quiet of speech but flowery withal, a fair seller of fine gloves. Out of the fork of this gentleman, from a tangled auburn bush, thrust and crowed a most importunate Adam. It was not he, it was not WS; it was some outlandish and exterior beast to which he must needs, and all unwillingly, play host. At it, WS watched, as it were, this other one, astonied, hearing him cry with some other's, stranger's, voice, yet aware of the rhythms of his need as starting in iambs and ending in spondees. And then the great vision glowed, its feet set on the fiery ball that made ready to go underground. But the goddess was greater fire, consuming the world as the sun died. He made haste to possess her, through the dark-flued country priestess who lay beneath him. He cried aloud, pumping out his life for her. But this time she laughed, mocked.

The world collapsed into mockery: heaps of old sacking, twigs scratching bare thighs; shame not at an act of sin but at bidding so much (that word 'love', for instance) for so little, questing crawlers in the grass, the whining country voice of Alice Studley unsatisfied. He saw the mockery of a whole life expressed in the disorder of clothing – tapes to be tied, the affects of promised ecstasy to be stowed in shame, an eternal hell of buttoning. And all else, too, of the Stratford glover's life marched gloomily through the void that now presented itself. The surfeit of ale, the vomit, the riot of frighting the ancientry after dark with Dick Quiney and Jack Bell and the fool from Kineton, the loud empty laughing of wasteful sport, the guilt of life brief and naught done.

'Love,' she whined, still lacing. 'Love, tha said love.'

'It is, in a manner, love. But I promised nothing.'

'Tha said of getten wed. Tha did promise.'

'A man will promise much in his heat.' And then: 'Though I am not yet a man but a boy still.'

'What tha has there is enow like a man's.' In the growing dusk she made herself prim and tidy; like seed, a great pity pumped and pumped from him; he must beware, lest he call that also love. Brutally he said:

'That you will know, doubtless. It is not just your dad's you have seen, peering through a chink in the door.'

'Chill tell my dad all, that tha did force me unto doing of it.'

A great weariness mantled him, another, swifter, dusk. 'As Ben Lovell did and Gervase Black from Blockley and Pip Gaydon and the rest. Forced, is it?' She wept. Pity advanced him to her, to take the soft slack body in his arms, to taste in pity the rugosity of pimples on her left cheek, the black loose

12

hair sucked deep, as he kissed, into his mouth. He saw, in one consuming moment, how pity might undo him quite. He took her hand gently and set her on her way. She grew soft again at parting, saying no more of complaints, glowed in a dulcet good-night of pigeon-kisses, waved, turning, walked into the moon.

And then the father and mother came, in hot August, but there was nothing to prove. They were doing their rounds of all the houses where young men, swelling in flesh-fed lustihead, skulked (too much meat in that diet, too little of the allaying cabbage-leaf), collecting here a tester, there a groat, to shut their loud mouths withal. It would not be hard to find a husband for Alice, eyes in bushes watching the unwary youth yielding to her open bosom, untrussing, caught in the act. It was ever thus. They went away, whining like their daughter, a coin clutched tight in the mother's sweaty hand, and then John and Mary Shakespeare turned on their eldest son. Shame, disgrace, sin, uncontrolled libidinous wretch, down on thy knees to pray to be made clean (John Shakespeare veered to the new pure faith of tradesmen and merchants). WS spake back pertly; it was the mother, lady Arden, that struck. He left the house burning.

He would go, he would be on his way that night, he would seek out his gold goddess. A night promising fair, scented, the moon in her third quarter, nightingales in the wood, WS, in worn cloak against the morning's chill, empty scrip and purse, taking the road. Whither? South-west, into the wind's mouth, to Bristol. Evesham, Tewkesbury, Gloucester. A march of a day or so, rewarded at last by salt on the lips and masts in the harbour. And then?

No, no, it could not be, not yet. He needed time. He be-thought him of the oracle that dwelt in an old woman's body, Madge Bowyer, who was called Old Madge and sometimes witch, in her hovel at the town's end. She had spells against warts and would guess at the future, but they were often good guesses. Her cats were fat and blinked in the sun; her house

13

smelt of no devil's compacts, but of pungent herbs, foul linen, and a woman's old age. He walked, calming himself, through the odorous dark, came to her cottage set away among docks and nettles on a side-lane, saw dim light and knocked. She came with a lantern, her pegless gums mounching away, knew him and bade him enter.

He coughed at the smoke. A cauldron of stew bubbled on the fire; from the low rafters hung hunks of nameless flesh, their shadows swinging on the walls from the draught of his entering; a cat suckled her brinded kittens and purred. The kitchen was in great disarray – a tumble of unwashed clouts, pots unscoured, a dish of sour curds on the rough table, a loaf grown all mossy and too hard for her to mumble. A wise goat peered in at an open window, chewing roundly, wagging her beard. A yellow-and-white cat mewed at WS to be picked up and fondled, and pity at its trust swooned through him. So it was with those calves he would have no hand in killing. He saw, in one of his fiery instants, all beasts that ever were, torn, hunted, baited, betrayed, bleeding; their cries seared his brain. Madge said, 'What would you know then, boy?'

'I will bring you a penny tomorrow,' he said. 'I would have one pennyworth of the future, whether I am to take a long journey or no.' He sat at the table on a three-legged stool, moving a greasy washing-clout from it first; the cheesy smell of curds rose at him like a small grey spirit. She mounched away at nothing, bringing cards. He knew these cards, though not the manner of telling them. *Cartomancy.* He thrilled at the word. These were not for an innocent game of trump or ruff; they were antique pictures, as old as Egypt (so she had told him), of towers crumbling to brick in a lightning-flash; of pope and empress; the moon all blood; Adam and Eve; the rising of the dead, sleepy and naked, at doomsday's trumpet.

'A journey,' she said. 'We will see of a journey.' A cat leaped on to the table, as it would itself see, and was pushed off with a distracted hand. She fumbled the worn reechy cards. The thin light, the shadows, gave a sort of small

majesty to this old lined crone, her wretched filthy hair, the
sack dress stained with years of unhandy eating (annals of
grease dropped from a trembling horn-spoon), the torn nails
with their margins of dirt. She told on to the table, at random
it seemed, an outer paling of seven cards, an inner lozenge of
four. Her trembling claws upturned them, her lips gibbering
strange language: '*Hominy pominy didimus dis dis genitivo tibi dabo
auriculorum.*' WS saw the calm fierce pictures look up at him;
there were dogs baying the bloody moon and a crayfish
sprawled in the waters below, the stars with the naked girl, the
juggler, the man hanging from a tree by his heel, Death the
skeleton mower, the woman with a leashed lion, a chariot.
She rocked, crooning; she delivered:

'You will go on no journey yet. Here you must stay to find a
woman that will drive you to it. And there is also the Seven
Deadly Sins.'

'What woman? Will she commit those sins?'

'It is a fair woman. The sins will be brought here and you
will go out with the sins.'

'I understand nothing of this.'

'You are here to be told, not to understand. And you will
take your pen and write like a clerk. You will be pushed and
hurried and told to write with speed.'

His heart sank. 'Is there naught else?'

'I will give you a fair rhyme, but that will be another
penny.'

'Twopence tomorrow then.'

She cackled, coughed, choked, sprayed his face with toad's
wet, and the cats looked up, unfearful. 'This is the rhyme.
Mark me.' Then she gave it as though reading it from the
dark wall behind WS:

> 'Catch as catch can.
> A black woman or a golden man.'

And would not say more. A poor twopennyworth?

III

THE GODDESS CALLED FROM THE SEA, and he could not answer; she called inaccessibly from dreamed golden bodies. He must close his eyes to the beckoning arms from the spice-bed, except those eyes of sleep, seeing most when they wink; for the visions of travel, he descried that they meant most when most cocooned in words. But would not words chime the goddess away for ever? He did not know yet.

Hoby, ere he died – as he did of a fever that clasped him to its hot body while he slept drunkenly in the rain – would talk sometimes soberly of ships and the sailor's life. He told of vessels high charged, high at stern and bow for majesty and terror of the enemy, for now was general talk of an enemy. Sail-trimmers at their work on the waist between poop and fore-castle, where too were stowed pinnace and skiff. The gravel-ballast and cable tiers; the outboard-thrusting beakhead that cracked the seas as the ship plunged. The hold below the orlop where the rotten beer and crawling cheese were stored. Foresail and foretop sail on the foremast; square course and topsail on the mainmast; the mizen mast with its lateen or mizen yard; the bonaventure mizen; drabler and bonnet. Calivers and arquebuses, the gunner with his linstock, the aft and forward slueing of the carriage, the quoin.

It was all words. And, anyway, to become a swabbing younker in wet and filthy dark would bring him no whit nearer to the goddess. With words there was a realm; more, if he practised the art of words, that vision of old Madge would not necessarily mean what it seemed to mean – the labour of clerking in some worm-eaten chambers of the law; it could mean noble lords saying hurry hurry hurry, the birthday ode must be ready soon for Her Majesty. There were books in the house of Bretchgirdle, the parson. He would lend them to polite youths. WS read Ovid, in the English of Golding, or he would pick out the Latin – with more relish than under Jenkins at the school – word by slow word, as an unskilful lute-player plucks out painfully his air. Ovid was divine. Could he not be Ovid, though in an English way?

> Fair is as fair as fair itself allows,
> And hiding in the dark is not less fair.
> The married blackness of my mistress' brows
> Is thus fair's home . . .

It was after dinner. He was quietly shuddering within, for that night he was to go forth to help bring in the May out by Shottery. His quill squeaked out the lines among the un-cleared trenchers, in the smell of the saffron and garlic that had given a savour to their dull veal (he had refused to help kill the calf), the green spitting elmwood of the fire, the sweating of a too-warm room (but his father felt the cold), tempered by the chill of a woman's contempt. He was enditing a sonnet to another black-haired girl, all her hairs black, all, the sonnet's shape that first made by the Earl of Surrey, English having too few rhymes for the more strict Italian form. But, he was learning, you could not write verses of the one and particular but only of the All or Universal (so why then did Plato cry out on the falseness of poets?), and the All was figured or incarnated in a new One, and what name could you give to that One but divinity?

> . . . for fair abideth there.
> My love being black, her beauty may not shine
> And light so foiled to heat alone may turn.

Meantime his mother, greying frizzed, with scanty brows of strong ginger colour still, railed at his father in fine Arden lady's fashion, and Joan – sole daughter now with poor Anne

17

dead these three years – neglectful of her table-clearing duty and the crumbs for the pigeons (ah, the Wilmcote cotes), stood by her haughty skirts, grinning. His father, merrily red-cheeked in his misery, sat hunched by the smoky coughing fire, gnawing a little-finger nail.

> Heat is my heart, my hearth, all earth is mine;
> Heaven do I scorn when in such hell I burn.

On the floor crawled little Edmund, his two-year birthday that month. Gilbert and Richard were without, and Richard was playing, shouting. Joan was all Arden, grinning there, siding with her virago mother.

'And now your talk is of selling my silver, so we shall be like the truly low, God help us, and end with digging hollows in the table as in some filthy rogues' ordinary, an we are kindly let to keep the table, and the broth slopped therein and we must needs fumble at it with greasy fingers. Oh the shame, the shame that we should ever come to this, I would all my children were safely buried like poor poor Anne, so they might not live to see what shifts we are coming to . . .'
Little Edmund gurgled toward WS's crossed feet. He uncrossed to give a privy kick but then thought better of it.

> All other beauty's light I lightly rate.
> My love is as my love is, for the dark.
> In night, on night, enthroned on night . . .

'And a promised a new gownd for Whitsun.' That was whining Joan, sharp-faced and mean-eyed. 'And now a says naught of a new gownd.'

> Enthroned on night I keep my something state.

'New gowns?' said his mother, with woman's ready pluralising. 'Look to thine old gowns, girl, lest he sell those

18

slyly to some rogue pedlar or belike change for a boy's whirligig to play withal.'

'My throne is night. Night is my throne.' So WS murmured involuntary.

'And there sits he,' said his mother, 'with idle versing and naught else in his head. What money will that ever bring in?'

'Many a man,' said his timid father, 'has known preferment through timely verses.'

> In night enthroned, I ask no better state,
> Twin-orbed and sceptred . . .

Too gross by far, that would not do.

'Will is crazy and lazy,' went Joan. WS made a speedy contortion of his face at her: squinny, cheeks finger-bunched, horse-nostrils. Then it came:

> . . . I ask no better state
> Than thus to range, nor seek a guiding spark.

And now the clinching couplet, whose work was full seven times more than all twelve precedent lines. But his father said:

'If it be work that is wanted, then we had best get back to work.' And he rose sighing from his fireside chair. 'Come thy ways, Will.'

> And childish I am put to school of night.

Right light fight wight tight. WS pondered, eyes trolling like tennis-balls at the low rafters.

'Am I nowhere to be obeyed?' His father was at last in one of his rare rages. 'Nor here in the house nor in my workshop neither?' WS, O foolish boy, sat on, chewing the gristly quill, tickling his gum with the soaked feathers. Johan giggled. Will said:

'This one moment. The poem is near done.' His mother said:

'Oh, he is going the way of preferment. He will be making a leg before Her Majesty, poem in hand, what time we are all begging for crusts for want of men in the house to work.'

> And childlike I am put to school of night
> For to seek light, for to seek light light
> light . . .

His father, with weak mottled nief, did a bold thing then, one that made the mouth of WS to gape, the chewed quill-feathers to dribble to the board, unregarded. He seized the paper with its fair script, unblotted, and made as if to tear it. WS was quick to his feet, he would have none of this. And it was then as if the goddess reappeared, rushing down the chimney in a wind, making the fire flare gold, and smote WS hard on the back, thrusting him into fight (For to seek light, and for that light to fight) against father, mother, sister, all one, enemies. And now he wrestled with his father for possession of thirteen lines (a sonnet thus incomplete being most unlucky), and then the paper tore and Joan went whoop with laughing. WS, in poet's frenzy, would have struck his father dead, but Joan was a child and easier game. So he flapped four stiff fingers crack hard on her cheek, crying words like FOR THEE, BITCH, and she howled like a hound, hellishly. Then came the last line:

> For to seek light beyond the reach of light.

WS glowed in anger and poet's triumph, but no shame or fear. There was loud protesting in the room, directed at him. Little Edmund set up a bruit. WS stood proud above all, and would – like a Roman conqueror in laurels – have placed his foot on Edmund's crawling body had he not crawled under the table. WS stood head-high, like some warlock that had conjured a storm of wild waters. A passer-by, hearing loud angry words, peered in through the casement. He had no nose, love's disease. WS cried to him:

'And, childish, I am put to school of night
For to seek light beyond the reach of light.'

He went on his way, a warning. And this magical incantation
put a good black blob of a period to the raving. His mother
crossed herself. She stared, holding blind hands out for crying
Joan. Softly she said:

'Come then, chuck, to it mammy. There there there there
there. Thou, Jack, touch him not, he is a devil, no son of mine.
He is but a beast, there is bad and wicked blood, it is the lowness of devil's stock coming out. There there, wipe and blow,
chicken, thy brother is no brother.'

His father bit his bottom lip, looking now on his son, now on
the rent and deformed sonnet: beauty's light for the dark
enthroned guiding spark heat heart hearth earth. (He hath a
good wit, God help us, and I have deprived him of his
schooling. I am to blame, wherein have I failed?) Then
Gilbert came in, the family idiot, saying:

'God. I ha' seen God with's hat on, a-walken down Henley
Street.'

His father seemed now as he would fain weep, wresting the
lachrymal torch from snivelling Joan. Joan's face shone
greasily.

'Aye, marry. And I did fall and did sleep a space and then
did rise. Aye.'

His mother turned wearily to him to say, 'And where is
Dickon? What is Dickon doing?'

'Dick is all dirt and feared to come home. All dung is, aye.
Was pushed in dung by these fellows.'

'Which fellows?' Very loud now, but a tightening in her
weasand. WS looked steady at his father and his father looked
not so steady back, then one nodded to the other.

'Tom of the Hill that is called Tom Hill and him from
Upper Quinton that saith never aught. Aye.'

His father head-pointed toward the door while his mother
took breath. Dunghills, dung, she would say. Words she had

never heard, let alone encountered the reality thereof, ere she had married into (ha!) the Jakes peers. I am done, I can no more. I am full-fed with work and misery. I am at my wit's end here with you all. Go thou, Jack, and fetch the boy hither and clean him. Go thou and do somewhat to redeem thine idleness.

'To work,' said John Shakespeare before his wife could say these things. He pulled WS with him very fast, so that WS near tripped, on his exit, over little Edmund. Without, whispering, he said, 'There is little enough work to do, God help us. I have somewhere a fine piece of old parchment. Copy the poem fair.'

IV

I т was this sonnet, then, copied in a good hand with no blot, that nestled snug in his breast that warm evening of May as, with S. Brailes, Ned Thorpe and Dick Quiney, he walked or slued (a skinful of ale to enthrone boldness) westward to Shottery. These were good brown laughing fellows who knew little of bookish learning or of poesy either, but they dearly loved a jest, especially if it entailed sore hurt for others, as for example skull-cracking, jibing, making skip the rheumy ancientry, thieving, wenching and the like. But Dick Quiney had, hid beneath the outer garment of conforming boisterousness, a gentle soul; he had brown hound's eyes, not unlike those of WS, but more melting, devoted. WS had, while Jenkins the master nodded over his book in the hour for grammar study, told him tales of old time and also of his own making. But perhaps it was this dog's look of near-worship that told WS he was now wasted here. Thorpe and Brailes were singing under the green trees some bawdy ditty:

> To it and to it and to it again
> To bid his mistress come;
> But an she will not he gives not a jot
> For Rodney is all shot home.

The heart of WS was high and fearful, aware of his lust for this black one, her hair's and body's scents a torment to be whipped away in steady lashes of a rod to spare not. For golden-haired girls he could feel nothing, nor for carroty ones – too like the Ardens, too like that Maundy Thursday discovery. Perhaps only in hate might he. But he did not know what hate was. Pity, yes; resentment; contempt perhaps of

23

himself for mingling with these rough red roarers, each carrying his gross share towards the midnight feast to be eaten about fires in the clearings – a bit of brickish cheese, pulse-bread, a leveret and a brace of stolen fowls, some filched cider in a bottle. Each with a ready rod.

As for that other and symbolical rod, the Maypole, there would soon be no more bringing home of that in Warwickshire, what with puritanical sourness and cries of out-on-idolatry; the Maypole, for all its decking with sweet-smelling nosegays and herbs, called a stinking idol. The times were on the change, the old free days being whipped fast out. But this delicate night would know mirth and, next morning, the bringing home of the great wreathed god-rod drawn by oxen, each with flowers nodding on his horn-tips. They were to go forth in small companies, into the groves and coppices, and then each group to break into primal twos, and she would be awaiting him by the cross. It was twilight, the western sky all burning argosies, the night at their backs advancing.

Noise greeted them, laughter, the thudding of an old drum and a fife's squeal, a Robin Hood horn being winded (well, here was Will the Scarlet). They were going off with their baskets and kindling and old cloaks. He saw some whose names he knew: Tapp, Roberts, little Noone, Brown, Hawkes, Diggens, and a girl for every man. But where was she?

She was there, she saw him, she was on another's arm, she laughed, waved. WS knew him, a golden youth – Brigg or Hoggett or Haggett – a baker's or miller's son or some such thing, as good any day as a young glover, though with a groom's face gilded with sandy flue, mouth a roaring O, eyes swine's eyes. The sonnet burned the breast of the sonneteer in shame and anger, his heart had dropped and shattered like a cold stale pasty dropped on to the kitchen flags. He tore away from his companions. They called: 'Aha! He cannot wait! He hath spilt all already!' But Dick Quiney followed, crying his name. He had seen what WS had seen, had seen him see what he had seen. 'There is a plenty more,' he said. 'She is but one.'

24

'Leave me.'

'I will go with you.'

'I want nobody.' He wrenched his buttons to draw out the wasted sonnet. 'Take this. You may join her list, you may buy her favours with it when she shall have done with this one.' Dick Quiney took it, wondering. WS ran. Dick Quiney called his name again but did not follow. Where could he run? Not the woods, not the church, not the duckpond, not home. The alehouse offered. He had money in his purse. The dark grew closer, the slain west's blood dripped to the nether world. The alehouse was full tonight, choked with the low and their stink, bad breath, black teeth, foul loud holes of country mouths. He saw, of a sudden, an image of proud high London, red towers over a green river with swans. He pushed himself room on a settle next to an old smocked shepherd who reeked of tar, his nail-ends swart crescents, crying rough speech in this blanketing thick air and noise to one who squinnied, thin, ancient, nodding, chumbling gum and gum ('And then what dost think a done? A laid all on board and quotha, "A groat an inch in warranty," quotha, main.') The girl who brought for him had a may-sprig in her bosom, fat, spongy tits thrust high as they were sacks on a man's back; she leered at him with country teeth. He drank. So kind, the glove-buying gentry, with a there's-for-thy-pains, the disdainful clink of wren-coin, I-thank-your-worship-and-thereto-I-touch-you-my-forelock-God-bless-your-worship. He had drunk; he would continue to drink; he had sixpence and would drink it all.

Drink ale fat growl mistress Hercules grave slue flow London dark gaggle crop. There is one that will crop no barley more. Dead of a fistula, aye. Or of a quinance, I know not certain. Fetch, I would fain. What would fain? Faith, it is all a great cheat and lie. And so saying he lets forth a rap nothing faintly.

> With that, he comes to Pluto's nether gate
> And Hold, saith Cerberus, what seekst thou here?

25

Him of the ships, saith he, and all his crew
That, bedded in the horse in Troy's confines,
Did did did

'A horse will have worms, aye, as well as your even Christian.'

He went out to piss and near fell over a dribbling drunkard who lay snoring at the moon. The moon had risen, then. He saw them in his mind's eye, buttocks moon-besilvered, rising and falling. The roar of the ale within, rage athirst for enactment, he would rail, send them on their ways stark naked, lash them with a birch-bough, sob, plain at unfaith, tear, kill. But he would drink first, drink out his sixpence.

Drink, then. Down it among the titbrained molligolliards of country copulatives, of a beastly sort, all, their browned pickers a-clutch of their spilliwilly potkins, filthy from handling of spade and harrow, cheesy from udder new-milked, slash mouths agape at some merry tale from that rogue with rat-skins about his middle, coneyskin cap on's sconce. Robustious rothers in rural rivo rhapsodic. Swill thou then among them, O London-Will-to-be, gentleman-in-waiting, scrike thine ale's laughter with Hodge and Tom and Dick and Black Jack the outlander from Long Compton. And here was one that was back to his heath after a year away, a *miles gloriosus*.

Hast a privy for a gob, thou, with the shit in't. Sayest? Not one fart do I give, nay, for all thy great tally. Wouldst test it, then? Thou wouldst not, for thou art but a hulking snivelling codardo. I have been in the wars and do speak the tongues of the Low Countries. *Ik om England soldado. U gif me to trinken.* Who saith a liar? I will make his gnashers to be all bloody. I will give him a fair crack, aye. You are but country cledge, all, that have seen naught of this world, and this one here, who is but new-wiped, he is a dizard. Thou yeanling, thou, had I my hanger I would deal thee a great flankard. But I have but my nief and that will I mash thy fleering bubbibubkin lips withal.

26

Loud mouth and oaths, offering to fight any there, much shotten. In galligaskins and filthy leather, his hat lost, his hair all elf-locks, he staggered toward WS. WS smiled loftily. Then with a clumsy belly-blow this bragger struck. Of a sudden, WS felt as it were a heavy-caparisoned trainband of ale given the order to march from his guts north to the moon and the gatekeeper to open up for its passage. His mouth face cheeks eye-flesh bulged bunched. And he had drunk but threepenny-worth. Nay, but there was before . . . Bunched, butched, birched, birled, swirled over and out. The deck was awash. Ho there, swabbers. And thou there, avast heaving.

He was not well. He was in pain. Great seas roared inboard, the ship staggered. Ahoy, sea-room. He fought his way out, sober WS aghast at drunken Will, but he was prevented. They thrust him all about, wide black holes of laughter, to force him to return doglike to it. In his emergent poet's brain, which grew like a toadstool Jove out of that fuddled head of WS, what time shamed Will staggered and thrust to be out and off, set upon by these stinkards, verse spewed steadily forth, the spouting goddess aloof above the body's wrack.

Anon he trinks him in his jewelled garb
And decked with flowers whistles the long way out
Till that he sees the steadfast pole above
That pins the wandering heavens . . .

And there he was, one that acts drunken in some silly morality, pursued by laughter as he makes his exit. And yet the act goes on offstage. He yawed and rolled, his aleship, under that very star, and saw there his own stars, his drunken initial, Cassiopeia's Chair. He lurched, and the second cohort bugled to gallop forth from his belly to the postern, out. Mewling and puking, he cried, prolonging his constellation, his unruly feet scrawling vee after vee after vee on the road: 'Mother mother mother.' It was a perilous cry.

Yet, an eternity of nothing after, he woke warm. The dawn

birdsong was deafening. He smelt grass and leaves and his mother's comforting and comfortable smell, the faint milk and salt and zest and new-bread odour of a woman's bosom. He sighed and burrowed deeper his head. His mouth was foul, it was as if he had licked rust. He squinnied, frowning, to see that the ceiling had become all leaves, that the house-beams had returned to their primal tree-state. There was white sky, in leaf-beguiled patches, over. He gave in wonder to this world a pair of tormented eyeballs. She smiled, she kissed his brow in gentleness. Her shoulders and arms and bosom were naked beneath the rough coverlet, a pair of cloaks. Beneath was some hairy blanket-like protector against the ground's damp, through which odd harmless needles of roots and stubble pricked. He was in his clothes, though they were unbuttoned, untied, in disarray. He dredged memory and found naught. It was the wood, it was Shottery, but what woman was this? To ask, when twined so in early morning and near-nakedness – would not that be ungentle? He must needs smile back to her smile and murmur some formula of good-morrow. It would come out, he would learn all if he waited. In God's name, though, what had he done in that great void of unmemory? Never never never never never would he come more to that. He would be a moderate man. But then she whispered, in a fierce sort, 'Anon will it be full light and all stirring. *Now.*' And she lay upon him, a long though not a heavy woman, and it was in vain for him to protest that his mouth was not yet, not till some cleansing and quickening draught had done its office, at all ready for kissing. And so he sought to avoid her lips, lithely (though with aches and dumbed groans) turning her to the posture of Venus Observed and giving his mouth to her left breast, his stiff and wooden tongue playing about its rosy pap till she panted hard like poor Wat pursued by hounds. He arose for air, his hand now at work in darkness, an eye on each finger-end, to observe with his true, though cracked, eyes this country Venus-head, its straight bound red-gold locks, brow deep and narrow and bony, twittering scant

28

pale lashes, the mole on the neck's long pillar gazing steadily back at his wavering light-wounded wonder, Will at work, WS thinking that perhaps he knew her (since she must belong hereabouts), though certain he had not, in the other sense, known her before. Was she not approaching carrotiness, Arden pallor? But, as the early light stretched and yawned, time spoke of the need for but one thing, and the ale's residuum, like lusty flesh-meat, fed that cock-crow Adam to bursting. ('This,' he told himself, 'is hate of her, that other, faithless with her roaring miller's son'.) And she made him like a madman, for she gripped him with powerful talons and let forth a pack of words he had thought no woman could know. So then he cracked open, going aaaaaaah, all in the tender morning, and loosed into her honey his milk, shuddering like a puppy, whinnying like a horse.

He felt, to his surprise, no shame after, no *tristitia*. They lay quietly as the morning advanced its little way, hid snug in their greenwood coïgn. She talked and he listened, ears pricked houndlike for a clue of the quarry. '. . . So, saith she, if Anne will not then mayhap one of the boys, her brothers . . .' So she was Anne, then, fair and English, smelling of mild summers and fresh water. She was not young, he thought: past twenty-five. She was no plum-plump pudding of the henyard, roaring the health of burning air and an ample plain cottage diet, nor was there in her voice the country twang of such as Alice Studley. The thin song of would-be ladyship (she would turn her blushing face away, no doubt, from the cock's ʿreading) beat smartly in her neck's pulse as he fingered it. It in no wise congrued with her lying near-bare against him nor with that horrible steaming-out, some few minutes past, of a mouthful apter for a growling leching collier pumping his foul water into some giggling alley-mort up by the darkling wall of a stinking alehouse privy. What could he do but smile in secret, still queasy as he was? But he must be on his feet soon and away, saying I-thank-you-perhaps-we-may-meet-again-Anne. But he said 'Anne' softly, to taste that

29

name in an unsisterly context, though posthumous, posthumous. . . .

Speaking her name, it was as if he spake pure cantharides.
'Quick,' she panted. 'There is time before they are all about.
Again.' She thrust bold hot long fingers, lady-smooth, down at
his root in its tangled nest. 'If thou wilt not—' And she lay
on him as before, to woman him, her tongue's tip near licking
his little grape, her kneading fingers busy at his distaff which,
all bemused, rose as it were in sleep.

And so the Maypole was brought home.

V

He did not think, he would not have believed, not then, that that was she who would watch over him when he slept finally not from drunkenness but from desire of death, – else lay with eyes near-closed, sleep's feigning succubus, to watch her creaking down the stair, a groaning old crone about her housewifely tasks, busying herself with the making of sick man's broth, a cock in an earthen pipkin with roots, herbs, whole mace, aniseeds, scraped and sliced liquorice, rosewater, white wine, dates. An old quiet woman, a reader of *The Good Housewife's Jewel* and *The Treasury of Commodious Conceits* (how to make Vinegar of Roses; onion-and-treacle juice as a most certain and approved remedy against all manner of pestilence or plague, be it never so vehement), later to turn to Brownist gloom with *God's Coming Thunderbolt Foretold* and *Whips for Worst Sinners* and *A Most Potent Purge for the Bellies and Bowels of Them that are Unrighteous and Believe Not*. Her pots a-simmer, she would sit scratching her spent loins through her kirtle, mumbling her book.

He was in a manner tricked, coney-caught, a court-dor to a cozening cotquean. So are all men, first gulls, later horned gulls, and so will ever be all men, amen. It was easier to believe so, yet the real truth is that all men choose what they will have. After this May business he took cold and had belly-cramps and sore buttocks, and it was his body's moanings that bade him consign all of Shottery (Shittery) to hell and to say that perhaps they were right who termed maypoles stinking idols. But spring days grew longer and summer waxed and WS was ready for love again, though this time a pure love, a clean love, no more of this most demure skin or film masking a filthy bargee's lust. He threw himself at first into the work of glove-making, soothing and empty as cow's eyes, and to candled reading of North's Plutarch and Golding's Ovid and versing of his own – dull versing, he would admit, in galloping fourteeners about Romans brought low by treachery. But one day his father bade him go to Temple Grafton to buy goatskins.

'Whateley is the man. He reads much religion and is no fool. He is from Snitterfield, like myself. Go on Brown Harry, for his fetlock is better now.'

To reach Temple Grafton he must needs skirt Shottery. 'Anne Anne Anne Anne,' the starlings scolded. He shivered on that summer's day. He knew now who she was: dead Dick Hathaway's daughter of Hewlands Farm, restive at this posthumous life of being reduced and humbled by those who were not her own kin – the widow Joan her stepmother and three growing and bulky and bullying half-brothers. Thou art become a woman past thy first youth and yet unwed. Thou art stale goods, unwanted of any. Ho, serving-wench, fetch Harry here sweet water from the butt. WS could still feel that tenfold dig of her talons. Yet he was safe, he knew. No man, so he thought in his innocence, can be made to do what he will not. As for paternity, that risk is nulled by being shared. There was no virgin knot he had had the cutting of, unless perhaps in that dark intermission of oblivion. But that could hardly be. She had comported herself like one that knew all.

And then he found that the bird-cry of 'Anne' followed him to Temple Grafton. There, in Whateley's house (Whateley was a skinner), Anne awaited him, Anne to drive out any lingering vestiges of that other Anne, for this Anne, seventeen summers, was spring's distillation, her hair rich black and shining to mock – in such gentleness – the brow's snow. Her eyes were black, but they were trustful, like Dick Quiney's eyes.

'Anne,' called Whateley, yawning, flat-foot in his slippers, 'give him some wine. He is Jack's boy,' he said to his wife,

32

'Jack that was in Snitterfield.' And the wife, who came in cool from her dairy, smiled, a ripe and plump redaction of her daughter.

Anne, an only child, for a brother had died at birth, cut off from the world, timid, yet her eyes wide as she listened to this swift-tongued, spaniel-eyed poet-glover, walked with him in the garden (her parents looking on through the window, smiling, nudging: there now, he will do well, she could do worse) on his second visit. And what call you this flower, and this? Some have many names. This flower like I not, it has a smell of graves. Oh, you are too young to talk of the smell of graves. What, then, am I not too young to do? That I know not; see, I lower my eyes in bashfulness.

Is it on the fifth or seventh or ninth visit that the father and mother leave the two young people alone a space? He takes her hand, which is long and cool, and she does not ask him for it back. He sees her young breasts swell and there is a film of blood an instant before his eyes. No, not lust, not not lust. This could well be called love. He thinks: to fall in love will be Will's act, an act of Will, as to say: here I make my bed, here I choose the manner of my settling, this way I free myself from freedom's bondage, thus I escape for ever the harpy talons of lust and admit the probing of love's sweet fingers. She was untouched of man and so would remain till the clean sheets of the lavender-smelling bridal bed (and there would, he swore to himself, be no drunken snoring Toby night) should lap them both. Ah, long white hands and foot high-arching, gentle low pipe like a boy's voice. Were these, and the sweet breath of innocence, too much? If he had gone this way would he also have gone the other – dying in New Place not unhonoured, something fulfilled? But what was it that was to be desired in life, then? Reply, reply.

This marriage would, touching his father's foundering fortunes, have been salvation. Whateley would settle a fair dowry. And yet there rose, mocking from its darkness the sweet lover's words, prelude to all that was permitted (chaste kisses, no more), that tough demanding Adam, that inflamed and chastening rod. It will not be long, wait, wait. Till the spring only.

Ah, we are all damned. There is truly evil lying coiled in good; did not God create Lucifer and foreknow the colour and heat of the light he was to bear? So desire is part of love, and desire unacted is evil, therefore enact that desire – away, hid, indifferent, secret – and cleanse love as a well is cleansed. 'Tis but an easy operation. Wait, indeed, for love in the spring (it is her parents' careful pleasure, this long betrothal), but go now to Hewlands Farm – not straight and upright, though: peer about and skulk till she come forth to gather roses. And she came forth, that other Anne. It was an August evening. They lay in dry moss under an oak, WS feeling himself still but a boy and she all woman, and she would have this boy stripped to his very pelt, the sun to stare shocked at the white moving buttocks before going under for his night's journey in *terra incognita*, the while she lay demure from the waist up in her flowery gown. And, at the moment from which there was no turning back, for his seed had signed its conveyance, he was sure he saw faces peering and grinning from the hedgerow. But that was not all. Lightning wrote his name – Wlm Shaxpr – in the clear heavens of a sudden, all un-announced, and then thunder thudded like the stamping of a seal. She smiled, this one that would be both succuba and incuba on common land but (why had he not seen it before?) more comfortably on an indentured bed. And, crown of these prodigies, he felt his spurt of seed somehow enfolded within her and put at once to growth. If he had had any of the old religion of the Ardens in him he would have crossed himself then.

'Anne Anne,' chimed the clock, 'Anne Anne Anne,' the rooks scrawked. It was to pure Anne, sweet Anne that he rode almost daily, the pure cooled lover. But he felt (he had strange and frightening dreams) that they could not delay till spring. They must be married before Advent.

34

'Now what is this?' asked Whateley. 'What have you twain been doing that makes such haste your theme? For if you have done what I fear you have done, then by God I will take my whip to you both.'

'Ah no no no, nothing of that.' WS could afford, in his innocence, to smile faintly. 'It is that I would fain have her my wife ere the fates can stop me. For I dream of nothing but disasters.'

'Tut, lad, that is but phantoms of the mind, not to be trusted. Wait, then. Keep your blood cold and your heart warm. It is but a matter of some few months.'

And so he was still riding to Temple Grafton in cold November, winter's first harbingers biting. Hoofs rang frosty on the road. Hard by Shottery two men stopped him. They addressed him by name and bade him dismount.

'No. I am late. What do you want of me?' They were round-faced men, rough in gesture, much alike, yeomen, spade-bearded, dressed in leather against the chill.

'It is less what we want than what she wants and what honour wants. As for late, you are very late. I,' said this witty talker, 'am Fulk Sandells. This is Master John Richardson. We are kinsmen of Mistress Hathaway.'

'How does she?' said WS in his foolish manner. 'It is many a week since I – Is she well?'

'She is well,' said John Richardson. His left cheek twitched as though a fly tickled it. 'She is big and well and grows daily bigger.'

'Late,' said Fulk Sandells. 'Late is very good. You are late in asking, but better late than never. She awaits you now. She will chide you for your lateness, but there is no doubt she will say aye at the end.'

'Many a week, quotha,' said John Richardson. 'That is very good also. Many a month, he would say. Time enow for that pudding to grow kicking feet.'

'Let us have no riddles,' said WS, though his falling heart knew the meaning all too plain. 'Say what you will say and

35

then let me pass.' Fulk Sandells held the horse's bridle; Brown Harry did not like this man's smell and shook his head, whinnying. Sandells held fast to the curb strap, saying, 'There there, old nag as thou art.'

'Come your ways,' said Richardson. 'You are to ask that you may appear as the lawful father of your unlawful child. You are to dismount and walk with us. You have walked that way often ere now.'

'That is untrue,' said WS.

'Once or twice will be enough,' said Sandells, trying to hold Brown Harry's unquiet head in stillness. 'One August eve will be enough, under an oak-tree.' Of a sudden WS pricked Brown Harry's flanks hard. He rose on his hinder legs and, with a great shake as to say: 'Nay, thou shalt not', he freed his head from that constraining clutch of dirty fingers. And off galloped WS and left their waving fists and shouted threats behind, though their foul words were all too clear in that cold air.

So what was to be done was to be done quickly now, before Advent set in with its snows. Mad importunacy might help (I perish of desire, I cannot wait to hold thee, my naked wife, in mine arms) if it were but a matter of Anne, for what woman will willing put off a wedding? It was through the mother that finally he had his way. He cried, he near-swooned. Her smile was soft. In bed that night she must, on his behalf, have prevailed. He rode (thanks be to God, if there be a God) to Worcester on the twenty-seventh of November, there to procure a marriage licence. All was set down fair in the bishop's register. Rain set in. He lay that night at Evesham satisfied. In the Waterside inn, drinking ale, he was found by Fulk Sandells and John Richardson. They both said 'Ah' in greeting, shaking their dripping cloaks. They too sought shelter.

'So,' said Sandells, 'tomorrow we seek one reading of the banns, not three. We have forty pounds for a bond. All will go butter-smooth.'

'It is against the sanguinity,' said Richardson with pride. 'It is to condemnify the bishop.'

'I am but newly come from Worcester,' smiled WS. 'And you are going to Worcester too late.'

'How he harps on "late",' said Sandells. 'You must learn of the law, lad, and how the law is enforced.' He made a yeoman's brawny nief in threat.

'It is all writ down on a paper,' said Richardson. 'William Shagspere and—'

'Shakespeare.'

'Shakespeare, Shagspere, it is all one. And Anne Hathaway in the diocese of Worcester, maiden.'

'As maiden as your mother is,' said WS, hot. Richardson was nief-ready too at that, but he perceived his lack of reason. He said:

'Aye aye aye, that is the nub of it all. But thou hast made her what she is not.'

'So then,' said Sandells. 'Forty pounds is no trifle. It is no child's pocket-jingle to buy kickshawses withal. No matter of law shall hinder the wedding, nor no matter neither that is outside the pale of the law.'

'She is a good lass,' said Richardson. 'Something stringy, but enow to grasp a hold of. She is not so young as she was but hath a light hand with a pasty. For her bedwork you yourself shall best speak.'

'Enough of that,' said Sandells. 'We are selling him no goods, not now. He did his buying in high summer. Now it is but a matter of the delivering.'

'That is the right word,' said Richardson. 'It will be a spring babe.'

'And if I say a fig,' said WS, 'and spit on your poxy noses?'

Sandells shook his head in calm regret. 'Oh,' he said at last, 'there is many a dog with a stone round's neck in a river. As it might be here. Oh, there is a many a bag of kittens in the millpond. Knives draw blood when they are sharp. You cannot scape your your your—'

'Destiny?' said WS, ever a word-boy.

'Aye, destiny. That is what you may call her.'

37

VI

ANOTHER little drop. Delicious. Well, then.

AFTER THE WRANGLINGS, family tears and rages, Anne Whateley's swoons and sending-off to kinsfolk in Banbury (Master Bustin and his daughter), after first tongues' then eyes' reproachments, he climbed to his old bed with his new bride. How doth WS the married man? He had but half of that bed now, and the familiar rest he sought, in so great need, so worn, was less than one quarter of what it had formerly been. He moved not forth, nor had any great desire to, to a new world of his own sheets and kettles; rather to his boyhood's home was admitted a fresh female conspirator, well-armed with the vinegar ladyship of his mother. The two old women, indeed, recognized kinship and later kissed night and morning. The household's lack of an Anne Shakespeare was thus proved but temporary. For the rest, his father, disappointed in a dowry, continued morose and merry-cheeked and went little, for fear of creditors, abroad; Edmund vomited on the floor amid the rushes, sick infant Moses; Richard was pushed much in mire and cried home limping: Joan grew greasier and sharper; Gilbert saw more of God and God gave him the falling-sickness.

Soon to his boyhood's chamber was imported from Shottery a great bed apt for the spacious galloping of four bare legs, or five. And, near up to the May-birth of Susanna (begotten in lust), there was galloping, trotting, cavorting enough. Nor was it all in bed. She had great gifts, that one. Hate was a sharp sauce to the part of WS in the games she devised. There was no tenderness for there was no love.

Anne would be all above love or hate, acting the queen. In her wedding finery she would stalk the chamber, bid WS lick her shoe, walk on him as on the carpet of her triumph, order his instant beheading. Then, so the grim sport went, he was to seize her by force, she protesting in a royal voice (though subdued, for there were others sleeping near by) and crying out out treason, the while he growled, 'By God's body I have you, Your Majesty, and now I call you thou and thee like a sloven and will wreak my dirty will all over your finery.' (So was he called Dirty Will.) Then he disrobed her in great difficulty, for she scratched and fought, and he was fain to desist from such fatiguing play. But once she said she would call in some other to help with the holding her down an he lacked force to do it alone; nay, even Dickon and poor Gilbert – in default of one lusty man – should be waked from their thin boys' snores in the neighbour room to assist at this treasonous rape. And then, aghast at the mere conceit of the counter-rape of innocence, he struck her a damned blow in the chaps and went hard at it, so that she cried both aye aye aye and her fear of harm that might chance to the child in her belly.

Often she said, when the queenly mood was on her, that this act of *laesa maiestas* showed to poor advantage in that small bare bedchamber. There should be her court all about her – her great men of state and chamberlains and maids of honour and even, as at some progress, the base commons – to witness the gross defilement of beauty and majesty by the meanest and most despised of all her subjects. And sometimes, in the approach of her dying scream, she would talk of their clipping naked at the window in full day and view.

She would act the queen otherwise. She would be the descending goddess to woo one who would feign to wish none of her (was it feigning?) WS must be adamant in his nays and pout, a lovely boy. She would have his beardkin off, she said, and eke all the hairs of his body saving his auburn crown. Then she would be at him with goddess strength, big-bellied naked.

After Susanna's birth – and she bore Susanna as easy as any sow – she was restored to her slenderness. Then it was her fancy

39

to be herself a lovely boy and, with Susanna crowing in the cradle, to steal Dickon's clothes from the press (they were much of a size) while the two unlovely boys, side by side in the spring night, entertained their innocent dreams. Then, decked as a pretty page, she would taunt him and simper before him and say: 'Take me, master, in whatever way you have a mind to.' This would fill his whole head with beating blood, so that he was blind and went for her blindly. She was, he saw, hunting out corners of corruption in his soul which he had hardly guessed at before. She would even make for him, grinning, with a dildo or *penis succedaneus*, and he was shocked to know she had such a thing in her chest of stored belongings.

How could all this expense be supported, work to be done, his eyes heavy and limbs drooping in the morning, head dropping to the bench two hours before dinner? She, mean-time, remained fresh and singing over her pans, bidding his mother rest, she had had a hard life, here was come a new daughter to halve all her burdens. Bless thee, Anne, thou art a good lass. Besides his work, he had the duty of teaching dull and godly Gilbert the glover's craft, and Gilbert would cut his hand and drop foaming at the sight of blood or else cry loudly on his brother for the strictness of his rule and say, 'I have spoke to God of thy naughtiness.' And WS would reply, 'Well then, ask God to teach thee of tranks and gussets, for, by God, I have had enough of it,' and then Gilbert would fall, going hud hud hud, and near upset the workbench. To be added to the agents of discontent was the antiphonal wailing of Susanna and her nuncle Edmund.

But most was his wife's scolding, for she more than mur-mured of his untimely tiredness when it came to the time for climbing to their creaking and bouncing Shottery bed. He would say:

'Not this night. The day has been hard and hot. One night's holiday will not harm.'

'So,' she would reply, 'thou callest it work, then, that thou callest not doing of it a holiday. Thou wert ready enough that

August night of my undoing.' And then she would prate of his effeminate unmanliness and take it beyond the confines of love to the manner of their life, how she would never at this gait rule her own hearth nor have fine gowns like Mistress Whatyoucall an he did not seek some better mode of employ than boy to a poor gloveman. 'Thou art weak, thou art all water, I have married but a poor thing, I, that could have had great Worcester merchants for the asking but took pity on one that seemed, with strong wifely help, like to promise fair. Thou wilt, I see it, become like thy father, a mewling shrode, naught of the ambition that should be in a man at all in thee.' There was no ho with her, so he would escape, crying creak, to his slumbers. But one hot night, in that bedchamber, he took quill and paper to set down some lines that had come all unbidden that day at his work; he had said them over and over in his head and now would see them in some more sempiternal form:

> Backward she push'd him, as she would be thrust,
> And govern'd him in strength, though not in lust.

These lines seemed to be part of some story which, by gentle thinking on, might be teased out. But then she said, her dress already off her dancing bosom:

'You have time enow, oh aye, for the miowling of kitticat poetry like a struck fool, but no time at all for your wife and her lawful pleasure.' So he replied coldly:

'For one line of verse I would trade thirty such scolds as you.'

'Aye, thy little thing is shrunken to a nib. Dip it in ink as a tool to write withal. I will go find me a man.'

'You will be long finding. You were so before.'

'Your meaning?'

'You were out to catch and it was I was caught. But I was, God help me, drunk at the time. It is a warning against drink.'

'I could have had all I wanted.'

'Aye, and did have, doubtless. But I was your true woodcock. Do you not say I was the first, nor even the twenty-first.'

41

'It was you that did it, you.' Her dress was now fallen to her hips but he sat on, monumental, the stone poet with poet's quill. The quill, though, quivered. 'You defiled me like some drunken beast and then came back to do it again sober. I was a virgin untouched ere all that.'

'As a Coventry cockatrice.'

She came for him at this, her talons ready. He marked, a poet, the beauty of her white flesh, the long arms a-shiver, the breasts' bell-tolling. 'Scratching cat, wouldst thou then?' he said, seizing one near wrist. Womanlike, she saw that she would win by feigning that this was a struggle he had begun and yielding, in her own time, to him. Her panting, after but a half-minute of her seeking to free her wrists (for he had put down his pen to seize the other), became the panting of abandon, and he thought he would then, fully clothed and sweating as he was, take her naked against the wall. But hatred rose in him like black vomit, seeing that she had turned him into manner of a whoremaster, so to wish to go to it, she mother-bare and he ready to be so in some inches of hard flesh only. In her surprise (far otherwise had been her expectation) she staggered, hobbled by her down-drawn gown, and fell against the crib wherein Susanna lay sleeping. The child woke in deadly fright and howled loud as to rouse the town, what time this bare mother cried, 'My babe, my babe, my honey lambkin!' and plucked her up. Susanna held her breath and gaped in the candle-shadows and they both were in an instant's sweat of agony knowing not what to do, and then the child loosed all screaming hell, so that Gilbert seemed to start some exorciser's cantrip in his next-door sleep and WS heard his father cough and mother murmur. Then the babe recovered calm, soothed with Anne's lulling and rocking, then given a good suck of the pap that had been exposed earlier to a far different end, the wife and mother speaking low loving words of nonsense for this her womb-fruit but flashing toledo hate in the eyes for the seed-sower. The seed-sower? And then, for the first time, he was assaulted, the

42

fool, by great lubberly doubt. He knew now what the bride-knot-cutter need never, kept he but his wife in reasonable bondage, know – the cuckoo-fear that may never in no wise be resolved. Susanna might be his and then again she might not, and this, fool, he had not thought on before. The love he owed that child could not be diminished because of this doubt (indeed, it must – through pity and the loosing of pure animal blood-ties – be in a manner augmented), but he might justly, he saw with wretched glee, jettison all responsibility for the mother. He would not speak on this, not even, he vowed, touch on it in the course of other angers, for it would be the beating of sparrow's wings in an osier cage, the trudge of the chained bear round and round at the stake, for he could never know. Nor she neither, nor any.

But to him it seemed right now that he should leave and re-enter, after so brief a bed-slavery, into the manumission of his old bacherlorhood. It would be wrong, in this lack of love, to live a whoredom there in his father's house; he must forsake the bed that was hers. And to leave to seek other employ would appear duty too in another sort: Gilbert could make gloves after a fashion, a fashion of infra- or supernumerary fingers, for he could not count well, and oft no thumb, as it had been bitten off, but he would learn; Joan could help too with this work, as her kitchen-helping was less than before, thanks to her new sister; even Richard, now nine years old, might be pressed into some service of limping delivery. It was right that WS go to some other town, to fatten, however thinly, the poor Shakespeare fisc. But he delayed, he delayed. There was a fascination in hate; more-over, it seemed to him that, in those shameful bedchamber antics he could not leave off, he grew, at the moment of annunciation, somehow close to that goddess he had all but neglected (there was a dark way that was shown to him, but he was fearful of entering it wholly; he knew not properly what it was but it was to do with evil). This was especially true of some of Anne's new inventions, which entailed kneeling and a show of pious prayer. So summer died and winter lashed in, and he heard that Anne Whateley had married in Banbury.

That winter Gilbert dreamed a dream and came to his breakfast on a grey frosty morning to relate it, saying:

'I ha' seen heads, aye, all cut off and bloody, and great birds that did come down to peck at now one eye now another eye, aye.' Joan laughed sillily. Gilbert shook into an unwonted fury, spilling his little boy's pot of small ale. WS shivered, he thought not for the cold. 'Aye,' cried Gilbert, 'in London 'twas, and he is a ligger that saith I lig, for it was on like spikes these twain heads were and I did see all. And there was waters and a great bridge behind, aye. And one head was like unto her head here.' He looked on his mother as she were a stranger. None laughed, not even silly Joan now. Their mother had grown very pale. She said:

'God help them that are left,' crossing herself. In their father's voice was the thick redness of blood. He said:

'So will it be visited on all the Ardens. They are fools to cry up the Old Faith by dying for it. A man will best keep his faith alive by himself keeping alive, not by this hatching of plots that are found out. Now, trust me, there will be a harrowing.'

Anne smelt the fear round that table, for she clasped her husband's hand and her eyes had grown large. WS knew this plot his father spoke of to be one in which the Arden family had made a part, and of those two heads visioned by Gilbert one was doubtless that of Edward Arden, who had stopped once in Henley Street for a cup of wine on his riding south and had spoken fierily against the times and tyrants and usurpers. For it had been noted then how the Arden colouring and bones could be deduced from a comparison of this cousin and their mother. The other head, as news by Christmas was to tell, had belonged to John Somerville. WS shuddered, at that morning table, to see in his mind the tugging by greedy scavenging birds at the loose skin and flesh (a bird perched,

44

eating angrily of a chap, on a wall near which a rosy housewife hung out clothes, singing) and then the eternal terrible truth of the skull disclosed at the feast's end.

'My Lord of Canterbury will remember well who he knew in his old diocese,' said their mother. 'And he knew no harm of any Mistress Shakespeare. Thou need'st not fear any visiting of this house on mine account.'

Their father bit his lip, his rose-mottled cheeks according ill with his troubled eyes. But two years back he had been crushed with the burden of a fine of forty pounds (he had sold a messuage to find that sum) on account of a charge of recusancy. One hundred and forty Midlanders summoned to the Queen's Bench in Westminster on that same charge, but John Shakespeare doubly recusant in not appearing (Edmund's birth had been a difficult one). And now, in bow-ye-down-and-lick-my-dirty-shoe elevation at Canterbury but newly this year, was that Whitgift who had been a double scourge from that see of troubles Worcester, a whip in either gripe – one for the Papists, the other for the Puritans, a voice quacking of eternal fire through the gate of temporal fire for all that followed not the Holy Middle Way of the True English Church, God being an Englishman. And John Shakespeare favoured what he termed the cleanness and honesty of the New Faith (bishops, also, had ever been Antichrist), a religion for good men of trade. It was a time, that winter, for gloom and fear and stirring not much abroad; they hugged their comforting, not punishing, fire.

But WS kept quiet about his own weak faith in anything, except perhaps what might be found after crawling through a dark and narrow tunnel.

VII

THEN SPRING RETURNED to prove winter but a bad dream, and once again the roads beckoned. But still he delayed. He descried in bitterness that he must be pushed to everything, all will relegated to his name. He came to his morning's work (or lack of it sometimes) weary as though she had sucked out his very marrow. And one day in June it was made clear to him that she was with child again. This time, he felt, he could be sure of his paternity, though he had not had (as he had had that time in August of shuddering memory) the sense of a catching and holding fast of his seed for planting and growth, and all this bred in him a conviction that the beloved Susanna (and was she not perhaps the real reason for his loathness to depart?) was not his.

One day in late June a gentleman riding home to Gloucestershire from Warwick called, being in need of riding gauntlets. 'After this model,' he said, showing one. 'The other I lost on the road. I have been directed here by one I asked on Stratford's outskirts. Master Shakespeare, is it not? I have a kinsman in Ettington to visit, some two days only. May the gauntlets be brought to me at the house of Master Woodford?'

So. Master Woodford, that disbarred lawyer and decayed gentleman, a widower of a few acres.

'My own name is John Quedgeley, Justice of the Peace.'

'That,' said WS, 'is a place in Gloucestershire.'

'And my name derives from it,' said Master Quedgeley. He had a full black beard and a wet red nether lip; he was above forty, old, yet big-shouldered as a smith and near two yards tall. He had bright brown though grave eyes. 'Some remote and all forgotten forefathers did formerly live there. But now we are near enough to Berkeley.'

'Where there is a castle.'

'Where there is a castle. Well then, this you know. And what more do you know?'

'Of Gloucestershire?'

'Of anything.' He smiled at WS as if he in some sort despised the pretence of a mere glover to have even the meanest learning outside his mean craft. 'You are, then, a young man that has travelled.'

'I have travelled in books, sir,' said WS, in too loud a voice. 'I have read of matters bigger than where castles may be and whence a gentleman's name may come.' Then he recollected his place and blushed and was silent.

'And Latin, too?' said Master Quedgeley. '*Eheu fugaces, Postume, Postume*. I love the sweet tunes of P. Vergilius Maro.'

'Horace,' said WS, 'as I think, sir, you must know.' Then he must perforce smile at the other's smile, for this seemed in some sort to be a test.

'Yes, yes, Quintus Horatius Flaccus. Well, would mine own boys knew as much.'

John Shakespeare had come back to the bench with skins to be chosen for cutting. 'My son here is a good scholar and also a poet. He has writ fine verses. Show the gentleman some of your verses, Will.'

WS blushed again. He would not. 'He is come for gloves, not verses.'

'Yes. Well, then,' said Master Quedgely, 'when he brings my gauntlets he may bring also his verses. And with that I give you good day.' So he left. But, when WS took the Banbury road on foot the next afternoon, he carried gloves only. Ah, he dreamed an instant, that other Anne, my former beloved now another's, lies at the end; I will walk to her. But he turned into the court of a tumbledown gaunt farmhouse, much punished by weather and disfigured with unhinged doors and swinging windows. Two farm-men were lying idle on straw in the good summer sun, their eyes closed to it: swine nuzzled and honked at rubbish; a cock ran treading his dames, but his crow was a desolation. A chewing servant in a foul smock came to the ratatat, a mutton-bone in his dirty fingers. He stood sucking out the marrow. Then he said:

'Aye aye, thou wilt find 'em both in one room or another. Me and my fellows, today we make holiday.'

'What holiday?'

'I know not the saint's name. Saint Turd, mayhap, as this is Turdsday. Every day there is some saint.'

'You were best to watch your manners.'

'My friends brought me up as they were able,' he said, in a mincing way, hand on hip. 'When manners were in the hall I was in the stable.' And he bunched his face up and belched and left WS with the open door, returning to a dark region at the corridor's end whence came the sound of bucolic merrymaking. So WS went in and two little dogs came at him yapping as they would tear great collops of flesh from his calves an they were bigger, and their master, this decayed and grey Woodford, came out tottering. WS told him his mission; he bowed WS drunkenly in, saying:

'Here is Liberty Hall, where all take liberties. Down thou, down, thou great beast. What, Bell? How, Grinder?' And he aimed jocular kicks, missing, while the dogs barked, tails mad with a great joy and love. WS followed man and beasts into a dark chamber all dusty, folios and harness and stags' antlers sitting on chairs like Christians. And there was this Master Quedgeley, unbuttoned, waving a spilling pot and droning. He called:

'Ah, it is the gloveman that knoweth all Gloucester and environs. Good, we are three gentlemen and may troll a catch now. This fellow here is too low to sing with esquires, begging his pardon and his master's. Fill our glove-poet a quart of cider, thou.' A misshapen leering rogue limped from the room's dark corner with a jug. WS demurred, stammering.

48

He was not well, he had done with drinking, he had made vows, it did his stomach great harm . . .

'Take,' said Master Woodford, 'for this is heart's ease and the lover's – I would say liver's – joy. More, it is all we have. How, are you so nice that you will sniff at it, wishing sack and canary in a poor man's abode? You are too good for us, then. Odd's my little life, how they start up at their betters.' And he handed WS a great pewter pot, all greasy without, and he must needs drink to avoid offence. 'Nay, all down in one gollop,' cries Master Quedgeley, as comfortable as this were his own home. And then he started a catch and Master Woodford broke in, cracked as a crow, as *vox secunda*, and then both stopped and shouted for WS to follow as *tertia*. So follow he must, though this was a rude and poor catch he had not heard before:

> 'Pox take thy ballocks, thou reechy varlet,
> Thy dad a cuckold and thy mother a harlot,
> And squeeze the cheese from thy filthy nog.'

The apple-vinegar like gut-needles made WS go shudder shudder, but it allayed the dusty thirst, thirsty dust of his brief drouthy journey. He had more. At one point, later, he was standing on a table and declaiming lines of Seneca:

> *'Fatis agimur; cedite fatis.*
> *Non sollicitae possunt curae*
> *Mutare rati stamina fusi . . .'*

'There is words,' nodded Master Woodford. 'There is orating, what the Greeks called rhetoric. Now, that was plays that were read before the patricians, and good plays, not like the stink and ordure that passes for plays in our shameful time. Poor vagabonds all. Ah, long long agone. But there were two, and things once promised fair. Aye.'

'Well, then,' said Master Quedgeley, far gone in his cider, 'let us have ancient Rome here and now. Let's call in your girl

49

Betty or Bessie or whatever her name is and have somewhat of an orgy. God help me, I must be back shortly to behave cleanly, as fine a husband and father and justice as ever shivered in his short shirt of a frosty morning.' Then he looked up at WS, who was still upon the table, sighing: 'Aye aye, a life's but a span. But these young bullies will carry on my name. Yet what's the use? They will not learn. A name's but a name when all's done.'

Master Woodford said sharply, 'You, sir, down from there, you are no centrepiece.' So WS leapt down, very merry. 'The two I spake of were the two Toms. Give us somewhat of *Gorboduc*. They were,' he said in explication to Master Quedgeley, 'Tom Sackville and Tom Norton, and that was done, as it might be for a sort of latterday patricians, in the Inns of Court. The inner Temple it was, and some twenty years agone. Before, I daresay, this young makeshift or hockey-eater was born. I was there, by Jesus' mass, I saw all. They were our English Seneca.' To this he drank. WS said pertly:

'Two Englishmen to make one Roman.' For he believed then in his heart that there was naught in English plays but poor ranting and sorry bawdry, and all in the open, in sad rain or word-greedy wind. He had seen in Stratford but one play that had set the flue on his body to bristling, and its name he had forgot, though not the company, which was the Earl of Worcester's Men, nor the chief actor, which was Alleyn, and he two years younger than WS. Now he said to Master Quedgeley: 'Berkeley. But this last year there were Lord Berkeley's Men in Stratford. And so I know of the castle.' But now Master Woodford was on his feet, peripatottering in drunken discourse:

'I say again this. I say that if there is to be an English poesy worthy the name then it must be framed of true sounds, the throat all open, and not of mumblings in chambers or the impostures of the eye. It is the ear that is poesy's organ. And so, an we would learn, we could turn that freshet of the two great Toms (it was but abortive, that I admit, aye, abortive) into, into – what did I say then? Aye aye aye, a great rolling river of words.'

WS smiled at this, in youth's superior wisdom and the effects of the cider. Master Woodford saw the curl of his lip and turned on him as to belabour him, saying:

'Fleerer and mocker, what dost thou know in thine ignorance? Country hilding, that hast never seen the flower of cities nor the glory of sweet words in a great hall with a great fire and all light blazing.' It seemed then that he would weep, as remembering a past much different from his present. WS said, bold cider-boy and crony of justices and scholars:

'Words in such form surely I would not see but hear. As for acting, is it not all lies? A boy is made a woman, a short man will add a cubit with stilt-shoes—'

'Chopines,' corrected Master Woodford.

'– A living man will say he is dying. Now I grant that in Seneca there was none of this, for his plays were not acted but read aloud.'

'Oh, God preserve us from cheesy cant,' said Master Quedgeley. 'That is Banbury talk.' WS saw at once that it was, that it was his father with his Geneva Bible and not the sweet Hellenic scense of Plato. 'Life,' so went Quedgeley on, 'is in a sense all lies. We watch ourselves act every day. Philip drunk and Philip sober. One is inside the other watching the other. And so I am John Quedgeley and Jack Quedgeley and Jockey Quedgeley and Master Quedgeley, Justice of Peace, and all. It is all acting.' And WS saw that this was true, revolving it in the murk of the bottom of his cider-tankard. Had he not himself watched WS and WS watched Will? Where was truth, where did a man's true nature lie? There was, as it were, an essence and there was also an existence. It was, this essence, at the bottom of a well, of a Will.

Things became all confused thereafter and he woke to hearty kisses and face-licking from the little dogs, himself groaning from deep cidrous sleep on the floor. Somebody had let in these little dogs. They saw him eye-rubbing and heard him painfully gape and smack at his mouth's horror, then went to the other two, who were sacklike in chairs, dead men save for their antiphony of cracking snores, and they responded not to the licking nor to the barking. WS rose in great pain and guilt and limped out of the chamber. It was light still, but there was the sadness of summer evening in the light. In the corridor outside the chamber a serving-girl met him with ready bare bosom and blackened smile (yes yes, of course, he knew her, but not in that other sense). He groaned and shook his head and left by the open front door. The walk, he hoped, would shake him sober.

Well then, another holy vow never to carouse more, a meek face to Mistress Virago, and an end to Master Quedgeley. But he was already home and undressing himself to the pipe and tabor of Anne's complaining when he found the gauntlets still lying snug buttoned in his bosom, the true office of his going unperformed. So next morning Gilbert, his elder brother being in a foul crapula, was sent thither, though only after much repetitious instruction and even the drawing of a map. He returned late and hungry, having belike met God in a coppice, and to him it was given to speak the next stage of WS's destiny.

'Aye, then 'tis all done, aye. And here is the money for the gloves and for myself a penny. And the man saith he will come for thee early the morrow as the riding will be a long one, aye.'

It was to WS he spoke. 'What,' said WS, 'is all this of a long ride? Let us have all once again. And which man dost thou speak of?'

'Him of the gloves. Th'art going with him, so he doth say. Th'art to be as a father to's childer, aye, and teach them, and thereto is signed an adventure.'

'Indenture?' WS frowned, he could remember nothing of this. His father approached, wiping his hands on a napkin, Anne came with Susanna in her arms, greasy Joan listened, his mother was nowhere about. 'Where, then, is my half?'

' 'Tis here.' And Gilbert pulled from his bosom the zig-zag-edged paper that made one of a pair of indentures. WS took and read, incredulous. He had bound himself to Master Quedgeley for a year as tutor to his boys. His own signature was there, though cider-sprawling. He could not remember. He just could not remember. 'He is to go teach Senna and Pluto,' Gilbert told everybody. 'Aye, to all his childer.'

'Oh, a secret man,' said Anne. 'He plans to run off in the night and say naught.' Then she started.

' 'Tis in the morning,' said literal Gilbert. 'Early the morrow, aye. He did give me this penny to buy suckets withal.' He showed it to all with gravity.

Was he, then, wondered WS, to have his life's course writ for him behind his back, each several stage announced by bravos or idiots? 'There is payment,' he told his wife. 'I am not being sold in slavery. See. I will send you money home.'

But the great scolding went on. 'Amen amen amen,' said WS to himself.

VIII

'*LUNA fuit: specto si quid nisi litora cernam*—'

He had not thought his escape would take such form, though truly what form? He had (agreed) agreed in his cider stupor to be tutor to five young Quedgeleys, teaching them chiefly Latin and receiving in return bed and board and payment of ten shillings each quarter. It was no dizzy sum to take home at the end; he was not there in Gloucestershire to make his fortune.

'– *Quod videant oculi nil nisi litus habent*—'

For the house, it was new-built, of Henry the Eighth's reign, and as near Sharpness as Berkeley, so that he could see the Severn and dream again of ships; for the household, its lady was Mistress Quedgeley (the master's second wife), a sharp woman who could be more content with eisel than sack-and-sugar, the master himself no longer the jolly unbuttoned fellow that had cidered it to insensibility in Ettington but a grave man, much the magistrate, in black. The servants thought at first they would have WS as a butt among them, laughing at his Stratford twang, jeering at hing hang hog, but he was tart from the beginning with the swaggering butler and cold at the hip-swinging maids. He requested, and was granted, a chamber to his own self, near to the boys' rooms.

'*Nunc huc nunc illuc, et utroque sine ordine curro*—'

For the boys, his pupils or disciples, there was Matthew, the eldest at fifteen, then Arthur, thirteen-and-a-half, then John, twelve years – all by the first Mistress Quedgeley; the second had achieved twins – Miles and Ralph, ten or just under. There had been two daughters, with their mother's vinegar face to judge from miniatures ill-done by some Gloucester painter, and these had died very early – at seven and eight. So there were left these sturdy grinning youths, five brains to be charged with Latin and but four faces beneath them.

'*Alta puellares tardat arena pedes*—'

Divine Ovid rendered dull and sleepy in the sleepy afternoon of late summer. A bluebottle buzzed in through the open casement, their eyes followed its flight. They would not learn. It was as if the twins deemed it sufficient in life to be, as it were, a genetical prodigy; the elder boys yawned and stretched and kicked, groaned at Ovid and Lyly's Grammar, sometimes shouted and fought, threw inky pellets and drew dirty pictures covertly. For WS they had little reverence. Did he address Ralph, then he would be told it was Miles, and also the other way about, and the elder boys would abet this. At times their father would test them for what they had learned, but what they had learned was never enough.

'Why then,' growl-squeaked Arthur, whose voice was on the break, 'is it *tuli* and *latum* when it is in the present *fero*? It is all nonsense and I will have none of it.'

'You will, by God, have what you are given,' said WS, whipped to ire.

'You swear, sir,' said Matthew in holy shock. 'You take the divine name in vain.'

'I will take your breeches down,' cried WS, 'and not in vain. I will take a stick to your buttocks.'

The twins giggled at this mention of taking breeches down. Why?

One autumn morning Master Quedgeley said to WS:

'Well, my lord Berkeley's players are home. They have played, though of course in English, the *Mostellaria* at the castle.'

'The comedy of the haunted house.'

'It is that. And I think my boys will best learn out of themselves Englishing some Plautus that they may act it. Each one to English his own part. They will learn best out of pleasure – not the pleasure of noise and fighting (you need not deny that your classes are full of this), but the lawful and *useful* pleasure of working to a delightful end.'

'But there is no poetry in Plautus.'

'No, but there is wit and ready cut-and-thrust. Sticho-mythia. It is good for those who will study law, as Matthew and Arthur must. You will take the *Menaechmi*. Therein aré parts for twins. You will buy copies at Master Cunliffe's shop in Bristol. It is many years since I acted myself in it, at school, in Latin. I mind well the pleasure of it.' He said this in some-thing like gloom.

So WS rode to Bristol on a gold October day. Berkeley and its castle. Woodford, Alveston. Almondsbury, Patchway, Filton. He was mounted on Master Quedgeley's chestnut gelding. Leaves gold and brown lying like fried fish; birds twittering like rats in branch-companies, ready to leave the sinking ship of summer. He rode shivering, gold in his purse (a fine purse made by his father), an old cloak about him. The gold was for books and his simple dinner at some ordinary. He had no money of his own.

Bristol. He greeted Bristol in something like fear. Bristol, bristling with masts at his mouth open in wonder; he could smell salt, see sailors whose tarry trade was not in doubt (alas poor inland Hoby, now in earth). The streets rang with work and drunkenness and the bells of the slavetraders' chapels; barrels were trundled merrily over the cobbles; he grew affrighted and shy at the sight of so many sea-folk, some strange in colour and dress, at the earrings of gold the sun answered, sun glowing from skin tanned and burned by sea and far places of nothing but the sun. And his mission was, God help him, to buy books of a Roman long-dead, to pay, eat a frugal dinner, then turn his back on life again.

'We have here,' said Cunliffe the bookseller, '*Menaechmi* and *Mostellaria* and eke *Miles Gloriosus*. Oh, you can have five of any one and your own teacher's copy for three-quarters the price. Of others there are none.' He was an old man, chinny and chewing, and his shop was dark and smelt of the grave, which was to say of books; but on his money-table there was a skull (ah, those gnawing greedy kites) and he said, holding it in his right hand, that it was the skull of a black man, a slave, that had been beaten to death. Outside was the noise of sailors (yarely, my hearties) staggering from a tavern, and also the tang of brine carried up this other Avon, the brailed, or furled, masts. 'Nor,' said Cunliffe, 'wiww you find 'em in aww Bristow ewsewhere.' That was his way of speech (it was *Mostewwaria* and *Miwes Gworiosus* he truly said). Then a coach, drawn by a cobble-clattering pair of greys, went goldenly down Broad Street. 'Not aww the bwack be swaves,' said Cunliffe. 'She in there, hid by those curtains is bwack, or brown perhaps you would say. They do report that she was brought back from the Indies, aye, a smaww girl, a chieftain's daughter, and that she was made one of that famiwy out of pity. But now she is a fine haughty Christian dame with her thick mouth, though not many have set eyes on her.' WS followed that coach with hungry look to its point of clattering round the corner. 'In Fishponds,' said Cunliffe, nodding and chewing WS out of his shop.

WS, books stringed together in his oxter beneath his cloak, wandered, still in wonder, among the back streets that were like serpents or twisted veins. And it was then a voice summoned him. From an open doorway it called:

'What cheer, bully! Dost dou seek a bert?'

He turned, his heart near fainted. Dressed in a fair loose gown of virtuous, though dirty, white, her shoulders and bosom glowing to the empty street, she leaned, her arms folded, at ease against the doorpost, smiling. If Englishmen were white, he thought, then must she be called black; but black she could not in truth be called, rather gold, but then not gold, nor royal purple neither, for when we say colours we see a flatness, as of cloth, but here was flesh that moved and swam on the light's tide, ever changing in hue but always of a richness that could only be termed royal; her colour was royalty. For her hair, it coiled in true blackness; her lips were thick; her nose was not tightened against the cold air, like an English nose, an Anne nose, nor pinched as at the meagreness of the sun, but flat and wide; her brow was wide too, though shallow. And so she stood, smiling at him and beckoning with her long golden finger.

With scant money (the ordinary's destined mutton-slice, enough just for that), he knew not what to do. Surely it must be gold for gold, an angel, say, for this proffer of new heaven, yet had he never before paid (save dearly, or cheaply, with his freedom) for the act of love, and something within him shrivelled at the thought of haggling now over the price of entering this house of gold by its little hid gold door. But, first, the tumbledown brick house, a vista of darkness down a corridor, noises of lust and release. He stood undecided and she smiled still, then said: 'If'n d'art comin', come now den.' He mowed and grinned and muttered, opening out the fingers of his right hand to show an empty palm, and then she laughed in a fracture of strange crystal.

As he tottered towards her his calves were emptied of muscle and filled with water. Smiling, she beckoned him to follow her in. He entered darkness that smelled of musk and dust, the tang of sweating oxters, and, somehow, the ancient stale reek of egg after egg cracked in waste, the musty hold-smell of seamen's garments, seamen's semen spattered, a ghost procession of dead sailors lusting till the crack of doom. Noises came from the chambers on either side of the corridor – laughter, creakings in rhythm, a deep male voice ejaculating as in prophecy: 'Let nameless fall and all done.' And there was one chamber-door standing open, and WS saw what went on within. There was a low pallet with filthy blankets, bloody clouts on the floor, but it was against the wall that the act of lust proceeded, a ride now reaching, in sweat and curses, the destination that was a broken city, a voyage to a shipwreck. The woman was black, shining, naked, agape, thrust against the wall as though at bay, and there rammed and rammed at her a bulky seaman, in unbuttoned shirt and

58

points loosened for his work, whorls and bushes of red hair showing, his beard red, his head bald save for odd plastered tendrils and filaments of red. The companion of WS smiled to see all this, while he himself felt a sickness, an excitement, a disgust he had hardly known before, not even on those bizarre nights of Anne's madness; he even flushed in shame and fear, strangely fain to run blubbering to that known white body, the thin lips and sharp nose, burrowing into her, his coney, for comfort. But he followed his companion to another chamber, this time empty save for those ghosts of past doers, all grinning at him from walls, tiny rat-sprites peering from the folds of the crumpled dirty bed-sheets, a dead hairy arm gesturing from under the bed. He stood; it was still not too late to retreat. She pulled her gown swiftly down further from her shoulders, disclosing nipples black as ink-blobs; she came for him smiling, her arms held out. He dropped his stringed copies of Plautus to the floor and, his cloak still on but thrown back, he embraced her golden body trembling. She said naught, he kissed what words she would utter fiercely back into her mouth and, in that soft strange contact, felt as if he were starting some strange Hoby-voyage to lands of men with dog-heads or plate-feet, carbuncles and diamonds to be raked from under the golden-egg palms. Rocks, the oven-sun, fish that talked, the toothed waves. Then she drew herself away brusquely and held out her palm for money.

'I have but—' He showed. At once she grew angry. She beat at him with her black fists, what time he tried to force her back to that time-dissolving hug. She called a strange name. An older woman shuffled in, black, gross, smelling of grease, chewing something that had made her fat lips all purple, her unbusked bubs swinging – under a loose stained red gown – almost to her waist. They talked loud in their own language; they beat at him, four-fisting, shouting. He backed stumbling, his forearm to his eyes, for they would scratch him too, and, as he was thrust down the corridor, his couple of copper coins tinkling and rolling on the floor, an untrussed white man

59

looked out from a room, saw, then opened a mouth of rotten teeth to roar his laughter.

He fled, that laughter following on the wind that was of a sudden strongly arisen in the street, scarred with humiliation, blindly seeking Broad Street among cloaks blown by the wind, hats chased to urchins' laughter, under swinging inn-signs all creaking, looking, whipped to his knees by shame, for that Rose where a lad was holding his master's restive chestnut for a halfpenny. He would not stay for food in the loud smoky ordinary – indeed, he could not, for he had no money; nay, he had not even the halfpenny to pay this sniffing ragged boy. 'Take this,' he said, and he handed him his empty purse, the piece of fine leatherwork done by his own father. The boy opened his mouth, taking it, turning it over and over. WS mounted and turned his shamed back on Bristol, leaving Severn's mouth and returning to its source without, he soon saw in renewed shame and some fear, the books that had been the sole end of his coming hither.

IX

Aℕᴅ ʏᴇᴛ ᴛʜᴀᴛ ᴠɪsɪᴏɴ of the golden trull, the black nipples, the flash of breast-muscle, even the fierce small fists upraised, haunted his sleep and oft, in the dawn, lashed his seed to cold and queasy pumping out. In the daytime he lashed out another sort of seed, out of necessity, for if Plautus's *Menaechmi* did not exist (and it did not, not in this household: he searched Quedgeley's small library diligently when Quedgeley was out), why, then, it must be invented. Epidamnus? Epidamnum? He could not be sure of that town where the twins, separated in infancy, came together in a comedy of errors in later life, unknown to each other. As for the names of those twins, he knew that one was Menaechmus. But what was the other? Isosceles? Sophocles? Sosicles? It was many a year since he had seen a copy of that play. WS must be Plautus, not Ovid. That was a part of life's irony.

'A surprise,' said WS to his master. 'We shall be ready by Christmas. Ask nothing of their progress. Such foreknowledge must dull the pleasure to come.'

'Well then, if you will have it so.'

'It will be like My Lord Quedgeley's Men.'

'Aye. Aye.' He enjoyed the savour of that. '*Aye.*'

And so WS wrote:

> There had she not been long but she became
> A joyful mother of two goodly sons;
> And, which was strange, the one so like the other
> As could not be distinguished but by names . . .

Vile, vile – he saw that. It hid its rhymes ill. Could English, with its lack of tunes, bear this blankness? But, he remembered, these were meant to be lines translated from the Latin

61

by Matthew, who, being the eldest boy, should play the father of the twins, Ægeon; they must not glow with the burnishing of any expert hand. Blot no line: let it come, pumping out.

'And the twins,' he told his class, 'are called both Antipholus, though the one is of Syracuse and the other of Ephesus.' That would do, that name, those places would do. 'And the wife of Antipholus of Ephesus is called Adriana.'

'There is to be a woman, then?' growl-squeaked Arthur. 'Is our mother to play that part?'

So, then, for all their father's grunting against Banbury talk, they had not yet seen a play. 'Boys,' said WS, 'take the parts of women and ever have done, for it is not seemly to have women as actors.'

'But,' said deep-voiced Matthew, 'it is not seemly neither that there be love between boys and men, even in play.'

Something tingled within WS. He was pushed, impelled. He said: 'Oh, the ancients accounted that no sin, for the noble Athenians had their catamites, so they were called, that name being but a form of Ganymede, the name of Jove's cupbearer. For women they saw only as the bearers of their children, while for true pleasure of mind and body it was their own sex they sought. A sweet and lovely boy was all the desire of these bearded men. And so it is to this day with the Moors.' Father forgive him, he had strayed all from the path, but their eyes were bright as they listened. Then Arthur growled:

'Is not that against religion and the teachings of Our Lord Jesus Christ?' WS felt that Arthur and his brother Gilbert might belike make fast friends. He replied in his foolishness:

'There are some who say not so, and that He Himself did practise this sort of love with His beloved disciple John and that Judas was jealous and that no woman save one, His mother, is called to the Kingdom.' Then, in sudden fear of their blabbing this to their father as his own sentence, he added, 'It is false and wrong, yes yes, but there be some that have said that. And now turn we to our grammar-book.'

What was this? Why had he said that? Was it nerves struck

to jangling by frustration? Had his inner being revolted against women – white and nagging, black and punching? He threw himself into his re-making of Plautus:

> She is so hot because the meat is cold,
> The meat is cold because you come not home,
> You come not home because you have no stomach,
> You have no stomach, having broke your fast;
> But we, that know what 'tis to fast and pray,
> Are penitent for your default today.

Ah, these clumsy lines, each pinned to each by a device out of Seneca, not Plautus – were they not saying something of himself?

'Ralph,' said Miles, 'did not break his fast. His tooth aches very sorely.'

'So,' said WS, looking at Ralph, who, in a boy's dribble, thrust a new clove into his mouth, 'so now I know which one is which. It is Ralph that has the toothache.' Ralph whimpered. 'And what of the town toothdrawer?' asked WS.

'He is down with an ague. Our father is away today. He says he will take him into Cambridge tomorrow.'

'Cambridge? That is a long way.'

'*Our* Cambridge, fool,' said Miles, smiling. 'Gloucestershire Cambridge. Not the London Cambridge.'

WS said nothing in rebuke of that 'fool'. And he thought that Miles must surely know what he did when, that night, he came to his tutor's chamber and his bed. He shivered; it was frosty. He said:

'Ralph is crying with the toothache. I cannot sleep.' The twins shared a bed. WS listened; he could hear no crying. He said:

'Come in, then. Quickly.'

The next day Ralph had his tooth drawn. Miles came no more to the bed of WS, but he simpered in his presence like some girl, taunting and teasing. And then one day WS seized

63

him when he came, first and alone, to the lesson-room, but, God forgive him, it was not Miles he seized but Ralph. Ralph screamed worse than for the toothache. His father and mother ran in, both open parent mouths showing breakfast bread chewed but yet unswallowed. There were loud words; there were very nearly blows. WS, though, thrust out the quill-knife in defence. Mistress Quedgeley cried:

'He will murder us. I always knew this would happen. Villains picked up in outlandish parts.'

'Hold thy tongue, woman,' boomed her lord. 'For you, sirrah, out of this house instanter. Filth and corruption of the young and innocent. Out.'

'The lordly cider-swilling justice groweth all moral. Man, proud man. What now of Roman orgies?'

'Out, I say.'

'I want my money.'

'You will get no money. You will get instead my stick on your shoulders if you are not out at once.' The mother soothed Ralph, hugging him with a there there there, but Ralph was bright-eyed and attentive. He knew all, he knew what it was all about.

'There is a small matter of an indenture,' said WS, seeing distractedly the knife flash in the weak winter morning light.

'An you will have the law, you shall have it. Corruption of little ones. Vilest of sins. Out, or I will call the servants to throw you out.'

'I am going,' said WS. 'I feel defiled.' (A good phrase, he saw that: a field defiled.) And he went up to his chamber to roll his dirty shirts in a red neckerchief. Miles came up, running, panting. He said:

'We shall be sorry, then.' And he threw on to the unmade bed a few copper coins. 'These are mine. It is a gift.' Then he kissed WS clumsily on the cheek and ran off. More leisurely, WS left the house; the butler, leering, watched him go; a maid (Jenny or Janny or something) stood peering round a door, giggling. He would, by God, be avenged. He would, by Zeus

64

and Isis and all, prevail over these slaves. The roads rang with frost, but he was hot enough within. He had no horse, for it was on a nag bought by Quedgeley for his son Matthew's use that he had first ridden into Gloucestershire. Whither now? Not Bristol, not not Bristol. The western skies were a perpetual burning sunset of shame and humiliation. He took the long road north-east. A man so prone to sin had best go back to his family (soon, he counted the months, to be augmented), to dwell harmless in its bosom. He carried with him some little new experience of life, a memory of Berkeley Castle with its haunting martlets, and a few hundred lines of pseudo-Plautus.

> A heavier task could not have been imposed
> Than I to speak my griefs unspeakable;
> Yet, that the world may witness that my end
> Was wrought by nature, not by vile offence,
> I'll utter what my sorrow gives me leave.

But the utterance was to be much delayed.

At Whitminster he ate in a frowsy inn. He fell in there with a kinching coe whose trade was false dice. WS was mumbling bread into well-watered cullis when this rogue accosted him. This was no inn for gentlemen, and WS had the look of a gentleman; argal, in the kincher's syllogising, he must be one like himself – a smooth one, bowing, smiling, without scruple taking where he could. The cove was a thin man in a great black hat like a Brownist; he spake swift like a juggler. 'That broth,' he said, 'fills no bellies. In Gloucester we could eat mince-pies with flawns to follow. And what is your trade, sir? The trade goes badly by the look of things.'

'I am, I think, a poet. I was, though briefly, a schoolmaster.'

'Briefly, eh? Aye aye aye. Well, there is trades honest enow but there is little pickings there. I am called to Gloucester for the practice of a different trade, and profitable. Let us walk thither, but first let me say what I propose to you, who look a brisk enough fellow.'

65

Briefly, they were to enter an inn severally, WS first to call for ale like a gentleman, this kinching coe to follow with his rattlers. He was to invite play and WS was to go first and win, this other then saying, 'Nay, sir, go to, you are more than my match, yield place kindly to some other.' And then he would ruffle the innocent and reap.

They walked under a frosty sun, and, as they passed Quedgeley, WS spat. The other talked of his craft, whose mysteries would fill a book, what with the barred cater-treys and the barred cinque-deuces, the bristle dice, the contraries, the graviers, demies and fullams. And he told of other rogueries a man might meet in a fair town – the dummerers, who sought alms for pretending muteness, and the priggers of prancers, or horse-thieves. Then, there were abrams, swadders, jarkmen, dells, morts, uprightmen, glimmer-women. It was a new world, and WS felt himself already committed to it; was he not a cheat, a whoremaster, a corrupter of boys? But he felt also fear of what other things might be within him. He did the bidding of this kincher in Gloucester, at the We Three, which had an inn-sign of two fools, and took silver on his way. He lodged cheaply at another inn and next morning set off for home, his heart beating faster.

But he delayed at Evesham, seeing in that riverside inn where he had once dreamed of one marriage and had another announced to him a cry of players in the inn-yard. He saw with a new eye, he that had these lines of pseudo-Plautus in his traps. The players performed unhandily, with their cart at one end and their hillock of boxes up which they stumbled to make their entrances. Their audience was small (it was a cold, though bright, afternoon) and given to jeering. Whose men these players were he knew not, some petty lordling's belike or even, with counterfeit liveries, masterless men. They were out of what he knew to be the fashion; it was some morality they did of Prudence and Patience and Temperance, all in vile rhymes, and their play took life only when the Vice and his zany tumbled on. These were what the beholders

66

loved, and when Vice was sent packing to Hellmouth, leering, winking, unrepentant, they roared their displeasure and hurled flints they picked up from the yard. But when Vice and zany rose from the dead, as this were some Easter mummers' play, and rattled their boxes for money, the crowd gave a few small coins, they that had them, and WS himself, lordly kincher's accomplice, contributed a whole halfpenny.

He lodged there that night, and when he left Evesham next morning (wet and windy, his cloak well about him), for some reason plays and players were in his mind. The Inns of Court, he thought, and the courts of inns; was there not perhaps some decent middle way, where poesy might be shouted at the world like truth itself? And then he saw that this was not a gentlemanly thought and abandoned it. Yet it was to blank verse his feet tramped, tired and tender now, into Warwickshire, beating out the feet of tragic speeches:

> And for that sin I did I am cast off,
> Embracing now my hell with stoic soul.

Near Temple Grafton a devil-raven on a bare elm-branch croaked: 'Anne Anne Anne Anne.' Then it flew before him on his Stratford way, screeching 'Anne Anne Anne Anne' like a harbinger.

X

Railings, tears, embraces, eventually appetite: so much for
big-bellied Anne. Why am I back? I am back because I was
lonely for my wife and child, for my father and mother and
sister and little brothers. Though none could call Gilbert little;
a man now, he had shot up to slouching boniness, growling
about God; when he fell in his falling-sickness the house
rumbled and the pewter sang. Richard, still a limping boy,
yet had settled into his face a mature and foxy look. Susanna
had grown. For the rest, things were much as they had been
(after all, it had not been many months); Stratford was
Stratford yet. His father's fortunes had not mended; garments
were patched; the thatch of the roof was brown, burnt, thin,
rustling at night (an adder's nest?).

'Well,' said his father, 'thou art home in a good time, for
Master Rogers was but two days agone saying about his need
of a clerk and how such as thyself would fit to perfection.'

Henry Rogers, the Town Clerk, was a decent tooth-sucking
man who smelt musty and, indeed, had a relish for death and
dust. Well, that was right, for was not the law a raw head and
bloody bones haunting the living? A man could oft, through
the law's mediacy, rule stronger from the grave than in life.
Did not the rule of, say, William the Conqueror grow more
hard and firm on them year after year? William the Non-
Conqueror, nay William the Conquered, saw sourly again a
fresh rearrangement of his life. And so to learning the high
terms and rites of the law's creaking workings, the quiddits
and quillets, statutes, recognizances, double vouchers,
conveyances. It was putting calfskins to another use, for
were not parchments made of calfskins?

'Amen amen amen,' said WS.

68

'Feet of fines,' tooth-sucked Master Rogers. 'He to whom the land is to be conveyed must sue the holder for wrongful keeping of him out of possession. It is a legal fiction, that is what it is called.' His chambers smelt of dead and lively law, ruling from the mad and reasonable world of the dead. 'Then the defendant acknowledgeth the plaintiff's right. Then this compromise is to be entered into court records and all set out in the threefold indenture, at the foot of the fine.'

'But what is this fine?'

'A fine is the compromise of a collusive suit as a mode of conveyance, all ordinary modes being unsuitable. It is part of our history, it is from Richard the First onwards.'

'Ah, words. It is all words.'

'This realm is ruled by words.' WS seemed suddenly to see the light. Words, pretences, fictions. They ruled. 'You must learn the French language,' said Master Rogers. He gave one vigorous tooth-suck and turned to his loaded shelves. So there was the Conqueror again. 'Here is a merry and bawdy book,' he leered at WS. 'It is Rabelais, a tale of giants. We will read it together each day after dinner.'

Oh, the grey days of winter, Anne growing daily greater and greater, that extra mouth to be fed soon to blare forth its greeting to the dirty world. 'To be born,' sucked Master Rogers cheerfully, 'is to start to die. You are condemning a soul to death.'

Gargantua, after this disgusting stuff of arse-wiping with a live goose's neck, is sent to a great sophister-doctor called Tubal Holofernes. WS was learning no French; Master Rogers sat with the book, reading it, roaring, out in English. ' "Afterwards he got an old man with a cough to teach him, whose name was Maître Jobelin Bridé, that is, the fool with the muzzle." But we must skip all this and come to more bawdry. This is all for your education, young man.'

Christmas over, Anne grown large to prodigy almost, WS settling to the bowing, smiling, hand-rubbing effigy of small law clerk, kind husband, lullaying Susanna on his knee of firelit evenings. January limping along, each dull day a candlemas in the dark chambers, and then, at true Candlemas, Gilbert came to call him from his conveyances. Master Rogers was gone for a long costive séance in the privy, belike with a live goose. It was a stormy morning, the rain beating without as if it were mad, dripping (spies to the great battalions) from the ceiling and, jump on Gilbert's entering, blotting the name WILSON that WS had just engrossed. He knew what it was, Anne's pains being on her that morning ere he had left; he rose and reached for his cloak, nodding, before Gilbert could speak. Then Gilbert said, rumbling:

'They are come, aye, both. From their mother's belly, as it might be. God hath sent them for a sign in Israel.' He stood there in his kersey cloak, a rain-pool forming round his boots, drip after drip dropping stately from his nose-end.

'*Both? Them?*'

'Aye, of each kind one. A girl and a boy.'

'*Two? Twins?*' That word had meant only bitterness. And then, 'A boy? A son? I have a son?' A son; he had begotten a son, a man-child. He looked down at his parchment, at that name the rain had smeared.

'And now,' said Gilbert, 'th'art as Noah in all this flood-water with three childer.'

'Sons,' smiled WS. 'Noah had all sons.' He smiled (still, that fact of twins rankled, as though God and Nature knew, noted, minded, cared, thrust back to stain joy, a son.)

'That I know,' said grave Gilbert. 'There was Sem and Ham and eke Japhet, aye. That is a S and a H' (he finger-scrawled them in the dust of Master Rogers's table) 'and there is the other letter I know not.' (He meant it was I or HI or J.) 'And thou hast a S.'

WS marked his brother as he were an oracle. Susanna, yes, his purity, pharos in lust's sea. And his son should be Ham, nay Hamnet. And there was himself, WS, but some few months a poor Holofernes, like that schoolmaster in Rabelais's bawdy book, and his second daughter should be Judith.

'Oh,' said WS. 'The mother. Anne. My wife. How does she?'

'Well. Very well. She shouted and cried much.'

'So, then.' WS smiled ruefully. 'All is as it is always. Let us go see mother and twins.' They wrapped their cloaks closely about them. 'Our respects and our homage.' They sailed out into the flood . . .

And for ourselves (this first bottle is showing its bottom), it is time we loosed our pigeon to seek the settled dry land of a career that ended in— We shall see what it ended in. He has done all he can in Stratford, or nearly all, and the horns wind and bells ring for him, the sails belly in the land-breeze. We have but to open a door that any key will fit.

Let us say midsummer, '87. There rode into Stratford, each actor on his ass, the Queen's Men. It was a dry and dusty summer, dry as a bleached bone on a bone-white beach. What were these coming, this laughing dozen, boasting in the inn that they were Grooms of the Chamber, all, throwing carelessly around the name Tilney and eke Walsingham? Rain, what was wanted was rain; they were not bringing that. As God had once flooded the earth for man's sins, might He not now be proposing to cast them into an oven? Sin, sin, sin. It had been hammered at them from last Sunday's pulpit. And who was the worst sinner among them? But here was a man jigging about with a flat face, squashed nose, squint, in russet suit and cap with buttons, short boots strapped at the ankle rustic-wise, leather money-bag at's waist, squealing and thudding, in a kind of weak gnat-music, on pipe and tabor. Behind him there waddled another, younger, his zany, and he had a board on which was engrossed THE SEVEN DEADLY SINS.

That is Dick Tarleton, those that knew said. Hast not heard of Dick Tarleton? And that with him is Gemp or Camp or Kempe or suchlike, trill-lillies jinging round's calves. This Tarleton was once close to Her Majesty but (whisper it) he hath incurred her displeasure with some impudent mock about

Sir Walter Ralegh and the Earl of Leicester. His eyes are not merry, look, though his tongue quip never so.

Ho there, all, give ear to your betters. There is one blats like a flayed pudding and, by Godspod, I shall be after him with my little whip. Hark, all, your doubtful worships are royally bidden to a feast of wrongdoing (oh, you will like that well enough for all your long faces) and thereto will be added for good measure a good measure, nay a treasure of good measures, viddy or skiddy lissit a jig, aye, a jig. Here is your only jigmaker. And it will be tomorrow, you whoreson scurvyrumps, you cheesefoots, you heavenhigh stinkards and cackards.

They pranced, jeering and calling, against the drop-curtain of a fiery sunset, Jehovah's terrible wrath. Rain, when would the rain come? THE SEVEN DEADLY SINS. A jig to follow. There was song and light in the inn, the trolling of a ditty of love over the ale-pots:

> And so, my dearest heart,
>   Though yet I know
> That we must part, must part,
>   Say thou not so . . .

'The heat,' said WS, naked at the open window. Susanna now slept in Joan's chamber, as once before that other Anne. But the twins were cradled here, sleeping now. And Anne too, slender, carrying no further child, sat naked as her husband. The night air crackled with a sense of something to come – the moon to draw nearer the earth, Antichrist to caper over the cobbles. Well, thought WS, as for sin it is long since I sinned; they can make no scapegoat of me. He heard in the distance other, not singing, voices. Perhaps it was a company gone to pray aloud at the edges of the fields, asking God to flush green the dry brown meadows.

> Farewell, farewell, my blessing,
>   Too dear thou art

For any man's possessing;
And so we part . . .

He looked at his wife's slim moist back, its comely tapering
to the waist from the fair wide shoulders. Hearing that song, he
felt a regret he could not name nor place. She was reading a
small book, holding it close to her eyes; she was growing near-
sighted. He looked over her shoulder at the tight-knitted print.
'So then he did fare forth and wander many a daie till that a
fairer face than hers should greete his eyes, yet fairer face
sawe he notte and in his hearte he then knewe that none other
mighte haue all his loue . . .' Some little tale of venery, then,
delicate and meet for a woman. In pity he bent to kiss her bare
shoulder. She was both surprised and ready. She was speedy to
put down her book. Body against moist body kissed. I am doing
right, thought WS; here is no sin. Arms snaked and stroked.
    What was this noise outside in the street? It had come
nearer. It was no noise of praying but of jeering. The naked
man and woman on the bed looked up, he more distracted
than she from work that had not yet become urgent. There
were blows and buffets along with the jeers; dogs barked;
Hamnet and Judith grew restive in their sleep; Gilbert in
the next room murmured; WS heard his father cough. WS
got up from the bed, his rod sinking, and went to the window
to see. He saw, under the midsummer moon, a mob of
Stratford citizens driving a whimpering old woman before
them, Madge Bowyer, cat-queen, cartomancer. Seven deadly
sins. Black. Gold. What had that been?
    'Witch! Bring the rain back!'
    'Unholy spells, and her cats be devils!'
    'Strip her to her skin!'
    'Lash the evil out!'
Some youngsters were beating her with sticks; her gown was
torn, brown old dried flesh peering in the moonlight; she wept,
she panted as she would die, trying to run from her tormentors;
she tripped and fell; they laughed, whipping her up with

73

birch-boughs. It was like a deadly parody of Tarleton and the prancing players.

'On thy feet, witch! Out of town with her!'

Anne came from soothing the twins, both of whom had awakened crying. 'What is it? Let me see.' She brought her heavy breasts to the sill. She saw. 'Oh,' she said, 'they are killing her.' One young man carried a torch; he waved it about old Madge till she screamed in fear; her rags caught alight and she beat and beat the grinning flame out, yelling, then breathless, ready to drop. 'Now,' said Anne, panting. 'Now, at the window.' WS looked at her, sick, incredulous. 'Now, now, oh, quickly!' He shrank away from her, into the room's shadows.

'No!' Here was the witch, here. The driving mob passed on raggedly, beating, jeering.

'Is it the players?' called his father from the corridor.

'Yes, yes, the players,' WS replied.

The voices were more distant:

'She hath the Seven Deadly Sins! Beat her to church to pray!'

'How, devils in church? Burn her!'

WS trembled, picking up his clothes from the chair where he had laid them. She was still at the window, moaning. 'The end,' he said, retching the words out, 'that must be the end.' She came staggering towards him in her nakedness. He cringed from the threat of her touching him. He dressed in a hopping fumbling dance, like a dressing Tarleton, comic, the jig after the bloody play.

At the street's end the mob was quietening, shrinking away from what it, a thing, had done and tried to do, murmuring, breaking up into family pairs, companies of three. Some graver men and women had come out, some wrapped in their night-gowns. WS saw that it was Alderman Perkes, a bulky man, that had lifted Madge Bowyer. Her slack arms were swinging; her head lolled, tongue out, the moon showing blood on her mouth. And now the beadle in his shirt had appeared, driving the mob home with his staff of office. WS foresaw that house of hers, dock and nettle high around it in summer, forlorn at last in winter, the swinging door fallen from its hinges, the cats having taken to the fields to eat shrews, the mice in possession till the last of the mildewed bread should be gone, the flour-bin emptied. If not now, then next time.

He returned home calm enough to find Anne sleeping. Well then, tomorrow. Tomorrow to take those few hundred lines of pseudo-Plautus to the Queen's Players, yawning in their inn, crapulous after their merry night but perhaps the less prone not to listen to the decently fashioned (though not in any fire) blank verse. He could not delay his growing up much longer, three-and-twenty, father of three. They might say no, they might laugh at him: canst act, lad? Wouldst be an actor, laddie? Aye, he might reply, the time is come for acting, no longer lying passive to wait on destiny to deal. He sat, looking out on the street now empty of people but washed all in a queenly dispensation of silver; he was sure as though there were a letter in his breast that tomorrow or the next day he would be off with the Queen's Men. From a queen to a goddess, though first the capering, the self-abasement, the crawling through a dark tunnel of shame to that dark underworld where snakes coiled, heroes lay, a single goddess presided. Well, was not fate once more dealing, busy behind his back, so sure he was? The play we act in is still busily being written in that dark room behind, the final couplet not yet known even to the cloaked and anonymous writer.

Anne had sprawled her bare limbs all over the bed; she slept heavily. WS loosened his clothes and prepared for sleep in the chair by the window. Sinking gently to that simulacrum in his skull of the dark world that lay beyond, out, he became Endymion.

The moon awaits your sleeping. Fear to be
kissed.

Tepid her light unblenching but will twist
Your features to strange shape. Though blind,
   those beams
Get in the mind's slime monsters for dreams.

He did not fear. He had no fear at all.

1592–1599

I

'THERE THEY GO.' said Henslowe, wrinkling his face (though not with sweetness) to an applejohn's. Kemp was still panting from his jig; he looked benignly out at the prentices brawling their way from the Rose. Perhaps they were off to tell their friends how good Kemp's jig was, and the play that preceded it – *A Knack to Know a Knave* – not too bad (though inferior to the jig, naturally) neither. WS nodded grimly at Kemp's crass back. A self-centred man; a man who would not learn lines; a man who would sooner or later have to go. Not, he hastened to tell himself, that he really cared. It was glove-making all over again, a craft only. Not, perhaps, so mean a craft but still a matter of fitting, taking orders – five feet instead of five fingers. And certainly a more corrupting craft.

'The Knight Marshal's Men,' said Alleyn. 'They should not have done it.'

'They are naught,' said Kemp happily. 'They are but a sort of lawful ruffians.'

'A sort of lawful ruffians that will have us closed down,' said Henslowe gloomily. He knew all about it; he could foresee how one thing led to another; he was a business-man. That morning the Knight Marshal's Men had arrested a felt-maker's servant and thrown him into the Marshalsea. He had done, so far as one could tell, very little. He had but made a face at these swaggerers: a bilious tongue thrust out, eyes squinnying, the momentary gibber of an ape; he had break-fasted too well on ale. And then they had leaped upon him, beating him with merry cries – a thud here and a crack there – and dragged him off. Breaking the Queen's Peace or some such thing. Causing a riot. And now he was in the Marshalsea.

'This is a lawful place of assembly,' said Henslowe. 'And now they can march off in a body. Hark.'

There were mock sergeant yells from without. Into line! Take that man's name! March! It sounded a ragged procession. They had drunk their fill not only of *A Knack to Know a Knave* and Kemp's jig but also of the ale the Rose sold. And, thought WS, was not the playhouse for the peaceful quelling of the riotous spirits that haunt man's blood, not for their further inflaming? So Aristotle had seemed to say. This, then, was not in the service of any true art, this inn where none could spend the night. He himself had had no hand in the making of *A Knack to Know a Knave*; he had said his few ridiculous lines (badly, he knew, for he could put no conviction into them) and gone off. But what of *Harry the Sixth*, which made his auditors shout against France? Well, France was the enemy as much as Spain. And what of *Titus Andronicus*, making men's throats gargle with blood, eyes gloating over rape on a man's corpse, mutilation, the flesh of boys served in a coffin of ground bones baked? Gratuitous, gratuitous. Well, no, the fashion (as with gloves). Out-kydding Kyd, so to say. 'I will go see,' he said now (gratuitous, gratuitous). 'Perhaps it will come to nothing.' He had promised money home. A trade was a trade.

'Aye,' said Heminges, 'we will both go.' He was a heavy man like a grocer, and he lowered himself from the apron to the yard by sitting on its edge and dropping his short legs to ground-level. WS, eight years junior, jumped. The money in his purse jangled. No longer a boy, for he had had his twenty-eighth birthday some six weeks past, he was still light and slim and quick. They walked through the yard to the gate, Heminges panting. It was a dry June day, the eleventh of a dry month, perhaps plague-weather.

When they saw the riot outside the Marshalsea they did not wish to get too near. WS took it all in – the impartial river with its swans, the indifferent sun, and, before the grey bricks of the prison, a prentice mob brawling, bawling, fist-shaking, picking up stones and loose gravel to hurl. Let him out! Release the prisoner! We want the prisoner! He nodded in something like satisfaction. This was the people, the plebs, the commons. They were not after justice but riot for riot's sake. He was confirmed in his view. True, the prentices were young, but they had been joined by grinning bravos of maturer years, stone-throwing, though many not knowing what this was all about. Let him out, whoever he is! It is not right that men be put into jail! How, a small matter of rape or theft or murder? Look you, we did fight King John for this, which is the rights of the subjects. You may not have his corpus. Let him out and we, if need be, will string him up. WS nodded again, noting the raw angry faces.

'Here be the Marshal's Men,' panted Heminges, sweating under the sun. And there indeed they were, striding burly from the prison with their truncheons and cudgels; one or two drew daggers, tongues of silver in the fierce light. Their swords were sheathed. What, waste our cutting edges on this filth? At them now, thudding, cracking skulls. 'We had best go back,' said Heminges, fearful when he saw blood. Some prentices, their lout-faces already turning to big yelling babby-mouths, tried to get away; one or two had gone down, clawing at the legs that trampled on them. A fat waddling boy ran about, holding up a hand that fountained red, howling, for a finger had got cut off. The mob growled. It advanced. There were not many of the Marshal's Men. Even though they started to draw now it was availing them little. Boys skipped away from the slashing (WS admired, coldly, the brightness of the swords; this was perfect weather for the showing of steel). Long laths struck at sword-arms. In a mad clownish tumble Marshal's Men went down with prentices, thin young legs and thick older ones kicking the air. One defender, swordless now, was dragged to the crowd's periphery; he cried himself, like any prentice, as a shag-bearded ruffian raised a stone to break his skull and send his brains spewing. Kites wheeled overhead. Then was to be

81

heard the clop of horses. It was the Mayor's men coming. 'We had best go back,' said WS. For these riders would trample everyone down, even the innocent watchers. But could any watcher be really innocent? We are all in love with violence and hate, he thought hopelessly. Only himself, perhaps, had seen all this truly from without – a scene from a story, a spectacle in red and silver, marking how sweat and blood will mingle, how a gash on one cheek was in the form of an L, how one man's points had been slashed and the golden hair of his rump disclosed to further gilding from the sun. 'Here is the Lord Mayor himself.' An angry man in the robes of his office, the indignation of a city disturbed. The horses shook petulant heads, steaming; one neighed at the smell of blood; hoofs stumbled, recovered.

There was another acrid smell, that of burning bracken blown on a dry wind, as they walked back to the safety of the Rose. My Lord Strange's Men would be out of work this summer, nothing more certain. Midsummer Eve was approaching, a time of madness, hallowed, Knight Marshal injustice or not, to the rioting of prentices. The Council would close the theatres down. Perhaps till Michaelmas. WS shrugged his shoulders. This was a less sure trade than the glover's. If fear of disorders did not close the theatres, then plague would. If the weather did not break, the sewers and foul alleys flush with rain, then plague would leer with broken teeth and strike. An uncertain life, but all life was uncertain. There he had been, with the Queen's Men, till poor Tarleton had jigged into his grave. And soon, perhaps, a quarrel with Alleyn or a harsh word of contempt to Henslowe with his eternal cash-book or Kemp saying that he would not learn a speech for any man, had he not always done all extempore and who had ever complained save the poets? But what were poets? Aye, soon he might be out of this company, tame word-boy to a loudmouth who called for more Tamburlaine fustian and the man who would soon be Alleyn's step-father-in-law, the brothel-keeper who would brood over a lost farthing.

He was brooding now when WS and Heminges found him, peering at his accounts in the dark and airless room at the back of the Rose. It was an old vellum book, foxed, that had been thrifty Henslowe's brother's; Henslowe had turned it upside down to make a new clean first page. He was back to this page now, brooding. WS saw: JESUS; 1592. Oh, very pious, this pawnbroker and brothel-keeper. WS told him what he and Heminges had seen.

'Well,' said Henslowe, 'nothing could be more certain. The Rose shut for the summer, and what do I do then?'

'What do the Men do?' said Heminges.

'You can take your plays into the country. I must bide here and wait till better times come with the autumn. See what expense I have been put to this year, what with the making new of the Rose, a new thatch and the stage painted—' He mumbled on. 'One hundred pound, all told.'

'Turn but a few pages,' said WS quietly. 'To that part that begins with the holy words "In the Name of God".' Henslowe gave him a sharp look. 'Talbot has done well enough for you,' said WS.

'Talbot? Aye, Talbot. *Harry the Sixth*, that is,' said Henslowe, sighing. 'Well, there is no man like Ned, nor ever has been, Roscius nor anybody. Aye, Talbot brought them in.'

'It was as much my Talbot as Ned Alleyn's that acted him.'

'We shall see,' said Henslowe, appraising WS (the forehead's height? his chances of longevity? the strength of his writing fingers?). 'We shall see all, with Almighty God's help.' Such as how the bawdy-houses went when the town emptied for high summer. A busy man, he watched behind his eyes a holy trinity of figures dance; pounds, shillings and pence.

'Greene is naught, though,' said Heminges.

'Less than naught,' said Henslowe. 'Or soon will be.'

ROBERT GREENE was in the mind of WS as they rode out of town. They were taking their plays north in this continuing heat; the Court would soon follow, on progress. Behind the actors on their horses their cart trundled, laden with properties. The playhouses shut till Michaelmas (Henslowe had foreseen it all), the rats darting through the filthy detritus of a close narrow city, the plague announced in tender swelling buboes. They were well out of it, riding to northern country towns to make the hayseeds gape. Money must still be earned. Greene, decayed master of arts, master of decayed kidneys, must stay in London to earn it. WS imagined his late rising, cursing in crapula, from a bed soiled with his body's incontinence. Cutting Ball, the thief and killer that loved him, would be ready to fill a cup sour with last night's dregs from the Rhenish bottle, if the Rhenish had not all gone; if it had, then the pen must race at once, over a growling belly, through the first pages of some new coney-catching pamphlet, these to be hurried to the printer as an earnest of the whole, Ball the messenger to translate at once the meagre advance into wine. In the corner, surrounded by filthy clouts, Greene's blowsy mistress, Ball's sister, would nurse the yelling bastard brat Fortunatus. A foul life, and WS was surprised at the whiff of envy that arose each time he caught an image of the wrecked poet and scholar, bloated with drink and disease but still rufously handsome. Why there should be even a scruple of envy he did not know. Because Greene, having no cheesy Puritan qualms, went one way or the other, embracing his fortune with a ready hug? Because, to fall, a man must have a height to fall from (master of arts, gentleman)? Because, most obscurely, Greene had failed as a playwright because he was truly a poet? His work was clogged with poetry: poetry held up action, drove all differentiation from the characters: all mouths became lyric bird-beaks. WS admired more than he would say that failed *Friar Bacon and Friar Bungay*; there was poetry in it; the silliness of Margaret of Fressingfield, a mere dairymaid, purling a lyric stream about Paris and Œnone – was not this somehow transcended in a beauty higher than any one could catch in a truer mirror of life? Greene was no

84

Marlowe, but he was closer to Marlowe than he, WS, would ever be.

'88. He thought back to that year. Prentice acting with the Queen's Men, a patched play, and then Tarleton's death, the company's confusion, himself following Kemp's waddle to Lord Strange's Men. A lost Armada, the news of victory beacons, all men Queen's Men. But, more than anything, *Faustus*. A play, yes, a mere play, but the smell of truth in it – not the truth of the present feel of his horse's hot flanks, the sweat running down his nose, Kemp's droning song, but the bigger truth that lay behind this painted curtain. Greene embraced ruin and (it would come soon) a pauper's death; Marlowe would embrace hell itself, if hell were all (and he seemed to believe it was all) that the curtain hid. If *Tamburlaine* had been one big empty boastful shout, yet *Faustus* was a true voice crying for damnation as though damnation were a mother. 'My dam, damnation . . .' No, not that. No mean quibbles in Marlowe. WS shuddered. He had been once, along with Marlowe, to a meeting of the School of Night. Sir Walter had drunk smoke and been reasonable (may not the mathematics be a way to God as sure as prayer? And yet we will end this night on our knees); Marlowe had raged against Christ as a charlatan saviour and mocked at the soul's existence, daring God out of His heaven. Well, both Greene and Marlowe called on a dark goddess and expected some answer. They had no doubts. They marched, all or nothing, towards an all-consuming vision. That was true nobility of soul, despite the filthy lodgings of Greene, the bloodshot staring eyes of Marlowe.

And he, what did he, WS, desire? To be a gentleman, that, no more. A craftsman's son, he must proceed through the mastery of a craft towards the house, the arms of a gentleman. It was towards the slow amassing of money that he rode through the hot summer.

He left behind a manner of a necropolis. The city baked in its corruption; flies crawled over the sleeping lips of a child;

the rats twitched their whiskers at an old dead woman (shrunk to five stone) that lay among lice in a heap of rancid rags; the bells tolled all day for the plague-stricken; cold ale tasted as warm as a posset; the flesher shooed flies off with both hands before chopping his stinking beef; heaps of shit festered and heaved in the heat; tattered villains broke into houses where man, woman, child lay panting and calling feebly for water and, mocking their distress, stole what they had a mind to; the city grew a head, glowing over limbs of towers and houses in the rat-scurrying night, and its face was drawn, its eyes sunken, it vomited foul living matter down to ooze over the cobbles, in its delirium it cried *Jesus Jesus*.

IN cooler autumn, with news of the plague abating, WS rode back to London to write a play. This long tale of the Wars of the Roses must be brought to its triumphant Tudor close. The rest of the company could do well without him, proposing a slow return from Northampton through Bedford, Hertford, St Albans. They might not, they thought, be back at the Rose until December, the provincial takings being so good. Alleyn, though, said he would be in London in October; he reminded all, winking, that he was to marry Joan Woodward. Well, thought WS, there was one way to transmute player to gentleman: marry the step-daughter of a money-lover like Henslowe. For himself, it was all too late; he had done his marrying long ago.

He met Henslowe crossing London Bridge, account-book under his arm. 'Greene is dead,' announced Henslowe, as a butler might announce dinner to be on the table. 'I was all too late to give of any last help, poor soul. Mistress Isam, his land-lady, crowned him with bays, and he lying there in her husband's shirt. They say his lice knew when the end was coming, for they all crawled off his poor stinking body. Ah well, it is a lesson and an example. These men Burby and Wright have seized all his writings to be printed, and Chettle is in on this too.'

'Chettle I know. He bows much.'

'Well, Chettle is putting some of his writings together in a book. He speaks out against players. I could find no play anywhere in his lodgings.'

'So you went to his lodgings?'

'As I said. But I was all too late to help. Four shillings for his winding-sheet and six and fourpence for his Bedlam burial. Poor lost soul, howling in hell now, belike for penny Malmsey. They say his wife came forward with money, though he had long abandoned her for his drab that gave him this bastard. God save us all from a like end.'

'Amen.'

And then the dead Greene rudely handed WS a mirror. In his lodgings one day, September growing to gold, mist on the river, St Olave's bell clanging for the dead, he sat down to read this posthumous pamphlet of Greene's: *A Groatsworth of Wit Bought with a Million of Repentance.* Here was some stuff cursing Marlowe as an atheist; the great Greene had turned traitor to his goddess at the last, breast-beating, going *peccavi* in fear of hell-fire. But there was the sin of envy here before the whinings to a merciful God. He resented the players; they had grown rich on his plays (but they had not, as WS well knew) and now in this burning plague-tolling empty London they left him to die penniless. WS, aghast, saw one player above all singled out: '. . . Upstart crow, beautified with our feathers . . . Tiger's heart wrapped in a player's hide . . .' (So Greene had remembered that line from *Harry the Sixth*) '. . . supposes he is as well able to bombast out a blank verse as the best of you . . . absolute *Johannes Factotum* . . . in his own conceit the only Shake-scene in a country . . .'

WS threw down the libel on his bed. He looked out of his window, seeing nothing of the rising mist, the towers, the river. A poet had died with that curse on his lips. Upstart tiger's shake-scene. But wherein had he truly offended? By performing as well in his new craft as in his old? *Johannes Factotum.* Jack Do-all. He had pretended to nothing except the

87

fitting of words like gloves to a story, but because of him a poet had died in bitterness.

And yet, cooling as the day warmed, he felt a strange shameful pride. His name, though deformed and mocked, was there in a book to be read by all London. He was noticed; a dying poet had singled him out for his spleen, the rage of the pain of his rotting kidneys and the humiliation of his dead ambitions. But (he picked up the book, flicking through the pages to read again) there were those words that stung: 'An upstart crow, beautified with our feathers.' The glover from Stratford who had been to neither university, presuming to the learning of a master of arts. 'Let these apes imitate your past excellence . . .' Was it Nashe he addressed, or Lodge – other failed playwrights who could read Greek? An ape. A crow. A tiger. He smiled coldly. A strange phantasma, indeed. A new sort of cockatrice. Well, he forgave Greene, but he would not forgive this Wright the printer, nor the hack Chettle who had put the poor angry book together.

He looked sourly down on the manuscript play he was working on. Limping Richard and the cool Anne (a fire within) whom he courted. Marlowe's Machiavel but none of his poetry. Oh, he foreknew, they would drink it down and chew the very cup. Down with deformed Gloucester; God save the Tudor line. But he would show dead Greene (he seemed to grin up from below ground, a corpse's sneer) that he was something other than an ape, crow, tiger. Something other, too, than a play-botcher, an exciter of groundlings, a poor stumbling actor. The time was come to show he was a poet.

LORD STRANGE's MEN were back in London for Christmas. Drink, toasts, maudlin clawings. By God, we missed thee, Ned. As for Alleyn, he smirked and pawed his new wife all over. Aye, we open then before the old year shall have ended. With *Muly Mulocco*. Well, it is a fair play for opening. And then Hieronimo and the Jew and Titus. *Friar Bacon?* Poor Robin

Greene. In memoriam, you might say. This new one of Kit's promises fair. *The Massacre at Paris*. They will take multitudinous bellyfuls of Machiavel. And who is or was this Machiavel? An Italian devil, that is called also Niccolo, or Old Nick. And there is Shake-scene reading all gravely with never a cup of sack before him. How dost thou, Johnny Fuckscrotum? Caw caw caw. What is this book he is agape at? Take it from him, Ned. Read us somewhat out therefrom to make us merry. How, will his little holiness have all up? He is not used to good Protestant ale, this Pope of ours. Read thou then, Neddy. Well, it is of Will here and it is called *Kindhart's Dream*. Oh, that we know. It is ancient fishy stuff. It is Chattle, Chettle I would say, with his Apostle or Epistle to the Gentlemen Readers. Nay, Will, an thou wouldst have it back thou must chase me for it. Whoop, round the table. La la la. Hold him then, lads, for all must hear. Hem hem. Moyshelf have sheen his (what's this word?) demeanour no less civil than he excellent in the quality he professes. Nay, let us verse it. Lift me to yon table-top.

> Besides, divers of worship have reported
> His uprightness of dealing, which doth argue
> His honesty, and his facetious grace
> In writing that approves his –

Well, then, amends is made. Will is no atheist, he saith here, and he is worry that he let dead Robin ever cry that out from his death-bed. Nay, it was never said that it was Will that was Godless; it was Kit that was the Godless one, and still is, God help us. They say he is having an atheist's Christmas, with a dog in the manger. No, it is Will that is the crow with the tiger's heart and the bombast. Look at him, sitting sober there, as quiet a man as ever fumbled at points. Kiss him, Joan, mount him, ride him. And so we give all a merry Christmas.

IT was a hard January, smoky breath steaming up from the

groundlings. These stamped and danced for warmth, beating their arms crosswise, blowing their nails. Still, they came to the Rose. Alleyn, as Guise in *The Massacre at Paris*, had to rant loud to be heard above the coughing:

> Now Guise begins those deep engendered thoughts
> To burst abroad those never dying flames,
> Which cannot be extinguished but by blood.

But they liked it, the out-upon-religion, the whisper of hell, the torture, the treachery, the poison, the bursting ox-blood bladders. Yet it was not to this but to *Harry the Sixth* that a party was come, towards January's end, to fill the Lord's room, masked, holding pomanders to their nostrils (the plague was coming back, despite the cold), calling for a fire, for wine. Henslowe rushed about as he were scalded. But who is it? There are two noblemen with a man in black and a pair of pages. I can see no livery. What of their barge? They were rowed hither by common watermen.

The play went not too well. The players were nervous, distracted by the coughs and laughter and talk that came from behind the closed curtains of the Lord's room. Kemp tripped over in the final jig. Rewarded by roars, he determined to keep in that trip in the future: much of a clown's best business came by chance. And then, after the prayer for the Queen, Henslowe came awe-struck up to WS in the tiring-house. He said:

'You are sent for. They are asking for this Master Shake-scene.'

'Who are asking? If it is to make sport—'

'Sport or no, you are sent for.' WS shrugged, put down the pasty he had been chewing (some little trouble with a back-tooth), brushed crumbs from his doublet, and went. The groundlings had gone fast, no weather for dawdling. But, from the Lord's box, there came the sound of clinking and laughter. They liked to sit on with their fire and wine. He knocked at the door, he was bidden jovially to enter. Two young men, in warm doublets and fine ruffs, silver and the flash of jewels about them, sat at their ease in the small close room, their brows beaded from the fire. They wore no masks now; WS recognised the elder at once.

'My lord—'

'None of that, not today. I am Master RD and this is Master HW or, putting his family first as he is told he must, Master WH.' And Robert Devereux smiled a loose tipsy smile. 'A glass of wine for Master Shake-scene.' Master HW or WH said:

'You are welcome hither.' He was young, hardly older than the two bobbed pages who, unawed, played a game of treading on each other's toes and giggling. Eighteen? Nineteen? He had a red pouting mouth and very white skin; his golden beard was sparse. There was something in his eyes that WS did not like – a slyness, an unwillingness to look boldly. But he was beautiful enough, there was no doubt of his beauty.

'If it please you, my lords,' said WS, 'I will not drink now. I have but a poor stomach for drink.'

'A good stomach for blood and horror, though,' said Essex.

'It was not this present play but that other that pricked curiosity as to what manner of man this Shake-scene might be.' And the eyes of Southampton still would not meet those of WS fully, darting from point to point as though they followed a fly's flight. 'That play wherein all happens that the most fevered dream of horror could make happen. The one with the black Machiavel and the boys baked in a pie.'

'*Titus Andronicus*,' said WS. 'It is good, my lord, to know the name of anything, whether a play or a man. I may shake scenes together, but my forebears shook spears.'

'Ah,' said Essex, 'so your stock is warlike. Yet you look mild enough, clerkly one might say.'

'I refer only to my name, my lord.'

All this while a dark Italianate man in black, standing behind Southampton, had been observing WS coldly, no shifting eyes here, rather the eyes of a hangman. 'A man must in time live up to his name,' he said. His speech was faintly accented with foreignness.

'Shake-scene or Shakebag or Shakeshaft, it is all one today,' said Southampton. 'Today is a nameless day. It is so cold and dull it deserves no name.' And he pouted at the dying fire. The dark Italianate man now said:

'Though perhaps it is from Jacques Père, a French name. Perhaps he is of French blood. He has a French look about him.' He looked coldly on WS as though he were a butterfly, something to be described, speculated of, perhaps caught and pinned to paper, but in no wise to be addressed directly.

'Oh, Florio here is mad on French things,' said Southampton, smiling indulgently. 'He has done all this man Montaigne into English. Give him a penny and he will dole you out a tasty gobbet of gloomy French wisdom any time. Is that not so? Give us something now and you shall have a penny when my mother deigns to dig into her fisc for my spending-money.'

'*La vie est un songe*,' said Florio promptly. '*Nous veillons dormants et veillants dormons.*' He looked WS straight in the eyes as he said it, but it was as if the eyes were already dead.

'Well, Jacques Père,' said Essex, 'will you translate for us?' His tipsy eye mocked.

'Oh, my lord, Devereux is an older French name than mine own. And your lordship is, I think, but newly come from France. Your lordship will know all about French penny-worths.' Southampton laughed, a girl's laugh.

'Life is a dream,' said Florio, without expression. 'We wake sleeping and—'

'Aye, aye, we know all that,' said Southampton rudely. 'We are tired of Montaigne.'

'As he was of the world. Well, he has left it now.'

'To return to your Titus play,' said Essex, ignoring Florio's epitaph. 'You had not, I think, quite everything in it. Neither, for instance, pederasty nor the raping of corpses. But you had all else. I have seen the Italian Seneca-men, but you went further. As for the French, Garnier and the rest – well, no matter. And we see you what you are, a clerk losing his hair but a pert enough clerk, aye. I will give you French penny-worths.' To his friend he said, laughing: 'Well, I have won our wager so now we may dismiss him back to his writing lair. These poet-players are a very special and new sort of animal.' To WS he said, 'His lordship here said you must be some great roaring ruffian like this Merlin or Marlin the atheist. Well, he sees now you are not.'

WS frowned. 'Where saw you this play, my lord? It has not, I know, been performed at court—'

'Ah,' said Essex, 'we must whisper now. There are ever spies among you. You can never know who will be walking among you in disguise. Or standing out there among your citizens. And who,' he said to Southampton, 'is the most comely citizens' wife of them all?' Southampton blushed. Essex laughed softly, a sound that made WS cringe a little. Southampton said:

'We had best be going back to Holborn.'

Essex yawned and stretched. 'I had best first go piss some-where.' Standing, he staggered. He was fairly drunk. 'I would piss out this fire,' he said, 'hated I not the noise of hissing.' And he went out yawning. WS gulped, suddenly delirious with an idea, and he looked down bashfully on this young noble-man who sprawled so carelessly, bored, pouting. He took courage and said:

'My lord, might I beg a favour?'

'Ah, Jesus, is there no man that does not want favours? Every man tries to use me. And woman too.'

'This is a favour that will cost your lordship nothing. It is even possible it may bring honour to your lordship. It is but a matter of accepting the dedication of a poem.'

'More poems. Always poems. Is it a good poem?'

'It is not yet completed, but it will be a good poem. It is the story of Venus and Adonis.'

'Old stuff always. Is there never to be anything new? Well,

93

Florio,' said Southampton, 'shall we say yes or have him join the long line of petitioners?'

'It can do no harm,' said Florio, shrugging. 'If it is a decent poem and not wanton.'

'Oh, it is not wantonness I mind but only dullness.' WS looked down bitterly on this Adonis, so languid, so satiated of all his world could give. He saw himself taking him and stripping him of his silk and jewels and then beating him till he cried. I will raise great weals on thy tender delicate skin, puppy. He said, with a sudden loudness:

'There will only be dullness in those minds that perceive dullness.' Southampton looked up, surprised. Then, in a quieter voice, 'I beg your lordship's pardon.'

'Aye, do beg. Well then, I am chidden.' Southampton let his foxy eyes shift. 'There was something about a player's heart in a tiger's hide, if I mistake not. Let us have this poem by all means, Master Shake-scene.' He clicked his fingers at the two grinning pages. 'And you *will* drink a glass of wine before we go.'

II

'And you, Will, drink a glass of wine . . . And thou, Will . . .'
He walked London in a February of unwonted drought, dreaming, shaking himself out of the dream to tease out a new stanza. He knew, anyway, the triple chime of his name's homonym from that lordly and desirable mouth. The lips' pout, the red tongue's lifting lazily. As for the poem, there was leisure to finish it, the Rose, along with all the playhouses to the north of the river, closed on Candlemas Day. That was the birthday of Hamnet and Judith; he had sent a loving letter and money to Stratford; there was money enough in his strong-box to tide him over a few months' closure, relieve him of the need to join the others in the wearisome clop-clop of a country tour (fresh straw every night, but the same fleas; veal over-stewed; landlord, your sourest ale, an't please you). Meanwhile the company waited, nail-biting, yawning, quarrelling, rehearsing languidly, hoping for the plague to ease any day now, the Council to rescind its hard but necessary order. Will Kemp fooled, like the fool he was.

'Ho, Ned, what is this in thine armpit? Beshrew me, but it sticks out a whole ell. Why, it is a great bubo.' And then he would prance and sing sillily: 'Bubo, bubo, buboooh.' Henslowe was thunder-faced, as he might well be. One bawdy-house door slammed tight, a cross on it, the sign of the cross brought back from the times of pre-Reformation among those superstitious croshabells: Oh oh oh, we have been visited, see, Jenny is stricken and carried forth moaning on a shutter; oh oh, it is for our sins of the flesh. Henslowe said:

'Here is no matter for japes and jokes. There be thirty plague-deaths a week still. You had best all be off on your travels and leave me to my pain.'

95

'We will wait a little longer.'

'Tarry if you please, but come not to me to borrow. I have, God help me, naught to lend.'

'Ah, Will, Master Shift-scene, a small bit of silver only. My mouth is parched for want of a cold pot. I will do as much for thee, that well tha know'st.'

WS would shake his head gravely, pen hovering above a troublesome stanza. 'I do not myself borrow, therefore I may not lend. Save,' he teased, 'perhaps on interest, say of a crown in a pound and a pound of flesh for the mortgage.'

'You are nothing but a dirty Jew.'

'Oh, a clean Jew,' smiled WS. 'See, I am new-washed all over.'

'Ah, what bed is he visiting?'

He was visiting no bed, no bed at all. He was done with women. Women were a deflection; he must push on to his goal. Meantime he pushed on with his poem:

> And when thou hast on foot the purblind hare,
> Mark the poor wretch, to overshoot his troubles,
> How he outruns the wind, and with what care
> He cranks and crosses with a thousand doubles.
> The many musits through the which he goes
> Are like a labyrinth to amaze his foes.

It brought much back from those early country days. It was not just a toy, a bauble of flashy stones on an old string of myth, of the pretty and laborious order of *Scilla's Metamorphosis* by Lodge, nor was it a wanton lyric gale like that unfinished *Hero and Leander* of Marlowe. In a double figure it presented both a country poet set upon by a love-mad older woman and a pampered godling of an English earl nagged to leave his sports and marry (marry; it is thy duty to beget heirs; here is this fine girl Lady Elizabeth crying for thy love). In this image two men, stripped of their clothes and rank, became one. Coldly for a moment he saw that if there was to be love it must be love with advantage. He had suffered enough.

It was in early April that he penned the last lines. He trembled with hopelessness and relief and fear. He read through the whole poem and was filled with such disgust at his own ineptitude that he was fain to tear it and scatter the fragments on the river (the swans would come, thinking it food). And then he grew calmer and thought: It is not good, but it is as good as many. I cannot waste my whole life in longing for this man's art and that man's scope. If I am not made, why then I am not made; I return to my craft of glove-puppetry humbled. And then he walked the streets composing his epistle to the noble lord. It was far harder than any poem.

'I know not how I shall offend . . .' Spring waking in London, crude crosses still on the doors, but the wind blowing in the smell of grass and the ram-bell's tinkle. Piemen and flower-sellers cried. '. . . in dedicating my lines, no, my unpolished lines, to your lordship . . .' From a barber-shop came the tuning of a lute and then the aching sweetness of treble song. '. . . nor how the world will rebuke, no, censure me for choosing so strong a prop . . .' There were manacled corpses in the Thames, that three tides had washed. '. . . to support so weak a burden . . .' A kite overhead dropped a gobbet of human flesh. '. . . only, if your honour seem but pleased, I account myself highly praised . . .' In a smoky tavern a bawdy catch was flung at the foul air. '. . . and vow to take advantage of all idle hours . . .' Pickpurses strolled among the gawping country cousins. '. . . till I have honoured you with some grave labour . . .' A limping child with a pig's head leered out from an alleyway. '. . . But if the first heir of my invention prove deformed . . .' A couple of Paul's men swaggered by, going haw haw haw. '. . . I shall be sorry it had so noble a godfather . . .' Stale herrings smelled to heaven in a fishman's basket. '. . . and never after ear so barren a land . . .' A cart lurched, rounding a corner; wood splintered against stone. '. . . for fear it yield me still so bad a harvest . . .' The sun, in sudden great glory, illumined white towers. '. . . I leave it to your honourable survey . . .' A thin girl in rags begged, whining. '. . . and your honour to your heart's content . . .' An old soldier with one eye munched bread in a dark passage. '. . . which I wish may always answer your own wish . . .' Skulls on Temple Bar. '. . . and the world's hopeful expectation.' A distant consort of brass – cornets and sackbuts. 'Your honour's in all duty . . .' A drayhorse farted. '. . . WILLIAM SHAKESPEARE.'

'STRATFORD, then, has made this book entire,' said Dick Field. He spoke still with the Warwickshire burr, standing there, grave and bulky in his apron, a smear of ink on his fat cheek. A man was busy at the press, quietly whistling; at a corner table a boy was learning how to bind. Field had done well; he had married the widow of his master, the Frenchman Vautrollier, and taken the business over. But he deserved to succeed by virtue of his own skill in the craft: that translation of *Orlando Furioso* (Harington's, was it not?) was a beautiful book to handle. All questions of local patriotism aside, WS had done well to bring his poem here. He took the volume reverently from Field, handling it with a proper mingling of pride, humility, wonder, fear, smelling fresh ink and new paper in a sort of small vertigo. A book, his book. There was no doubt of it: a poem in print was somehow a different work from the warm, fingered, crossed-out, pored-on, loved and hated sheets that held one's own nature in every line (one's hand was indeed one's hand, part of oneself). Here it was, *Venus and Adonis*, cast on the waters: 'TO THE RIGHT HONOURABLE HENRY WRIOTHESLY, Earl of Southampton and Baron of Tichfield . . .' There was no going back now; the ship sailed. This book, this exterior thing, must take its buffets from a world as indifferent as the sea, knowing and caring nothing of the author, making no allowances; no actor could mediate to exalt with his own music or diminish (earning all blame) with stumbling memory or false accent.

Here was WS in naked confrontation with the reader, with, above all, one particular reader.

'Yes,' he agreed, 'Stratford poet and Stratford printer. We will show London together what Stratford can do.'

Field coughed. 'They say you have left Stratford for ever. I heard talk of this at my father's funeral. I met your father at the inventory-taking. He said you had promised a twice-yearly visit.'

'A man must work where the work is. I cannot always be taking holidays. I send money home.'

'Aye, they said that too.' He coughed again. 'You have not thought, then, of setting up house here in London?'

'When I buy a house,' said WS, 'it will be in Stratford. London is for work. There will be time enough for sitting by the fire, telling my children stories.' He spoke somewhat sharply.

'Forgive me,' said Field. 'It is none of my affair. Well, may things prosper for you. May your book prosper.'

'It is your book too.' WS smiled. 'Even if the matter were all nonsense, it would still be a beautiful book.'

It was launched, it rode the waters. It provoked ecstasy among the young exquisites. It was in the mode – wanton and yet coyly standing back from wantonness, all in language that was pure candy with honey sauce. WS sat in a tavern with grumbling Henslowe; he heard a gallant whisper that that was sweet Mr Shakespeare. Oh, the commodious conceits, the facility, the facetiousness. And all the time he waited to hear word of what one particular reader thought. The book had been entered on April 18th; May came in and he still heard nothing. Alleyn said:

'There is no use in our further waiting.'

'Waiting? Waiting for what?'

'Calmly, softly. Your mind has ceased to be on the craft. When will *Richard* be finished?'

'Richard? Oh, *Richard*. *Richard* can wait.'

'But we cannot. The Rose will not open this year. We have

this licence from the Privy Council to play anywhere seven miles out of London. It is to keep us in trim for playing before the Queen next winter.' He put on, something ineptly, a hayseed voice: 'Aye, Hodge, they be not harlotry players but a sort of royal officers. We must go see them in manner of a bounden duty.' In his normal voice he said: 'It is but a small company – Will Kemp and George Brian and his little holiness Tom Pope and Jack Heminges. There will be little baggage to take. Will you make one?'

'No, no, I must stay here.'

'Well, then, we will have a good drinking night before we part.'

And then, on a day of bad news, he had a visit. It was news buzzed among the pamphleteers and petty playwrights. The Privy Council was heresy-hunting, special men termed Commissioners were searching in the lodgings of writing hacks for seditious papers. In the rooms of Thomas Kyd (and was he not a sort of god, had he not written *The Spanish Tragedy?*) they had found terrible words in black ink, something about Jesus Christ being not divine. Kyd, in a sweat of fear, had said Marlowe had written them. The end was coming at last for Marlowe; the end might be coming for all who had lived by the pen. We had best burn all, papers, notes, letters. Anything can be twisted to heresy and treason by those who wish it. Kyd is already in Bridewell; some say he was put to the torture, six fingers broken, sweating and screaming.

To the lodgings of WS came a man in black. WS did not at first recognise him; he prepared for interrogation (what heresy, then, might be lurking in *Venus and Adonis?*). Then he remembered that January day, the Lord's room at the Rose. This man, who looked so gravely and coldly on WS, was called Florio, subtle Italian, translator of Montaigne. He said:

'May I sit?'

'I have here a little wine. If you would care—'

Florio waved the wine away. 'I read your book before he

did,' he said directly. 'It was too sweet for my taste, like a very sweet wine.' He looked sourly on the flask he had been offered. 'He could not at first be persuaded to read it. It was my lord of Essex who burst in, almost at dawn, to shout about its virtues, to tell him that it was he who was honoured and not yourself. My lord of Essex can move him to anything. So now he has read it at last.' He paused, sitting in gloom.

'And,' gulped WS, 'what says he?'

'Oh, he is on fire,' said Florio unfierily. 'He has sent me at once to summon you. Or rather I offered to come; he wished to send merely his coach and a footman with a letter. I offered to come because I wished to talk with you.'

WS frowned in puzzlement.

'I see your surprise. You are thinking that I am nothing more than a servant myself, a secretary and so somewhat intimate, but still no more than a paid man. In one sense that is true, in another not.' He crossed one thin black leg over the other. 'I am Italian-born, a stranger, an outlander. It is for this reason, perhaps, that I see the English so clearly. I have travelled, but I have not met anywhere the like of your English nobles. They are a kind of being that God would seem to have made for His own special pleasure.' WS settled, as to hear a sermon. 'If English nobles take pleasure in fine horses, God may be thought of as taking pleasure in such as my lord. Wealth and beauty and high birth, also a little learning, as much as he needs, also a quickness, a quivering as of a pure-bred horse starting at a fly or a feather—'

'You have certainly read my poem,' said WS, smiling.

'I remember your verses about the horse. You will then know my figure and my meaning. If you understand a horse you will understand what I am saying about my lord. He is all fire and air and water. He can hurt and he can be hurt. If you are to be a friend—'

'I would not dare to presume,' stammered WS. 'Who am I to ask that—'

'You are a poet,' said Florio calmly. 'There is perhaps

something of the horse in you, though you are only a humble man from a village.'

'Stratford is a borough.'

'A borough? Well then, a borough. That is not to our purpose. What is to our purpose is that I will not have him hurt. My lord of Essex is too much the soldier, the courtier, the man of ambition to harm him greatly. I saw in your eyes that day of our first meeting what you might do.'

'This is nonsense,' said WS, smiling uneasily. 'Might I not be more easily hurt? There is power, there is beauty, youth. I am, as you say, but a village man.'

'Borough.'

'If he calls me, then I must go, and gladly, humbly. But I know of the fickleness of the great.'

'Let me tell you about my lord,' said Florio. And then, as though he had just then taken in the words of WS, 'Yes yes, you will have read about fickleness in your story-books. Now, his father was not fickle but suffered for his faith in the Tower there, the faith that was my own before I read Maître Montaigne and learned to say "*Que sais-je?*" He died young, and my lord, at eight years only, had to become a court ward. My lord Burghley was his guardian, is still. Like a horse, my lord kicks at control. My lord Burghley, his own mother and grandfather, urge him to marry. If he wishes to follow my lord Essex into battle, it may be that he will be killed and leave no heir. Thus a great house will die. There is a bride waiting ready for him, the granddaughter of my lord Burghley – a beautiful girl with that cold-seeming English beauty that masks terrible fire. He will have none of her. He will have none of any woman. I think your poem may harm him.'

'But there, surely, it is but an old Greek story—'

'Oh, already he talks of himself as Adonis. Poets have more power than they think. I think,' said Florio slowly, 'that he ought to marry. Not only for the sake of the house, but for his own sake. There are corruptive forces at court, there are hot hands eager to lay themselves on his beauty. I think you, more than any man, might persuade him to think of marriage.'

'Come now,' smiled WS. 'If his own mother cannot—'

'His mother urges advantage and duty. You might urge advantage and duty also, but with you they would be different. They would, in that alchemy of poetry, seem a kind of vice, and vice attracts young men. He sees himself as Adonis, and that makes him also Narcissus. You might play on that.'

'You mean,' said WS, 'that I should write verses to him on this theme of marriage?'

'It can be made a commission. His mother would be glad to throw gold at you.' Florio stood up. 'I must take you now. He is very eager. I would esteem it a favour if you would say nothing of our words together. A secretary's office is to write letters.'

'And so then,' breathed WS, 'he likes the poem.'

'Oh, he is, as they say, altogether ravished by it. He swoons at its rich conceits, again as they say. And all this in a single May morning.'

Was there not already the scent of decay, of delicate corruption, in that boy's greeting? WS pushed, as it were, through the sumptuous wrappings that hid this jewel in the very core of the great house. Truly a Stratford bumpkin, he gaped at the profusion of concealing silks and brocades, a whole Ovid in the hangings, the carpets that muffled his feet like snow. Wryly grinning, but his eyes saturnine, Florio handed over this raw poet to the hierarchy of house-servants (gold chains, glittering livery, finally an ebony staff, silk-tasselled) that led him by the formal degrees of ceremony to a great bedchamber. It was a bedchamber that WS found overwhelming but curiously familiar; he remembered his boyhood's vision, the gold goddess, the arms that implored. But here was no goddess; that premonition had been false. In a bed of gold that seemed to float like a ship on a carpet that was all tritons and nereids, Master WH lay on satin cushions. He was resting, he tired easily these days. To WS he said:

'Come! Come here! I have no words, thou hast taken them all.' ('Thou': he said 'thou'.)

'My lord, I humbly—'

'Not humbly, never humbly anything. Come, sit here beside me. Be proud, but let me be prouder. I have a poet as friend.'

'Dear my lord—'

III

'Dear my lord—'

'I will be called by my name.'

'It is not seemly that I—'

'Oh, it is for me to say what is and is not seemly. And I will say that it is not seemly for you to go moping about with this long puling face on so bright a June day. I keep my poet for my ape, not for my *memento mori*.'

WS looked at him with bitter love. The death of a poet was nothing to this lord who was as careless with his poets as with his gold (Pay thou this reckoning, Will; I have spent all I had with me. – But, my lord, I doubt that I have enough in my purse. – Aye, I forget that thou'rt but a poor crust-eating sonnet-monger.)

'I cannot be unmoved, my lord (Harry I would say), when I hear that my friend was stabbed with his own dagger and died in torment. His own dagger, straight through the eye, imagine. He screamed, they say, that all Deptford could hear it. The agony of suffering Christ could not be worse.' That news had come to WS late, cushioned as he was from the real world of ale and plays and lice by sumptuous satins and giddy perfumes. He had heard first the elation of the pious at the death of Antichrist; then the coroner's droning that Frizer had slain Marlowe in the defence and saving of his own life; last he had put together the ghastly scene in the room at Deptford Strand – Frizer, Skeres, Poley standing about, laughter then sudden rage from the poet lying on the bed, the flash of the dagger, the flash of the enemy hand snatching the dagger, and then – That line would not leave his mind, that scream of damned Faustus: 'See where Christ's blood streams in the firmament.'

'You may exult now, friend or no friend,' said his lordship Mr WH, Harry, 'that you are without peer. Now my poet is the only poet.' He was shrewd in some things, pretty pouting boy as he was. 'You may gladly lose a friend to know that.'

'He was not so close a friend. But there was no poet like him.' That was true. Still, he had seen his successor burst like a new sun in the very days of his daily summoning to the Council's inquisition about souls on the top of a pole and run God, run devil, have it who will (did you say this?), his own masterpiece unfinished.

'I should hope he was no close friend. Well, this may mean one more nail in the coffin of his upstart protector the tobacco-man. Sir Walter Stink. I cannot abide the oaf, what with his Brownists and atheists and wenching at court. You must write a play mocking him and all his black circle.'

Why this enmity? Had Essex been squirting poison in? Oh, the intrigues, the ambages, the labyrinthine plottings. As for the School of Night, WS kept his own counsel. This was a new life, post-Marlovian (a pretty coinage), dedicated to love and advancement and poetry. 'I have here,' said WS, smiling, 'a new sonnet.' And he took it from his breast, the black ink that had flowed so confidently scarce dry. ('. . . Thy love is better than high birth to me, Richer than wealth, prouder than garments' cost, Of more delight than hawks or horses be . . .' Was it not perhaps over-forward, after but a few weeks of friendship, this harping on love? But Mr WH, Harry, had said it first.)

'Oh, I have no time now for reading sonnets,' said Harry in petulance. 'I have still to read the first you gave me. Place it in that chest there.' It was a box of carven camphorwood, cool-smelling and spicy within, brought, he had said, from the Indies by a captain that had loved him but was now cast out. Jealously, WS saw other poems than his own, but, certainly, there was that first sonnet: 'A woman's face with Nature's own hand painted . . .' It was true, it was a woman's beauty, but there was the swooning delight of its being on no woman's body. Forward? There was not all the time in the world. He grew old, he would soon be thirty.

'Today,' said the lovely boy, 'we are to go down-river.' And the river it was, in joyful sunlight, paddling softly towards Gravesend, the grave watermen in livery, the barge new-painted with cloth-of-gold canopy above, the handsome laughing young friends of his friend deferential to this sober-suited poet who had taken the Inns and the Universities with his mellifluous conceits. Wine and cold fowls and kickshawses, and then, as the sun went in a space, distaste blew into the poet's heart like a damp gust, he seeing himself again truly as an upstart, without birth or wealth, one plain ring only on his hand, his garments decent but no more, and a different distaste at the sudden sight of the open laughing mouth of this lord they called plain Jack, the teeth clogged with a powdery sweetmeat. They were idle, they were dying of *ennui* (a fine apt word from Master Florio), they hid diseased bodies under silk and brocade. Then the sun came out again and they were transformed once more to air and fire, the flower of English manhood. They were swans, but like the swans that sailed in the barge's wake, greedy and cold-eyed. And the kites that flew to and from their scavenging in the June air, the ultimate cleansers of the commonwealth, they attested the end of all noble flesh.

'When will the playhouses open again?'

'Oh, the plague-deaths are still above thirty a week.'

'I care not for plays. They are all bawdry and butchery.'

'Well, there is always Lyly and his little boys.' A coarse secret laugh. 'Lily-white boys.'

'May not a gentleman rise above carnality – blood and panting and close-stools? As for love—'

He would give them what they wished, redeeming his craft to art. He saw in his mind's eye a fair-hung stage shut in from sun or wind, fair languid creatures like these discoursing wittily, no Kemp grossness, no blood-bladders or Alleyn ranting. He would provide, he would lend words to these elegant puppets. But he sighed, knowing himself to be caught forever between worlds – earth and air, reason and belief, action and contemplation. Alone among all sorts of men, he embraced a poet's martyrdom.

'Your sonnets harp more and more on marriage. Oh, it is nothing but marriage I hear from my mother and my grandad and my noble guardian that has a bride in store for me, and now you join them. My friend and own poet makes one in a conspiracy.' He pettishly threw the poem on to the table. It fluttered in the fresh autumn breeze from the casement and planed gently down to the carpet (dryads and fauns greenly embroidered). WS smiled, peering with eyes that were growing near-sighted at the upside-down lines:

> From fairest creatures we desire increase,
> That thereby beauty's rose might never die . . .

He had come, he considered, delicately and discreetly to his burden. Besides, it was by way of a commission, engineered by the subtle Italian. He was no lord with estates and retainers; he must earn money. Her ladyship, the handsome ageing countess, all of forty years, had embraced his hands painfully with hers sharp and crusty with rings. My thanks, dear friend, my most grateful thanks. A matter of the songs of Apollo after the words of Mercury. Carefully he said:

'A friend should speak what is in his heart, a poet even more so. It is waste I fear. Should I die now at least I leave a son. The name Shakespeare will not die,' he said confidently. But, saying the rest, he felt the old self-disgust of the actor; he was earning gold through eloquent pleading. It was for lying, he saw hopelessly, that words had been made. In the beginning was the word and the word was with the Father of Lies. 'But I am a mere nothing.' He extended his hands to show them empty. 'I fear so many things for you – death in the field, in the street. The plague took, this last week, over a thousand. And what then, with you gone? A few poor portraits, a sonnet or two. It is a perpetuity of flesh and blood that we beg for.'

'Aye, the family first, as ever.' He was bitter. 'Wriothesly before Harry. Mr WH.'

'There is nothing wrong in marriage. It is a thing a man will enter for his name's sake. He can still be free.'

'Are you free? If a man has to run away from his wife I see not how he can still be free. You dream in your plays of taming shrews.'

Aye, WS thought, I am always under-estimating him, *magister artium per gratiam* at fifteen, commended by the Queen herself for wit and beauty. It was the beauty got in the way. The Queen seemed to have stepped into both their brains, for Harry now said:

'As for wranglings about succession and great houses in an uproar, the Queen has set all a fine example.'

'The Queen is a woman.'

'Part a woman. If the Tudors will die out let the Wriotheslys also.' WS smiled at those heavy words coming from the pouting girl's mouth. He said in banter:

'Well, they say there is no worry over the succession. All will be taken care of.' And, stepping to the window, as though to look carelessly out, he whistled a measure or two from a popular ballad. Harry knew it: 'For bonny sweet Robin is all my joy.'

'You grow too familiar.'

WS turned, surprised. 'Whistling? May I not whistle?'

'It is not the whistling. Your whole manner is become too familiar.'

'I have been schooled thereto by your lordship. I humbly cry your mercy, my lord.' He spoke mincingly and ended in a ridiculous smirking bow. It was Harry who was ridiculous; he could be as wayward and petulant as a girl in her courses. 'Dear my lord,' added WS.

Harry grinned. 'Well then, if I am dear your lord let us see more lowly abasement and fawning. First, you may pick up your sonnet from where it fell.' He could keep no mood up for long.

'The wind blew it, let the wind lift it.'

'Oh, but I cannot order the wind.'

'Nor me, my lord.'

'Ah, but I can. And if you will not obey I will have you escorted to the dungeons to live with toads and snakes and scorpions.'

'I have lived with worse.'

'So. Well, you shall be whipped. I will apply a whip to thine ancient shoulders. I will raise first cloth, then skin, then blood. Tatters of skin and cloth and flesh all delicately commingled.' Even in play he had a certain lordly cruelty. Power to hurt and he would do it.

'Oh oh, whip me not.' He wondered at himself, ancient WS. A friend, a lover, he saw himself an instant as a father; he carried on those ancient shoulders more than the weight of ten years' difference. Falling into the game, he went down to the carpet creaking, going oh oh on cracking joints, kneeling. Harry at once was there, a delicate foot in delicate kidskin placed upon the sonnet. WS saw: '. . . or else this glutton be, To eat the world's due by the grave and thee.' Suddenly he thrust his arms in a tight hug round the slim boy's calves. Harry's voice, high up there, screamed. Then WS brought him down, not hard on that deep pile showing embroidered green wantonness, his arms striving too late for balance, laughing, breathless. 'Now,' went WS in mock gruffness, 'I have thee.' They fought, and the craftsman's arms were the stronger.

'No more sonnets on marriage,' panted Harry.

'Oh no, none,' vowed that practitioner of lies.

He could not altogether keep his old life out of this new.

When roasted crabs hiss in the bowl,
Then nightly sings the staring owl:

'Tu-who;
Tu-whit, to-who' – A merry note,
While greasy Joan doth keel the pot.

He could see her clearly, cleaning the trenchers in cold
water after the Christmas dinner. It should be a good one this
year: he had sent home enough sonnet-gold. He had not,
however, as he had promised, sent home himself. He had had
work to do, a resident playwright in a noble house, writing a
play about lords who vowed three years' abstinence from love
and the comedy of their breaking of that vow. 'How long will
it be?' Harry had asked. And he had answered: 'Three ells.'
And, as there was no company at all in London then (the playhouses still being shut, though the plague had much abated),
it must be a matter of lords playing lords. The first day of
Christmas brought My Lord Sussex's Men to the Rose
(Henslowe recording a God Be Praised in his account-book),
but that was too late. Lords must act even ladies' parts, all for
an audience of ladies, and Master Florio must do Don Adriano
de Armado, because of his foreign accent, while Holofernes
the schoolmaster was none other than –
(The twins would be nine years old at Candlemas. How fast
time flowed away.)
'. . . I marvel thy master hath not eaten thee for a word, for
thou art not so long by the head as hon- hon- honorif-'
'Honorificabilitudinitatibus.'
'Oh, I cannot say that.' This was Sir John Gerrald, whose
droll face singled him out for Costard. They were all remark-
ing on the wit and the learning, the pedantry even, even when
pedantry was not being mocked. This was what he wished,
directing his lordly cast in the fine heavy gown that was a gift
from his own lord, his friend. ('In your time, sir, perhaps
Oxford men were less sportive?' A smile, a shrug in answer.)
But, after a heavy night's feasting that he was forced into, for
he could not plead a weak stomach all the time, nor say he was
in pain or had work to do, he was sickened, veering from Arden

to Shakespeare and in a manner envying that Friar Lawrence that had already appeared, duly set in a new lyric play, out of some remote cave of his brain. To be cut off, to live austere, an eremite: he sighed for that. But then he remembered his mission here, the restoring of honour to a name that had lost it, along with family fortune. And there was this damnable love, this ravishment of the senses, bursting into jealousy that, in the quietness of his own chamber, he must unload into verse to be torn up after (Harry laughing with Lord This or Sir Such-an-one, hand-touching, hand-holding) or flowing in compassion, the manner of a world-woe, when he saw tears brimming down the soft, faintly translucent cheeks as a consort of viols or recorders discoursed. *Lachrymae, lachrymae.*

> Music to hear, why hear'st thou music sadly?
> Sweets with sweets war not, joy delights in joy.

'There it is again,' Harry scolded, 'finding a pretext for a marriage sermon in everything.'

> Mark how one string, sweet husband to another,
> Strikes each in each by mutual . . .

'Ordering my life for me, all of you. And yet,' said the cunning boy, 'what would you say if I did now go a-courting and spend all my time with Lady Liza? I do believe you would be out of your mind with envious rage.' WS smiled uncertainly. 'Confess now,' said Harry, leaping up with great nervous vigour from the couch where he had been lying. 'You shall confess that you do all this to please others and not yourself at all. Does my mother, then, come to your chamber and stand over you while you write, telling you to say this and say that, only, an't please your poetship, to use fine high phrases as befit a poet, and if you will not you shall out of this house and never see my son more, for, why, what art thou, thou art no better than a harlotry player?'

'*Harlotry* is good,' said WS, blushing.

'Well, is it true? Have I hit it?'

WS sighed. 'I have endeavoured to please all save you. I have done more sonnets on this same theme. I write many at a sitting but give you one only at a time. Well, I shall write no more.'

'Why why why? Why do you sing their tune? Nay, why do you make the tune for them to sing?'

WS extended his empty hands like, he thought, doing it, some usurious Jew. 'I did it for money. I must live.'

'For money? Oh God, for money? Do you not have everything you want? Do I not give you everything?' Harry stood, hands on hips, narrowing his eyes. 'For how much money? For thirty pieces of silver?'

'Oh, this is all nonsense. I must send money home. I have a wife if you have not and will not have. I cannot disown my wife, nor my three children.'

Harry grinned maliciously. 'Poor Will. Will the married man.'

'I have a son. My son must grow up a gentleman.'

'Poor Will. My poor, dear Will. Often I feel myself to be so very much older. I could speak to thee like thine own dad.'

'A son to grow up like you, though never to be a lord yet perhaps a knight. Sir Hamnet Shakespeare. I see in you what he may be. And often I feel that I may never live to see it, not in reality. Often I feel so tired.'

Harry came up to his chair from behind and embraced him, jewelled hands winking in the winter light as they lay crossed on the breast of his friend. WS took the right hand in his own and squeezed it. 'I shall write no more sonnets,' he said. 'You have seen through the poor trickery.'

Harry kissed his cheek lightly. 'Write me more sonnets,' he said, 'though not on that stale and profitless theme. And let us ride together ere spring comes to – to wherever it is thy wife and children are.'

'Stratford.'

113

'Aye, thither. And we shall take a fine present to Lord Hamnet.'

'You are kind. You are always kind.'

'But,' said Harry, breaking away and striding towards the window, 'thou shalt do something for me. Another poem. And let it be a revenge on women, the whole sex.' Rain had started to fall. It was a grey day. Bare branches tapped, tapped forlornly at the window. 'Especially on these women who are so holy on marriage and the sanctity of marriage. I wish to see another book and my name on it and to hear the congratulations of my friends.'

'What I have done is yours,' said WS. 'What I have to do is yours. But I cannot be altogether so harsh against women.'

THEY did not go to Stratford. Instead, WS worked at his poem of Lucrece and Tarquin, and Harry took to low company, drawn into it, in life's sly irony, by another poet. The poet was George Chapman, older by some four years than WS, and he had ventured on his first plays this rare time (rare in two years) of the Rose being open. He had done a ranting tragedy for Sussex's Men – *Artaxerxes*, in which Cyrus the Younger, second son of Darius, had raving speeches which smacked of WS's own Holofernes, though not in parody. Harry was much taken by his black-bearded loudness. Summoned to the Lord's room, as WS himself had once been, again in a frosty January, he tickled Harry by being most undeferential. Florio did not like him. As for bonny sweet Robin Devereux, Earl of Essex, he was busy with things other than the pertness of poets and players.

'Will,' said Harry, 'I am in love.'

WS put down his pen carefully. He stared for full five seconds. 'In love ? *In love ?*'

Harry giggled. 'Oh, it is not marriage love, it is no great lady. It is a country Lucrece in Islington. She is the wife of the keeper of the Three Tuns.'

'In love. *In love*. Oh, God save us.'

'She knows not who I am. I have been with Chapman. She believes I too am a poet. She will have none of me.' He giggled again.

'So the seed stirs at last. Well. He is in love.' Then WS began to laugh. 'And what thinks the husband of all this?'

'Oh, he is away. His father is dying in Norfolk, and yet he will not die. It is a slow quietus. I must have her, Will, before he returns. How shall I have her?'

'I should think,' said WS slowly, 'that your new friends will help you there. The Sussex men are, I hear, a wenching crowd.'

'They are not. They are all for boys. There is a house in Islington.'

'Well. Well, well. In love.' He picked up his pen, sighing. 'I have a poem to write, a commission of your lordship's. My mind is wholly taken up with the harm that comes to those who force the chastity of noble matrons. I should think like harm will come to the authors of lowlier essays.'

'You mock me now. Write me a poem I can give to her. You have written sonnets enjoining me to love a woman, now write one that shall persuade a woman to love me.'

'Your friend Master Chapman is perhaps less busy than I that he can take you drinking to Islington. Ask him, my noble lord.'

'Will, I have no taste for this mockery. George cannot write that sort of verse. She would never understand any poem of his.'

'Can she read?'

'Oh yes, and write too. She has a good hand in making out of a reckoning. And as for George, he too is busy enough with a poem. He is lodging at Islington, at the Three Tuns, writing it. It is far out, he says, from the distraction of those who admire him.'

WS was amused; disturbed, a little jealous, but still amused. 'The distraction of his creditors, he would say. I have a mind to come out to Islington to see this innkeeper's wife who has all my lord's heart.' He had a mind too to see this Chapman.

'Ah, she has such a white skin. And a very tiny foot. She has a waist a man could span his two hands withal. She is black-haired and black-eyed.'

'She is out of the fashion, then.'

'These great ladies chase a man. She does not. She thrusts me away. She thrusts all men away.'

'Including Master Chapman?'

'George is only in love with himself. That is why he amuses me. He too is writing a poem, as I say, though not to my commission. He says he will honour me with its dedication.'

So. He had very much a mind to see this Chapman. 'Well, when shall we go thither?'

'Tonight. This night. You shall see her this very night.'

It was a fair ride out to Islington, where Canonbury Tower was being new-built by the Lord Mayor. A cold ride, too, that sharp night, the road ringing. They were both glad of the warmth of the fire of the inn.

'Is she not beautiful?'

'Hm.' Her eyes accompanied, in merry mockery, the chaff she was handing back to a table of three guzzling citizens (they had ravaged two whole fowls between them and were tearing at cheese and black bread); she was country-whole-some, a new experience for his friend. Well, he must learn that he could not have everything he wanted. 'I would say,' he said, 'that she is any man's meat. Perhaps you are somewhat too young and pretty. Perhaps she will take better to an older, uglier man.' An older, uglier man came heavily downstairs, yawning, showing stained teeth, his black hair all a tangle. Jowled face, mean eyes. This was Master Chapman. He and WS eyed each other like fighting cocks.

'Ah, Harry,' said Chapman loudly. He took a seat at the rough well-scrubbed table near the fire, yawning. 'Poetic labour is hard labour,' he said. 'I have been taking a nap.'

'*Homerus dormitat*,' giggled Harry. 'Sometimes your verse reads like hard labour.'

Chapman ignored this. To WS he said, 'When comes Alleyn back with the rest of the Strange snipperados?'

'I hear nothing. I am cut off this whole year from playhouse news.' WS grinned. 'Snipped off, let us say.'

She brought sweet wine, glowing. She was certainly pretty enough. Harry did a furnace-sigh. Well, this was new: his lordship in love with an alewife. He must be cured; a good swift cure, like a Lowestoft herring's. 'This,' said WS, 'seems a cleanly enough inn. It would be cold riding back. Let us lie here tonight.' And he closed one eye at Harry. Chapman said:

'Your Venus poem had a good epigraph.' He mouthed the Latin loud, sounding round brown vowels:

' "*Vilia miretur vulgus: mihi flavus Apollo*
Pocula Castalia plena ministret aqua." '

Then he belched gently though long on his first draught of wine. 'Whether a man can maintain two writing sides I know not. One will corrupt the other, doubtless.'

'Perhaps the better will corrupt the worse,' said WS. Harry's eyes could not leave her. 'Well,' to Chapman, 'I am glad you at least like the epigraph.'

'Oh, the rest was well enough. There was a sufficiency of lusty country matter in it. Each of us has his own way. One way is not another. We must do as we can, remembering the parable of the talents.' He then took a large swig and, his mouth dripping, looked Harry full in the eyes and declaimed:

'Presume not then, ye flesh-confounded souls,
That cannot bear the full Castalian bowls,
Which sever mounting spirits from their senses,
To look in this deep fount for thy pretences.'

'You are welcome,' said WS, 'to my full Castalian bowls.'

117

'To Night,' said Chapman, raising his near-empty Castalian bowl. 'Night is my mistress and my muse. To her I drink.'

'To her I drink,' said Harry, flesh-confounded, languishing in ridiculous desire.

'We will go to bed soon,' promised WS, smiling.

THEY rode back to Holborn next morning in sharp sunlight, jewelled cobwebs on the bare branches, their breath going up, as they spoke, like the wraith of speech. 'Well,' said WS, 'I knew it would be easy for an older man. It is very much a matter of experience. Women will ever go for the experienced man. They can oft see experience in a man's eyes.'

Harry looked unbelieving, then aghast. 'But you did not. You could not. Her chamber-door was locked.' He was pale. 'No no no, you are joking.'

'To you it was locked, aye. I was not asleep though I snored. It was a fair counterfeit of sleep. I am, after all, a player.'

'But you could not. She would not open for any man.'

'I went out while you were sleeping fast.'

'I was not sleeping fast. I hardly slept at all. I thought you were going to the privy.'

Not the privy, not all the time. A quiet half-hour by the embers below. 'Oh, it was no trouble. I knocked and she asked who, and I said I was the Earl of Southampton, the older man who was growing bald. She opened at once. Ah, the bliss. Such warmth, such whiteness.'

'No no, you are lying!'

'As your lordship pleases. Well, I have shown you the way. All you need do now is to follow.'

That would teach the young puppy.

IV

' "... THE WARRANT I HAVE OF YOUR HONOURABLE disposition, not the worth of my untutored lines, makes it assured of acceptance. What I have done is yours; what I have to do is yours; being part in all I have, devoted yours..." '

Harry left off reading it aloud.

'And now,' asked WS, 'what of Chapman?'

'Chapman may stuff his *tutored* lines down a privy. This is better than *Venus*. I did not think it possible, but it is so.'

Yes, better. WS knew that, knew too he could go no further in that heroic vein. Restless, he bit his nails. The players were returning to London after so long a wandering absence. Alleyn had left Strange's Men and was, only figuratively as yet, flying the old Admiral's flag over a nearly new company; Lord Strange had become the Earl of Derby only to die of (so many said) witchcraft: Kemp and Heminges had come off tour to approach Lord Hunsdon for his patronage. Lord Hunsdon's Men. But Lord Hunsdon was the Lord Chamberlain. WS had a hunger for a tarter diet than this perpetual honey of overpraise. Those of Harry's friends who had read *Lucrece* in manuscript had swooned all about its author in a perfumed langour of adulation – oh, the commodious conceits, the mellifluous facetiousness. Now that manuscript had become proofs; in a week or so the proofs would be a book; the Inns and the University men would start their gushing. WS caught a momentary image of himself writing verse of a very different order: yes yes, it speaks well but must be cut, it holds up all action; I cannot say that, it is not in my character; what is this here? – why, man, they will never comprehend it. He had mastered a form, had proved himself to himself, but now

119

seemed called to settle to living in a filigree cage, fed on marchpane (his back teeth ached), turning out jewelled stanzas for the delectation of lords, a very superior glover. Spring always brought this restlessness. Stratford had been in his mind. Even in the writing of *Lucrece* there had come Stratford images. 'Back to the strait that sent him on so fast.' The strange back-eddy under the Clopton Bridge. And he had gone to see it again, showing himself, an earl's friend, in red cloak and French hat, mounted on an Arab.

Fine spring weather, the many days of riding – Slough, Maidenhead, Henley, Wallingford, Oxford, Chipping Norton, Shipston-on-Stour: many days for choice, to savour the leisured travel of a gentleman with gold in his purse. And then, gulping, Henley Street unchanged, his father and mother riper, Anne carrying thirty-eight stately years on her fine wide shoulders, Gilbert approaching thirty – still godly, prone to fall foaming, unmarried – and Richard a man of twenty. There were no children in the house now, only young men and women: Hamnet and Judith were nine, Susanna eleven, their uncle Edmund a sturdy voice-breaking youth of fourteen. Time churned steadily, silently, behind one's back. There was shyness in the presence of this Londoner with the tired eyes, hair receding, who called himself son, brother, husband and father. It was to Richard his own children ran, nuncle Richard.

'And so th'hast made thy fortune.'

'Not yet. This gold is nothing. The fortune is to come.'

'And when wilt come back for ever?'

'Soon. Very soon. And I shall never go away again.'

There was shyness between Anne and himself, back in that old bedchamber from which he had watched out on the beating and driving of a witch, in which he had shrunk from her desire. They had lain together in the bed from Shottery, but in no marital embrace. Something had died that dry summer night with Tarleton's men singing in the tavern, poor Madge whipped, sobbing for breath. Well, the wife had done the function she had pressed him to. Sitting up in bed in the morning, he told stories to his son, embracing the boy's thin body with hopeless love.

'And what is there in London?'

'Oh, the Queen is there and the Tower of London and the great river. There are very many streets, full of shops in which a man may buy everything in the world, and there are many ships sailing in from America and Cathay and Cipango and Muscovy where the Russes live.'

'Shall I go to London?'

'One day. Meantime there are duties here. Thou must look after thy mother.'

'Tell me a story and let me be in the story.'

WS smiled. 'Well, once there was a king and he had a son and the son's name was Hamnet.' He thought of Kyd's crude play; strange, this matter of the name. And of dead Lord Strange with his north-country voice: 'I'll play Amloth with thee, lad!' Meaning that he would go into a rage (it was with a servant, not a player) like the hero they half-remembered in Yorkshire from the old days of Danish rule, only his rage had been a feigned madness to discover who had killed – 'And the king's father died but his ghost came back to tell the prince that he had not truly died but had been murdered. And the man that had murdered him was his own brother, the uncle of Hamnet.'

'Which uncle – Uncle Dickon or Uncle Gilbert or Uncle Edmund?'

'This is a story only. The uncle wished to marry the queen and become ruler of all the land.'

'Oh, it would be Uncle Dickon then.'

'Why Uncle Dickon?'

'Oh, he says he is King Richard now that William the Conqueror is away in London. And Uncle Gilbert says that he should be king, for he is eldest, but Uncle Dickon says there never has been a King Gilbert, but Gilbert can be the, the—'

'Archbishop of Canterbury?'

'Aye, that. It is all joking. Uncle Dickon laughs because it is all joking.'

RIDING back, presents and money bestowed and duty done, WS saw the terrible mystery of fatherhood clearly in the spring weather but, more than that, the horror of its responsibility. An actor, a playwright, he turned himself into his son an instant, a sleeping being called out of the darkness to suffer, perhaps be damned, because of a shaft of enacted lust. Out of the urgent coupling, the stave, the chord of summer morning, the melting of the night island of winter heat, he came, crowned with more than was asked for. Only from them, the makers, was hidden the enormous pulse of the engines, whose switch they touched by an alien curse concealed in the fever of rose or apple or mirror. One would ask only a candle, whose doomed flicker was grateful enough; but that other gift embarrassed, fire that could not be handled or tamed to humble sufficient processes. With that passage from intolerable heat to water there was remembered the ocean in runnels, the ocean in the corn, in the fruit-skin's pressure, and death might be thought the desirable crown of the foul river. But instead it was fire that was found, ironically bestowed, waiting, rehearsing, with a smothered laugh, lurking in the comfort of light. The fuse of water sooner or later led to the ghastly miracle implosion which would not blast its frailest tabernacle. When the warning bell announced to the crouched hearers the wafer suffused by fire, there could be no escape, nor could the burden be purged in news (poets dead, thieves hanged, traitors torn to pieces) that cast no shiver over dawn sleep. Oneself was the storm's centre, the heart of the giant flower. The smallest room he could rent, though with only a single friendly door fronting the light and music of traffic or carnival, would at length – when the picture was burned, the mirror with its dream panorama shattered – still in a speck of dust open the desert and the howl of the time wind.

Calmly, he thought, before sleep in the inn at Oxford, that

all over Europe and the Antipodes and Cathay and Cipango and the fabulous Americas, the gods were detonating. Yet there was only the one personal burden of being the source of the whole, the centre of the projection of shadows into the real that, bigger and undying, yet moved as oneself moved, in the mock court of an endless sterile reign to truckle and mow.

He woke in the spring morning to clutch the receding dream: in all the wood there was one leaf or acorn which, touched or gathered, would release the spring that fired the great trees on the outermost ring, and the circled fire closed in to him, trampling down, dissolving to heat and light all but the finally known – that when flesh, heart, lungs were quite wrung to irreducible ash, the exact centre would be proved in a gush of water.

But the morning wreckage floated on the raw flood and the day probed and had to be answered, a nightmare of many parcels. Multiplicity was sickness. In either fire or ocean only rest lay, when the point of light could grow and renew the known globe of air. Blood and renewing cells and the body's river flowing over the stone of mole or naevus called to the dance and the climb or the descent, but the son, himself, was rooted in that dead tree, left arm stretched to a world it might be death to finger, right arm signposting to a new land. There the fiddler stamped on a floor where the wineskins were never emptied, where saffron ladies moved in a calm pavane, and tomorrow was certain as the grave and happy laws, and a string would strike always the note expected, the word flung in the pool pulse out its steady circles. His son, then, inherited the curse that stilled the present to a mouldering picture hung in every room, he hanging in that picture, caught in paralysis, the nerveless arms held on a crossbar flush with the river's flow . . .

'You are not well this morning, sir,' said the landlord of the inn.

'Bad dreams only. Bad dreams.'

'WELL, I must to court then,' said Harry, putting down the proofs of *Lucrece*.

The mock court of an endless sterile reign. 'Yes, we hear there is much going on at court. Alarms and excursions.' Incursions too. Harry, WS knew this, was worming into that delectable flower-bed of the Queen's pert Glories. It had to come. Life, after all, was not a limiting but an expanding. The love of men and the love of women could co-exist, nay had to.

'It is all this business of Lopez. Lopez is this physician that is also a spy, the Jew from Portugal.'

'Yes, I know all about who Lopez is. Even tame poets hear court news.'

'The Queen would not have it that Robin was right about his treachery. Well, she must believe it now.' There was excitement in his girl's-face, the excitement of one who was privileged to be near the centre of great things. WS felt very old, very weary, looking at him. 'He is condemned, and these two others, Tinoco and Ferrara, are condemned too. And yet, out of spite to Robin, she will not have the sentence carried out.'

'Before you go,' said WS slowly, 'I would beg one small word.'

'Well, quickly then.'

'I think I am no longer welcome here.'

'Oh?' Harry opened his mouth at him. 'Have I said aught of your not being welcome?'

'No. But I hear things from your secretary. I think he is disappointed in me.'

Harry laughed. 'Florio is disappointed in everybody and everything. Florio is Florio. And also my secretary, no more.' He pouted, quick in his moods. 'But I will not have this. I will have Florio in now.'

'No. No, wait. I think her ladyship your mother has been speaking to Florio. Has she also been speaking to you?'

Harry rubbed his chin. 'She has said some things, very

gently. She talks of time wasted on sonnets that seem to have persuaded me the way opposed to what she wanted. Well, she is a mother, only that.'

'A mother that no longer approves of her son's friend, not since he ceased to write sonnets on the duty of marriage. And I think that Master Florio, in his subtle way, knows of what we do together.'

'Florio is immersed in the dictionary he is making. I think you worry too much.'

WS took a deep breath. 'Everything points to my leaving. I have thought of this much. I do not mean my withdrawing from our friendship, for I will ever be what you wish me to be, since what you wish I wish also. But I have chosen a craft and, with the opening of the theatres again, I must follow it. Some, seeing me as a poet, forget I am a player. Well, a player cannot lodge here.' He extended his hands briefly to indicate the rich hangings, the crystal, the gold inlays.

Harry looked bored and tired. 'We will talk of this at another time. You are making a great ado about very little.'

'And I fear that you yourself may, one of these days, report to me the sneering of your friends at a player being close to you. And Sir Jack and Lord Robin will, of necessity, mean more to you than poor Will. I have to prove myself yet. To have a ready pen is something, but it is less than to have land. I must work to the having of possessions.'

'You have my love,' Harry laughed.

'I must pay for it. It is a dear thing to pay for.'

But summer came and *The Rape of Lucrece* raped the senses of its exquisite readers, overcame them in heady dispensations of rose-leaves and honeysuckle, though many saw in it a sterner moral core, a stiffer and maturer view of virtue (not the seeming virtue of the innocent but the achieved virtue of the experienced) than in the earlier poem. WS knew that the players who were once Lord Strange's but now the Lord Chamberlain's had united with the Lord Admiral's Men to act at Newington Butts, but he heard that things went poorly. His play of Roman atrocities and his play of shrew-taming had both been presented to yawns and near-empty houses. Cosily, he remained the poet; he stayed in his friend's house; the sheaf of sonnets in the camphorwood box grew thicker. Those were poems by which he would never make any public name as a sonneteer: they were for one reader's eyes only. Sidney had told the world of his wrecked love for Lady Penelope Devereux, bonny sweet Robin's sister, now poor Penny Rich; Daniel had published his *Delia* and Drayton's *Idea* was going from hand to hand; but, though there were rumours of Mr WS's 'sugared sonnets among his private friends', those rumours must never sharpen into exterior knowledge. There were some things that must remain secret.

But, one hot day in June, Harry said: 'We are to go forth together. I will take you to see the best play in the world.'

'A play?'

'You may call it that.' He was excited. 'No more questions.' WS had not asked any. 'It far outdoes any of your Senecan stuff. It has no title as yet. You and I will give it a title after.'

'Whose men are doing it?'

'Oh, you could say the Queen's.' He giggled. 'I have ordered the coach. Come.'

'I have but the final couplet of this sonnet—'

'Oh, that can wait. We must not miss the beginning.'

WS felt foolish, as he often did, trundling in the rich coach westward from Holborn, four greys prancing before. Curtains were drawn to keep out the peering mob as well as the sunlight that would burn off Harry's pallor. He pulled an inch of curtain aside. There were crowds scurrying west, roaring, chewing bread and bits of garlic sausage, some armed with bottles against the summer drouth, the plebs, the commons, the mob. 'It seems to me,' he said slowly, 'that we are going to Tyburn.'

'Ah well, it was not possible to keep it from you for long.

Tyburn today puts on a very special spectacle. Robin is puffed up as a pigeon, and rightly. He is shown to be right and the Queen admits she was wrong. Her little ape of a physician that everyone knew had received a great jewel from Spain. And those two that were sent to win him over. Well, there will be no more treason from any of them.'

'You should have told me,' said WS bitterly. 'I do not like to see these things.'

Harry laughed. 'Little innocent Will. He who makes Tarquin leap on Lucrece and everything the filthy world could dream of happen in *Titus*. Well, you cannot separate so your dreaming from your waking. If you would indulge the one you must suffer the other.'

'I will not look.'

'You will. You will drain it to the dregs.'

They moved with some difficulty over the cobbles of the narrow street with its toppling shops and houses; they could hear the confusion of the horses' feet, the crowd jeering, feel the coach jostled. The coachman lashed out at those who came near enough to scare the horses or finger the gleaming brass and polished harness; the footmen shouted abuse. There were cries of pain and growls, but the underdog remained under. At Tyburn they drew the curtains back to let light in and the vision of a grim holiday crowd that sweated and squinted under the light. Here was a whole clutter of noble coaches, on some of which the gaily and richly dressed had climbed to the roof or ousted the footmen from their seat; the soberer citizenry sat, more soberly, inside their sober coaches. All waited.

'That is Robin over there,' said Harry, dismounting. 'It is his day of triumph.' Well, so it was. It was Essex who, some four years back, had employed Lopez as his agent, for Lopez knew better than any in England what went on in both the states of Iberia. But Lopez had given his news first to the Queen, then to Essex, and Essex, monger of old information at court, had been laughed at. Then came his malice towards

Lopez, his accusations, and more derision from the Queen; more, the Queen's rebuke: so Dr Lopez was buying strong poison with Spanish gold, was he, bent on assassination? The poison was in silly and naughty Robin's own mind, not in the medicine-chest of the Queen's own little ape of a Jew. And so four years of hard and malevolent work, culminating, on a bright June day, in this. 'Triumph,' repeated Harry. 'I will go over to him.' Essex and his toadies were drinking wine and laughing, their raiment gay in the sun. 'Do you stay here and shut your eyes to it all.' And he grinned.

There was the tree. Crouched on the platform the hangman's assistant was securing a plank with busy hammer. The hangman himself, masked, with brawny arms folded, strutted like Alleyn, an Alleyn that needed no glory of words. The eternal kites wheeled above in the pure and blue and crystalline air, as yet unpolluted by men. From afar came a roar. The hurdles were approaching, dragged over dry ground, raising a coughing dust. One of the draggers, with a toothless idiot's face, greeted friends from a black and panting mouth. There were jeers, men spat on the still figures roped to the hurdles, a young woman in front of WS began to jump, partly to see better, partly in a kind of transport of expectancy. Children were lifted on to parents' shoulders. Some further hangman's assistants brought, severally, a great metal bowl and four steaming kettles. There were cheers as the near-boiling water was jetted, splashing, into the bowl. One kettle-carrier made as he would pour a scalding stream over the spectators nearest the tree; they retreated in a scurry, screaming their laughter to his grin. The hurdles had reached the end of their journey. And now—

That is Noko. What is his name? Noko, no, Tinoco. A foreign and heathen name. He is to be first. And now this Tinoco, a dark and shivering man in a white shirt, had his shirt stripped from him as he was roughly untied from the hurdle. The hangman presented his knife, new-sharpened, new-polished, to the sun; the mob went aaaaaaaah. Called the hangman, it was yet not his office to fix the long thin neck into the halter; the first assistant must do that. Tinoco, stumbling, falling with fear, and all to the crowd's laughter, was made to mount the ladder, rung by slow trembling rung. Behind him, behind the gallows itself, the hanger waited on a narrow crude podium, a platform mounted on a platform. He was a young man, muscular; his mouth opened in some ribald pleasantry to his victim as he secured the hempen noose about his neck. And then WS could see the lips of the victim moving, as in prayer; the trembling hands sought to join in prayer, but could not. Of a sudden the noose was tightened; over the momentary inbreathed silence of the crowd the choking desperation of the hanged could clearly be heard. The second assistant pulled the ladder away sharply. The legs dangled a second but the staring eyes still blinked. Here was art, far more exact than WS's own: the hangman approached with his knife, fire in the sunlight, before the neck could crack, ripped downwards from heart to groin in one slash, swiftly changed knife from right to left, then plunged a mottled fist inside the swinging body. The first assistant took the bloody knife from his master and wiped it with care on a clean cloth, the while his eyes were on the artistry of the drawing. The right hand withdrew, dripping, holding up for all to see a heart in its fatty wrappings; then the left arm plunged to reappear all coiled and clotted with entrails. The crowd cheered; the girl in front of WS leaped and clapped; a child on his father's shoulder thumb-sucked, indifferent, understanding nothing of all this, the adult world. Blood poured and spurted richly, the sumptuousness of heraldic bearings, glinting as the sun struck. And then (for the rope must be used again) the noose was loosened, the ruined body upheld while blood poured still, the tautness of the rope made slack again. The hangman threw the heart and guts into the steaming bowl, freeing his arms from the incrustations with quick fingers, drying them then, unwashed, on a towel. The crowd moaned its pleasure, its continued excitement, for were there not two more victims to come? The hangman was handed a hatchet, squat and dull compared with that quick artist's instrument but sharp as it cracked through bone for the quartering – the head, the limbs. A gaping torso was upheld a moment, then all these pieces of man were thrown into a basket.

Next came Ferrara, gross and heavy, the flesh shaking on his bare black-haired chest as he was lifted, his three chins wobbling to the crowd's pleasure, his eyes rolling like those of some insentient doll. Here was comedy, a sort of Kemp. Ferrara squealed like a swine, going *No no no no* nasally as he was thrust up the ladder, groaning dismally from his belly's depths as the noose went about his no-neck. This time the hangman was a second's fraction slow with his knife; Ferrara was dead already as the point pierced. But there was a great fat heart, crammed like a goose's liver, dripping treason treason treason; the entrails were endless, an eternity of pink sausage; the crowd was a-roar with delight at the comedy of the fatness of the chopped limbs.

And here, at last, was the crowning course of the rich dinner. Dr Roderigo Lopez, Jew, Machiavel, small and black and mowing and chattering like an ape. Let him not be granted the least dignity in his dying: strip all off. There is a fair-sized thursday for thee; mark, he is like all foreigners for the appurtenances of lust. Lopez prayed aloud in a high screaming voice, in an outlandish tongue, his own. No, it is to the Devil he prayeth, for is not Adonai the foreign name of the Devil? And then, in ridiculous foreigner's English:

'I love de Kvin. Ass mosh ass I loff Zhessoss Krist—'

The crowd split their sides with laughter but were, at the same time, most indignant: this naked foreign monkey praying, saying the Holy Name in his nakedness, screaming, with that smart filthy rod, of his love for the Queen. Despatch, but not too slowly. And then, *in articulo mortis*, his body spurted, but not with blood. Parents, shocked, covered the eyes of their children. Draw, draw, draw. The hangman's hands reeked. Then he went with his hatchet for the body as he would mince it fine.

As he had been foretold, WS watched all, drinking this sight of blood to the dregs. Then, with shocked eyes (shocked as if he looked in a mirror), he saw Harry laughing, miming that he was to go off to drink with his triumphant friend Robin, that he, Will, might proceed homeward in the coach. He was trundled off, numb, as to his own execution. The crowd was sated, spent, purged, cleansed, splitting up into decent family groups proceeding to the quiet of their houses.

WS awoke from a dream of Paris Garden, roughly jerked. There had been blood of yelping dogs that the bear mauled growling, a screaming ape riding a dog but caught by dogs and ravaged and gluttonously eaten, a little boy that a bear chased crying with the claw-marks on his head just about to well purple. Paris Garden was Paradise Garden, home of sweet innocence: so it was revealed to him in his sleep. It was Harry who pulled him awake, Harry drunk and laughing, sweet innocence holding a candle in a silver sconce. 'And so, old dad, how was't then? Didst like the free show from the Lord's box?' He placed the candle on top of the press. Dewy, irresistible, made by God before God made morals, he bounced on to his poet's bed, straight from Paradise Garden, unbuttoned. But WS could resist him tonight. He pulled the coverlet over his head, shivering, saying:

'I am weary. I am in pain.'

'In pain. Thou wilt be in pain. First the hanging, then the disembowelling.' He laughed softly. 'We have been with wenches tonight. But not in Islington, nay. Thou wert right about the alewife of Islington. And we were with these wenches and then I thought of my old dad here all alone.' He took a handful of the hair of the head of WS, silky and long still at the back, scanty above the brow. He tugged.

'Leave me. Let me be. I am in pain.'

'Aye, as I wished. And now in more pain.' And he tugged

131

again. WS writhed up to seize the hand that tugged. He said:

'There are times when I can feel nothing but hate. Hate and despair.'

'Aye, let us have hate. Hate only, without despair. Hate hate hate.' His nails were long; he dug all five of his free hand into the bare chest of WS. 'Let me claw out what is within.' And the five nails clawed down in a slow raking motion. WS yelled in momentary agony and seized this hand too. He held both delicate lady-hands in his, squeezing, saying:

'An I am not to be left in peace I had best go find lodging in some tavern.'

'Ah no, thou'rt to stay. I, thy lord, give this order.'

WS weakened, as he always must. And now Harry became a bold aggressor.

'To die, to die.' The act of dying would come later and, with it, as WS bitterly foreknew, a consummation of intolerable self-disgust.

V

'I SAID IT WOULD COME TO THIS. All along I said it. Yet you would not have it so.'

Harry screamed and threw the book to the floor. It was a thin book, ill-bound, the cover already coming away. WS, calm, in many ways glad, picked it up. It was an anonymous poem called *Willobie His Avisa or The True picture of a modest maid and of a chaste and constant wife* – anonymous, but he could guess who had written it or, at least, was behind the writing of it. It was not weighty enough for Chapman, slim stuff; belike he had sold the theme to some drunken hack, master of arts. It was sure of good sales. WS turned and turned the pages to a hunk of prose, as indigestible as cheese-and-black-bread:

'. . . HW being suddenly infected with the contagion of a fantastical fit, at the first sight of A, pineth a while in secret grief, at length not able any longer to endure the burning heat of so fervent a humour, bewrayeth the secrecy of his disease unto his familiar friend WS who not long before had tried the courtesy of the like passion . . .' It was not quite right, any of it, but there was a pea of truth beneath the mattresses of verbiage. The story was of a true and beautiful alewife, innkeeper's wife he would say, resistant to all onslaughts on her virtue. Who could HW be but Harry Wriothesly? And, to fix the identity of WS, there were sly nudges at the player's trade: '. . . see whether another could play his part better than himself . . . sort to a happier end for this new actor than it did for the old player . . . at length this Comedy was like to have grown to a Tragedy by the weak and feeble estate that HW was brought unto . . .' And here, surely, something more direct: '. . . the divers and sundry changes of affections and temptations, which Will set loose from Reason can devise . . .'

'You can expect talk now,' said WS, putting the little book down on the table by the casement. Outside the plane tree was yellowing. The swallows twittered in loud companies. Another autumn, a sere fall, but now perhaps the end of his servitude. Not of friendship, no. He felt himself as close to this lord as to a son, as to himself. But the end of hugging, of that secret love that June's frenzy and self-hatred had seemed to quell. He thought it must be so. As for Harry, he was more openly busy now among the Queen's Glories. WS twisted the knife in further. He said:

'My lord Burghley will be told, doubtless.' Harry gave a maniacal smile, saying:

'Oh, my lord Burghley knows everything. My lord Burghley has issued a table-thumping threat.'

'Threat? When was this?' For WS had been busy, these last weeks, with other matters, player's matters.

'I am given my last chance. Either I marry dear Lady Liza, God curse her poxy face, or pay the penalty. And the penalty is by way of a damages, for my guardian's ravaged heart and the time wasted in waiting by this pocked bitch.'

'A penalty? Money? You must pay money?'

'Five thousand pound.'

WS whistled in Stratford tradesman's vulgar astonishment. 'So what will you do?'

'Oh, I shall find the money. It will not be easy. But I will pay ten times that rather than mingle my bare legs with hers. I refuse to marry.'

WS spoke carefully. 'You may, if all I hear is true, be hurled still into marriage against your desire. Love is pleasant, but nature sees that it will have consequences that are naught, or little, to do with love.'

'Do not paste your own past on to my future. Because you were forced into marriage by the baring of a fat belly—'

'Yes? Great lords are different from Stratford glovers?'

Harry went to the wine-table and poured himself a beaker of the bloody ferrous brew of Vaugraudy; he liked it; these

134

days he was growing faint ruby with it; he did not offer any to his friend.

'I do not think you should speak so to me,' he said. 'There are times when I feel I may compass mine own disaster through over-much familiarity. Not through disobedience to them that are set over me but through mine own free behaviour with— Ah, it is no matter.' He drank thirstily.

'You have never had cause,' said WS, 'nor will you ever have cause to complain of any indiscretion of mine. I never took you tavern-haunting. I sought to discourage your Islington venture with a trick. I would never be so foolish as to place myself in a posture that could earn just rebuke. We are friends when we are alone, and when we are in company I am as tame an adjunct to your house as Master Florio. And now I cease to be that. This book tells me what to do.' He held *Willobie His Avisa* in both hands, as he would tear it. 'You need five thousand pound now, you say. Would that I were in a position to let you have it. It is not right that you mortgage ancestral land. I go now to seek the way of substance, and that lies not in pretty poetry. When we meet again it must be more as equals.'

'You cannot make such equality,' said Harry with a sort of foxy sneer. 'You will never earn yourself an earldom. Earldoms are not earned in playhouses or by the buying of flour against famine or by the foreclosing of mortgages. Degree remains and may not be taken away.' He poured himself more wine, but this time he offered a cup to his friend. His friend shook his head, saying:

'I foresee a time when gold will buy anything. Gold already rules this city. I foresee a time of patched nobles seeking alliance with dirty merchant families. As for myself, my way up leads to the estate of gentleman. For you, the way up can lead only to disaster.'

'Meaning?'

'I say no more now. But let us consider the example of my lord of Essex.'

135

'I will not consider his example nor anybody's,' said Harry in a sudden passion. 'I will not have country nobodies speaking of great lords as though they were subject to the rule of ordinary men. Play with your plays and leave state matters to statesmen.'

'So my lord Essex is no longer merely a soldier and a courtier but a statesman too? And what is the next step?'

'I think,' said my lord Southampton, 'you had best leave now. And take that filthy book with you. No,' he said, 'I will read it again. We shall meet this evening when perhaps we are both more in our right minds.'

WS grinned at that. 'Alas, my lord, I have other business. Player's business. But tomorrow I shall be much at your service if you would wish to come to my lodging. See, I have writ it on this paper, the house and the street. Bishopsgate is not far from Holborn.'

Harry threw the book once more, this time at his friend. The cover that had threatened to come away now did so; it was a piece of cheap and unskilful binding, not the work of Richard Field, that other ascending Stratfordian.

FAR from the river now. North of the divers fair and large builded houses for merchants and suchlike. North even of the City Wall and the fair summer houses north of the wall. Good air in Shoreditch. The Theatre a finer playhouse than the Rose. Burbage as good a man of business any day as Henslowe and an old player too, though, from what I see, of no great skill. But his son now, his son promises, this Richard. He may yet go further than Alleyn. Is that Giles Alleyn from whom old Burbage got the land of Ned's kin? It may be so. In '76 it was. A lease of twenty-one years. A mere patch with rank grass and dog-turds, even a man's bones they say. A skull grinning up at surveyors. And now a fair playhouse. Twenty-one years, let me see. To '98, which is but four more. Will this Alleyn renew? Were I he I would not. But it is the men more than the playhouse, sure. The Lord Chamberlain's Men. It hath a fine ring. Richard Burbage, John Heminges, Tom Pope, Harry Condell. As for Will Kemp, is that right? We have ever been together, two Wills. But he harks back to the old way, the ways of leers and the extempore fill-in for lines forgot or unlearned. He is somewhat too bawdy and he deems himself to be above the supererogatory fripperosities of poetlings. Yet will he draw them in. It is the drawing-in that is needed, blood and murder (well, it is there, it is the world, I would be what the world itself would be) for this Dick Burbage, for Kemp the low laughter of Launce's dog pissing against the heaven-posts. To get money from all, from the little lords too, scribbling my conceits on their waist-tablets. Now the Admiral's at the old Rose have still more an inn than a house built expressly for plays, yet have they a repertory – *Faustus*, *The Jew of Malta*, *Tamburlaine*, *Guise*, oh many. And mine also, *Harry* and *Titus* and *The Shrew* and that botched pseudo-Plautus and. It is a matter than now of working fast between now and Christmas. Waste naught, take all. If a poor Jew doctor remains their posthumous villain, why then – *Christophero gratias* – they shall have a Jew and set in Machiavellian Italy withal; and Italy will do for this warring family play (well, there is Brooke's poor poem as a base) which is also of Harry's friends the Danvers brothers and their war with the Longs. Aye, Montague will come into it, which is a name of the Southamptons. There is also LLL for comedy.

A player's share, a full player's share (they need me, do they not?), it would be a beginning.

LET me take breath, let me take a swig, for, my heart, she is coming. She is about to make her entrance. It was while he was walking off Bishopsgate – Houndsditch, Camomile Street, St Helen's Place, St Helen's Church – that he saw her. She stepped from her own coach outside a house near St Helen's, veiled, escorted by her unveiled maid. But, in the fresh fall wind, her veil lifted an instant; he saw. He saw a face

137

the sun had blessed to gold. Another autumn, that autumn in Bristol, returned to him in a gust of shame. Beaten out of a black croshabell's brothel for want of a little tinkling silver. It was different now. But this woman was, he thought, no tib, no purveyor of holy mutton. The coach was new-painted, the two roans well-groomed. The coachman creaked down in fat dignity. The door was opened to disclose a wink of richness – a gilt-framed portrait on the hall-wall, a table with a silver candlestick. And then it closed on this vision or fable from his own past. Had he imagined it? They were rehearsing *Romeo* at the Theatre when, in a break or brief ale-intermission, he asked old James Burbage. He knew of her; he knew all that went on in Shoreditch and environs. He said, in his quick breathy way:

'There be many tales touching her origins. Her own story is (or they say so) that she was brought back as an infant from the East Indies by Sir Francis Drake himself, in the *Golden Hind* that lies at Deptford now. It is said that both her father and mother were a sort of noble Moors of those parts and were killed by Drake's men in a fight they had there, then she was left all alone and weeping and so, in pity, was brought to England to be in a manner adopted. It is said also that money from the Privy Purse was given to a Bristol gentleman for her upbringing, so that she might be made into an English lady. Well, English she cannot be made, not by no manner of a miracle. As for lady—'

'Bristol? You say Bristol?'

'They say Bristol, but what can any man believe? It is certain that she lodged awhile in Clerkenwell, at the Swan in Turnbull Street, and that she has been friendly enough with some of the gentlemen from Gray's Inn. Now, she has money of her own, that too is certain, but how she came by it may be conjectured. The story from herself seems to be that the Bristol gentleman that was her adoptive father died and left her somewhat. Now this you may perhaps believe if you know aught of these Bristol slave-men. The adoption and the leaving of money might well be in the way of a what-you-call, a penance—'

'And what is her name?'

'Oh, she has some foreign or paynim name, a Mahometan one, but she goes under some Christian nickname here. I fancy I have heard her called Mistress Lucy. She has been to the Theatre here once only, with mask and pomander and all, curtained off like any Christian lady. She would be, as I guess, some twenty-two-or-three years old.'

It was not right that a past dream should waken for WS when he was so bent on securing the future. He could not, in his curiosity, prevent his feet from pointing her way when he went walking, teasing out in the morning autumn air some immediate problem of his craft. St Helen's bell rang reminders that she lived, a paynim or Mahometan, in the church's shadow. What was he being bidden, by some arcane and all-hid suburb of his brain, to do? What did this mean, the dark woman in the fair house? Perhaps his boyhood's timid lust for the wealth of endragoned seas and spice-islands. And youth, his own youth that he could only now live in plays and poems, obsessed him since his friendship with Harry – a youth purged of poverty and a struggling trade, an over-hasty marriage to a shrew. He saw himself in fantasy some ten years younger, sword flashing in passionate sunlight in a square where a fountain plashed, a handsome noble extravagantly in love. But the mirror in his lodgings showed a tired face, eyes most weary, and the hair fast riding back from the forehead. White paper flattered more than blue glass. He wrote his last scenes, the sheer lyric outpouring (ah, love, youth, love) clogging the limbs of the action. Well, that had been Greene's way, and Marlowe's, more the poet's way than the hack's, the mere play-botcher's. Did he want too much – to be poet and gentleman? A man could never, in this uncertain world, ask for too much.

He saw her again, this time unveiled, one early November day that was like autumn acting spring. He walked by her

139

house and, looking up, caught her face gazing out on the milk gold of the morning in a kind of wonder, the upper casement open, her elbows on the sill. Her bare arms were thin but shapely; her shoulders were covered against the brisk air by a shawl of white wool; the point of division of her breasts showed sharp and agonising above the low-cut bodice. For her face, there was the delicately splayed nose he had seen on that other one, the lips thick. Her black eyes were alert and merry but, WS thought, could melt swiftly to tears. She spoke to one who was behind her, unseen from the street, perhaps her maid. Her words could not be heard, but she smiled in a sort of malice. She was desirable, there was no doubt of her desirability. He stood, looking up glumly. Her eyes, that had been ranging over the few sights of the street (a couple of urchins playing, a fat man like a Turk on a white gelding, a chair-mender), met his; he tried to hold the gaze; she seemed confused, she laughed, she turned her look away from him; she shut the casement.

And then he did not see her again, not till Christmas was come and gone, but there was enough to distract his mind from thoughts of dalliance (still, passing her house in his warm cloak, he asked himself where she could be. Was she ill? Had she left for ever? Was it but a visit back to the West?): *Romeo* ravished the Inns, as he had known it would; Gray's had asked that *The Comedy of Errors* be given during their Christmas revels; the Theatre was commonly spoken of, in the extravagance of the talk of the exquisites, as the Temple of Sweet Master Shakespeare's Muse. And on January 4th (he had begun to keep a combined journal and commonplace book about this time, so he noted the date) he was visited in his lodgings by Harry.

'Oh,' said Harry, walking about the dim chamber, looking for the wine-jug, 'some sort of amity is restored between us. Dear Lady Liza is to marry my lord of Derby, God bless the two of them, they are well-matched for stupidity, so my burly guardian says less of five thousand pounds than he did. It is a good thing I was slow in finding it.'

The ears of WS pricked at this. Could he— Might he—

'He was high-flown last night at Gray's, the aged sinner. All were high-flown. There was this nastiness between Gray's and the Inner Temple, as you will have heard, for was not your own play wrecked on that Night of Errors, as they now term it?'

'I heard something. I was not myself present.'

'They had this mockery of a royal state with a Prince of Purpool at Gray's, and there was invited a sort of Ambassador from Templaria.— so they called the kingdom of the Inner Temple. But too many came and this sort of Ambassador was crushed and beaten. But last night there was a masque in which Graius and Templarius were friends again, very silly stuff. The Prince of Purpool gave many commands to the nobles of his kingdom, saying that they must all go to the Theatre to improve their brains with a course of instruction from sweet Master Shakespeare.' Harry laughed. 'Oh, there was drinking enough. I vomited, I could not keep their sweet wine down.'

'You look well, as ever.'

'Aye, but I would be better with my old dad to give me grave counsel.'

WS grinned. 'I am always here. Here, or in my workshop. You are busy at court these days, with little time for poor players.'

'There is, I will confess, one at court— But it is no matter. They are all false.' He poured himself some of WS's wine, tasted it, then said: 'This is harsh stuff. I must send you some Canary. It is not too sweet a Canary.' He drank, made a sour face, and said: 'Who is this Abbess of Clerkenwell they talk of?'

'Abbess?'

'Oh, there was something in the Revels at Gray's about an abbess who holds the nunnery at Clerkenwell. It was all foolishness. She was to find a choir of nuns to chant *Placebo* or some such nonsense to the Privy Chamber, that is of the Prince of Purpool on his coronation. Her name was given as Lucy Negro or some such silliness.'

WS did not like the sound of this. 'Negro? There is a lady, a girl almost, who lives by St Helen's. She is called—' He stopped himself. 'I know little about her. Black women there are, though, at Clerkenwell. Very old and dirty and poxy and not to be recommended. So I hear. I have not seen them.'

'You see nobody these days. You are working hard to make money.'

'We are both busy, each in his own playhouse.' He gulped. He said: 'There is this matter of my buying a player's share, as we call it. I thought once of coming to you for friendly help.'

'I know nothing of player's shares, whatever they are.'

'It is an interest in the whole venture of the playhouse, so that the investor or purchaser draws his proportionable share of the profits. The Theatre is doing well and will do better.'

Harry drained his wine. 'I am glad,' he said carelessly. 'I hope you will ever prosper. I must not forget to send you this Canary.'

WS spilled it out. 'It takes more money than I had thought. I did not know whither to go for the money. I need a thousand pound.'

Harry whistled. 'Well, playhouse business is no longer mere play. A thousand pound is a fair sum to look for on a winter's morning.'

'To whom can I turn save to you?'

'Ah,' grinned Harry, 'I remember talk of your making your own way and that sometime ragged nobles would seek an alliance with playhouse-keeping families.'

'I never said quite that.'

'Your new rich were not, I understood, to become so by begging from the old rich.'

'There has to be capital. Where can capital come from but the land? Who owns the land of this realm?'

'We own it that have it.'

'The land was in the beginning for all men. The Conqueror

142

came to steal it and to parcel it out. That injustice cannot obtain for ever.'

'You talk of injustice?'

WS blushed. 'So some speak. I accept degree and place and all else. All I do now is to ask humbly for help from a friend.'

'A thousand pound. Would that be a loan?'

WS spoke carefully. 'One does not willingly take a loan from a friend.'

Harry smiled and said, 'I would charge but very light interest – say, ten per centum.'

WS smiled back. 'With a bond made out for the security of a pound of flesh. And your lordship quite straight-nosed. Go to, I had thought your lordship a good son of the usury-hating True Church.'

'I doubt thou'dst have a pound of flesh there. Thou'rt grown thin out of my service.' He made a sudden thrust at WS with his jewelled hand, a young man who had revelled all night but was still full of sport in the morning. They tussled in their old manner; wine was spilt on the bare polished boards of the floor.

VI

January 4th

Madness madness all madness. After H departed there comes Dick Burbage all hotfoot and sweating spite of the bitter cold with loud news that the Men are commanded to play at the wedding of the Earl of Derby and H's cast-off Lady Liza. Things so coincidentally chiming ring like matter of a comedy, yet life is so, often grossly so, so that a playmaker feels himself to be a better contriver than God or Fate or who runs the mad world. The madness is in the brevity of the time. At the Court of Greenwich but three weeks from now. Well, let us lie back on the bed unmade for more to coincide, for H knocked books from my shelf and one was Chaucer that opened at the duc that highte Theseus and weddede the Queene Ypolita, and the other was this fire-new marriage-song of Edm. Spenser with his

> Ne let the Pouke, nor other evill sprightes,
> Ne let mischievous witches with their charmes,
> Ne let hob Goblins, names whose sence we see not,
> Fray us with things that be not

And so I lay on my back a space and watched the fire sink to all glowing caverns and it was like a dance of fieries, I would say fairies. And then came the name Bottom, which will do for a take-off of Ned Alleyn, so that I laughed. Snow falling as I sat to work (I cannot have Plautus twins for most will have seen C of E but I can have the Pouke or Puck confound poor lovers) and the bellman stamped his feet and cursed, blowing on his fingers. Yet with my fire made up I sweated as midsummer, and lo I got my title.

January 6th

Walking over crisp snow to my ordinary I saw her. She is

either newly back or newly up from a sickness. To such as her our cold must be all agony. She was all mobled up at the window, her tawniness flat and dull in this snowlight, and I felt pity. I cannot believe that she is more than mocked at by the Inn men for her colour, I cannot believe that she is of that Clerkenwell tribe. She is brown not negro. Boldly I waved my hand passing, but she did not see or she ignored. And so back to rhyming away at the lovers' scenes, wooden wooden wooden but there is no time for re-working. Well, I put the bad harvest in Oberon's speech and then thought for a fancy I would give my dark one in the window a womb rich with Titania's young squire. I do but beg a little changeling boy to be my henchman.

January 9th

At the Theatre in the mornings they are rehearsing already in their several groups, for that is the one way to deal with short notice, to write a play soft-jointed and separable out. And it was without the walls that I had the good chance to see her and, my heart beating unwontedly, even to address a word. I was leaving for my lodging and her coach was coming by. Then a gentleman appears from Spitalfields way and his horse slipped and slithered in all the foul slushy snowbroth so that her own two took fright and the offside reared and whinnied. It was I that nimbly darted, though panting much after, and seized his head, saying calming words. Her coachman got down and first her maid put out her face from the coach and then she on the other side, drawing aside her veil to see what was the matter. And so I went up and doffed my hat and bowed.

–All is right now. That horse slipped, see. He has ridden on and all is well again.

–I am beholden. I thank. Wait, I will give . . .

–Ah, madam, no. I am a gentleman. I am Master Shakespeare of the Theatre there.

–You are there? You are of Master Burbage's company?

How knows she of him? Her voice is prettily foreign. She cannot say *th* or *w*. I tank. Bwait, I bwill geef . . . I drank in her goldenness.

–You have seen Master Burbage act then, madam?

–Him I did see in *Rish Hard de Turd.*

And so I smiled, saying:

–The play of which I myself am the author. You are welcome any time at the Theatre. I will be most happy to offer you what hospitality the house affords.

But she smiled queenlily, saying:

–I tank you. Now must we on.

So saying, she bade her coachman continue on their way and left me there standing in the dirty snow. And I was aware that H has said no more of the £1000 and I remain the writing hack whom they will welcome as a whole shareholder can I but find the money.

January 13th

So cold and kibey a day that I laugh in scorn of our trade that we represent midsummer, all leafy and flowery. She has kept indoors, her house all muffled up with shutters as it too feels the cold. I am sick of these sugar rhymes. I dream after dinner (a drowsy one of fat pork and a pudding) that I am ass-headed Bottom in the bower of a tiny golden Titania. Thou art as wise as thou art beautiful. The mirror shows bad teeth and beard fast greying, a wormy skin. Old dad.

January 20th

Today I pierced that fastness. The bit-and-piecing of the play goes on in rehearsal but, hearing the set speech I have given Theseus on the lunatic the lover and the poet I, standing hand-rubbing oldly as Philostrate, was of a sudden filled with lunaticloverpoet's pride. I marched bold as a soldier to her house in the afternoon, there being no performance, and knocked and said to the maid, a long-nosed girl, that Master Shakespeare was come to deliver somewhat to her mistress.

Her mistress, says she, is occupied and cannot be seen, may-hap she herself can take. I say no, I am here on the Lord Chamberlain's behoof and will not bandy with servants. And she she she comes into the hallway to ask who is here. She sees me and says: Well, come in and let us know what is your business. So I leftright leftright to a fair panelled room and we sit. The somewhat I have for her is but a cordial summons to tomorrow's *Romeo*. Is Master Burbage in it, she would know, and I say aye. Ah, she is sorry then but she is promised abroad. You have then, madam, a large acquaintance in London? Oh, I am invited much. For mine own part, madam, I find a poet's life a surfeit of clawers and rubbers. I was but saying a week gone to my near friend Harry Wriothesly, the Earl of Southampton that is . . . He is a friend, you say? The Earl of Southampton is your friend? Oh, I have earls and dukes enow as friends; I was saying but this morning to Duke Theseus . . .

You speak English prettily, madam. What, though, is your native tongue? Say somewhat in it. She says (I write it on my tablet): *Slammat jalan*. What means that, madam? It is what we say to one who is leaving, it means: let your journey be safe. And so I am gently dismissed. But I kiss that wonder of a warm tawny hand before leaving.

January 27th

It was yesterday and I have scarce breath to write. Liveried barges to Greenwich and then the great roaring fires and braziers against the bright thin cold as we deck ourselves, wine too and ale and chines and boarheads and a tumbling profusion of kickshawses, then we gasp in to the Great Hall, the Queen chewing on broken teeth in her magnificence, gold throne, bare diamond-winking bosoms glowing in the heat of logs and seacoal, laughing lords and tittering ladies and the Queen's bead-eyes on my lord E, amethysts bloodstones carbuncles flashing fingers jewelled swordhilts the clothofgold bride and silken yawning groom. And so, amid coughs, to our

147

play, Will Ostler trembling and forgetting his lines and finger-clicking for bookholder to prompt but all else going well save for Kemp, impromptu king, who got not so much laughter as he thought his due and chided audience for this. Later almost to blows with Kemp, but he has a share and I am but a poet. So home in dead weariness (torchlight on the river as though the river burned). But in my cold chamber I am dragged wide awake by letter on table with H's seal. It is to be done. I am to have my share. In fever of delight and gratitude. So I go today to her house, clear flashing winter sunlight making a world all of tinkling money, and I am admitted at once, for all must go well for me now. I have a gift for her if she will accept it, it is no more than a dish of candy from the Court, but it is from the Court the Court, mark that, madam. Aye, my play was done before the Queen's majesty at Greenwich. Before the Queen? Aye, that. And what did she wear and what noble lords and ladies were there and tell me all all all. And so I told her all.

February 2nd

It is the birthday of Hamnet and Judith and I have not been home this long time. But I have sent news and also money. I am busy here, I am much occupied, I am working for them, am I not? Aye, much occupied; be true to thyself if not to others. I ask her about her present life but she will tell me little. What does she seek, what does she wish from this life? She does not know. Surely love, I say; surely we all wish love, the pleasure of love and the strong fort of love's protection. She does not know. I ask what name I may call her by now, for I cannot madam her so in perpetuity. Her true name, she says, is Fatimah. Kissing both her hands in leaving I let my lips linger. She does not draw her hands away.

February 6th

At work on this new play of *Richard II* and have Holinshed and Marlowe's *Edward* before me. Ah, dead Kit, long rotted, long worm-eaten. How long has any one of us? By the Minories this morning was found, thrown into the kennel, bloody, stripped, robbed, a man I have seen oft about, a decent merchant called Gervis or some such name, now dead and his poor body dishonoured. I take to the drinking of a little sweet wine to dispel the vapours that cloud my brains. Soon I am on my way to her, determined on boldness. The little wine has become much. I am come, I tell her, to read verse to her. She is in a loose lawn gown, her arms and shoulders bare to the great seacoal fire. She will listen. Listen, then. Here is the Roman poet Catullus. You know no Latin but I will English it. Let us live, my Lesbia, and love (who is dis Lesvia? – She is the poet's mistress.) . . . Suns may set and rise again. For us, when once the brief light has set, there is left for our sleeping the sleep of one endless night. Ah, the horror of that, Lesbia (Fatimah, I would say), is in the very sound of the Latin: *nox est perpetua una dormienda*. She shudders. So what den do dey do? Oh, he asks for a thousand kisses, then a hundred, then another thousand, then a second hundred, then another thousand again, then a hundred. Mx Cx Mx Cx Mx Cx. Thousands and hundreds of kisses in sweetest alternation. Dat is a many kisses.

–Do you kiss in your country?

–We kiss not as you do. We have what is called de *chium*. It is done wid de nose.

–Show me.

–Nay, dat I may not.

–I beseech you.

She shyly places her delicate splay-nose on my left cheek and ploughs up once and down once, as she were new-making the furrow already there.

–Ah, that is good, but an English kiss is better.

So saying, I seize her in mine arms and place my lips on hers. It is like no English kiss I have ever known: her lips are neither a rosebud nor a thin predatory line; they are full and fleshy, like some strange fruit or flower of her Indies. Her teeth are well forward, set like a palisade to forbid the melting of a close kiss. I bring my mouth away from hers and set it to kissing the cool-warm brown smoothness of her shoulder. But she will have none of this and yet she will; she pushes and pulls me toward-away from her. So now it is to me to say:

–I love thee, by God I do. My love my love I love thee.

–I love not dee.

And then she thrusts me away with more power and strength than I had thought possible to reside in such slenderness. But now I am whetted and will not desist. I clasp her and she batters me with little golden fists, crying at me in her own tongue. She cannot prevail and so she bites toward me, her tiny white teeth snapping at the air. So it is needful that I bear down upon her, drawing, as it were, the teeth of her biting in a great disabling kiss, the while I hold her to me as I would engraft her on to my body. And so soon she yields.

Soon? Very soon. I see soon that she knows all. She is no tyro in this game. I feel that disappointment that all men know when they discover they are not the first, and disappointment makes a kind of anger which makes a kind of savagery. But I possess her in a terrible joy, the appetite growing with the act of feeding, which astonishes me. And in the end I coldly see that I have a mistress. And a very rare one.

February 14th

This is St Valentine's Day, twittering feast of the low-bending blessing bird-bishop. Tawny bird with white bird on couch close-lying. Ah God, what fluttering tweeting tricks she has already taught me, lore and crissum and alula aflame. We fly, I swear we have flown, I swear we have taken wing and soared through a ceiling that has become all jellied air and floated then among puce and auriferous nebulae. It is the glorification of the flesh, the word made flesh. She calls down strange gods with strange names: Heitsi-eibib and Gunputty and Vitzilipuztli and the four archangels surrounding the god of the Musulmans. In a fever I take to my play-making and theatre business. I write my few lines of *Richard* in despair of the power of words. I force myself to a mood of hatred of her and of what we do together, making myself believe that I am brought low and soon must come to ruin. I cleave my brain, writing of England's past, a cold chronicler that sees how all this will fit the nation's present temper, and at the same time a silken Turk on a divan. Her servants leer at me, my growing thinness, the black shadows below my eyes. I ask her to come to my lodgings, it is better so. In her bedchamber (I remember that past August) I am too aware of padding feet without, fancy the locked door not truly locked or full of eyes in knotholes. She says she will come.

February 25th

Money money. My presents are not enough (the bolt of silk, the dress of taffetas, the mask encrusted with brilliants). WS, prospering man of affairs, gives gold. Prices are so high, she says. It is on account of the crops failing last year. What does she like best to eat? Mutton stewed tender in spices, coughing with pepper. *Odi et amo.* Her smell, rank and sweet, repels my sense and drives me to madness. (And all the time poor *Richard* jogs on toward his foul death. Roan Barbary I have called her: that horse that thou so often hast bestrid, that horse that I so carefully have dressed. Then I see the twoness. She harps still on Burbage, a proper man. Well, that Bolingbroke shall never ride her.)

March 4th

Lying on, in, under her, I pore with squinnying eyes on a mole on that browngold rivercolour riverripple skin with its smell of sun, or else a tiny unsqueezed comedo by the flat and splaying nose. Her breath was sour today, too many squares of powdered marchpane. She did not want but, chewing the honey almond stuff still, all careless of my madness, she careless let me do. Then I hate, then I would strike her down to grovel like a bitch on her belly. She poutsays I must take her to

151

fine places, go to feast as others do. But I am jealous; not even to the Theatre am I willing that she come, though masked and curtained from men's viewing. I question the wisdom of her coming now to my lodgings, though mobled up in her coach, her coach to return for her in two hours. Shall we set up house together, this lodging being small? She will keep her own house, she says, she would be free. I have not talked of my wife and children, nor she ever of marriage.

March 15th

I hear news from Court that H plays no longer about among the Queen's flowers, that he, in his great man's new-found maturity, himself now tweaks the pink peach-cheeks of a lovely boy. Ah, how love, in all herhis manifold guises, doth take hold on us and squeeze us of our pride and lustihead. I am besotted with her, would eat her like a butter lamb. I tell her of my near friend's pederastia, thinking it may make her mirth, but she says men go only so an they lack a powerful woman to keep them to the proper way God ordained. She tells me Tales of the Wise Parrot, which she writes down in her language *Hikayat Bayan Budiman,* wherein serpents bite the toes of great princesses and are left as dead till some magical prince cometh to kiss them alive again. And then she asks a piece of gold for telling of the stories.

April 20th

Sir Philip Sidney's *Defence of Poesy* is out at last as a printed book. Well, we have done better than *Gorboduc* in the years since he penned it. He would have right tragedies and right comedies and delightful teaching &c. Yet if we are to hold a mirror to nature (I thank thee, nasty Chapman, for that phrase) we must see all in one. Thus, gibbering in my nakedness and approaching her with my cock-crowing yard, I see I am a clown, I see I am also a great king that will possess a golden kingdom. Tragedy is a goat and comedy a village Priapus and *dying* is the word that links both. Cut your great king's head off and thrust him in the earth that new life may spring.

May 1st
We were together, she and I, in my bedchamber, she but newly arrived in a sort of hunting costume with feathered hat, then who should enter but H, whom I have but heard of these many weeks and hardly seen for any length of time since my few minutes of slobbering gratitude over the £1000. She drinks him in, I see that, this striding-about-the-chamber lord with his ringflashing hands beating time to his loudly elegant eloquence of that and this and what Lady Such-and-such said and what His Grace observeth of the evil times and the approach of HM's grand climacteric. He is full of French – *bon* and *quelquechose* and *jenesaisquoi* – so that she listens to him in wonder. He then, as she were a Bart Fair show like a pig-headed child, praises her strangeness, her colour, her little-ness. Oh bring her over, he says, we must exhibit her, my friends will be much taken. And all the time she quaffs him and, when he is gone, will not do what she is rightly come to do (or have done) but talks of his clothes and his deadgold swordhilt and his quicksilver words, Mercurio. He is gone now for his plump prostitute boy, I roughly tell her. Oh, dat believe I not, she answers, he is much a gentleman for de ladies; dat see I bwery clear.

May 10th
In fair spring weather he comes to say how faithless lovely boys can be. This one (Pip he calls him) that had all his heart has treacherously gone over to my lord T, drawn by some pretty bauble. But, I tell him, loving is all fear: from loving to losing is but the change of a letter.
  –Aye, with women too, he says. Merrylegs all. Your own doxy is only a unicorn for her colour.
  –Meaning? (A great fear blew in upon me).
  –We in Europe cannot govern what a woman shall do, any

153

more than a boy. The Grand Turk locks her up in his seraglio, eunuchs armfolding portily before the portal. We cannot.

–Your particular meaning?

–I thought I saw your Dick Burbage in a carriage with her. She cannot wash off that colour. Veiled, but a brown arm taking a posy from a flowerseller.

–This is a trick to make me jealous and angry. (I have de flowers on me; I cannot see dee today den.)

–Is she your wife? Have you claims on her?

–I give the false bitch money.

–My money that would be, in a manner. Well. But there is no signing of any indenture.

May 11th

To her to rail, beat, near-kill. She screams, her wrists cracking in my gripe, that she has done naught wrong but she will do wrong an she wishes. I rip at her bodice, tear, wrench, gnash, chew. Her maid, fearful for her mistress's safety, batters the locked door but I shriek terrible curses and she departs going oh oh, fearful for the safety of herself. The transports I now enter are a burning hell of pleasure. If before we have soared and flown, now we burrow, eyes and noseholes and snoring mouths filled with earth and worms and scurrying atomies, all of which are transformed to a heavy though melting jelly of pounded red flesh mixed with wine. We dig with pioneering wings down towards the fire that is the whole earth's centre, nub, coynt, meaning. At the seventh approach to dying, my loins scraped raw, she sinking to a howling sweat-gleaming brown-gold phantom, I fancy that the ceiling opens as by some quaint shutter-device to reveal a pearl intaglio heaven, watching, bright-eyed like a pack of foxes, God the Father beard-stroking (party-beard), saints with uncouth names like devils all about – St Anguish, St Cithegrande, St Ishak, St Rosario, St Kinipple, St Pogue, plumpy Bacchus with pink eyne. Leaping around the bed is a cherub-demon that is Mr WH, crying do this and that and more, I

154

would learn, I would be shown. I show him. And after, in a cold and rainy May evening, I sit in mine own lodgings feeling truly in a wretched dim hell of mine own making, spent, used, shameless, shameful.

May 14th
This afternoon I must to act. It is but the part of Antonio in *The Two Gentlemen*. Speaking to Proteus I say:

> Muse not that I thus suddenly proceed;
> For what I will, I will, and there an end.
> I am resolv'd that thou shalt spend some time
> With Valentinus in the Emperor's court.

And Proteus, my son, that is Dick Burbage, stands grinning there. I would shout at him: Tell me, tell me whether it be true. Here is the platform of truth and nakedness, I will have none of thy lying. Wert thou with her or no? And so I forgot the line following and must be prompted by the bookholder. Then my shame near makes me shiver with an ague. I look out on grinning faces among the groundlings – few, very few, they like not this play well – and up at the wooden heavens and back at the curtained study and think perhaps I am dead and already a ghost. Then I think I hear whispering and laughter from a sidebox: it is she, it is she with another. This will not do, it cannot be supported, I must purge her out. But I know I may not.

May 20th
Well, there is no way out, for I must obey my lord and ring-giver. She has been leaping and cavorting and high lavoltaing these last days with the knowledge of what she sees as her entrance into the great world now coming in a trumpet-and-banner and livery-glittering barge-feast, Harry and his friends and their ladies (ah, they have learnt; I taught them; LLL was Learn Learn Learn) swan-sailing Greenwichwards with

155

the kites soaring over in the unblemished May heavens. And so it is. Poor Will very sober-suited but she in a sort of flame-satin stepping aboard. Oh, Lord P and Sir Ned T and the Earl of K are much taken, the rose-and-cream ladies envious and shifting their best malice at this russet innocent from the land of four-footed men and women with their things cut at a strange slant. They mock her dis and dat and de udder ting, but she is brownly cool while they sweat. The lords surround her, bringing her slices of goose-breast in sharp sauce, veal-shape, a flawn on a silver dish. To H she flashes black eyes and teeth like serried snow-gems; his eye burns, drawn to, trans-fixed in, her brown bosom. I see his long fingers, all crusted fire, scratch at their palm. I see the two of them, in my fever, lying together, lordly silver moving in kingly measure upon queenly gold. He has not forgotten Willobie and his Avisa, the Islington trick; he knows he is at liberty any time to buy something with his thousand pound. Day's end in torchlight, the rowers' slower strokes, cob and pen and cygnets a preen or a sleep of silver, the kites no longer disfiguring the empurpled May heavens. The madrigalists sing of a silver swan, each voice married in perfection to a correspondent viol in a consort of viols. It is she has put hand in his.

May 25th
And yet the strangeness is that they may feed both my hungers best by showing those hungers so clearly separate and apart. For soul and body can never be fed together for all our pretence of the unity of love. For love is one word but many things; love is a unity only in the word. With her I can find the beast's heaven which is the angel's hell; with him, the body's hunger now able to be set aside, there is that most desirable of sorts of love, that which Plato did hymn. And then the devil within me says: Yet thou dost admire his beauty of form, it is an impure love. I dream of our somehow gravely dancing a pavane or sarabande, all three, in whose movement the reconciling of the beast and the angel may, in myself, be

156

accomplished. I would, in some manner, wish to share her with him, him with her, but perhaps only a poet may think in these high terms, not understandable of either the soul (giver) or body (taker). And so I wait to be told that I lose both a mistress and a friend.

May 30th

He will have her, he says, for her newness, for her unicornity. He asks not; he doth take. She is ready to be taken. Take too, I say, what I have writ for her, by her unread. Add them to the odorous fellowship of that spicy chest. Take this sonnet also, of the perils of lust (hark to the dog's panting: had, having, and in quest to have). I am aware of a manner of glee in all this, the glee of the wronged man; it is a sort of cuckolding. The trick is to be glad and noble and to smile; better far, it is to wish this loss and conceive it as the child of mine own will. He will tire of her, and I must force in myself a willingness to take her back. And then I see myself as ageing, bald, rheumy, three teeth but newly drawn, a man who should think it foul shame to drivel and froth so in youth's lust. And more than mine ageing I catch a picture in sun and dust of the squalor whereto I, and all men in me, am condemned by reason of time and flesh and indolence: a louse I but now caught in the grey hairs of my chest, the Fleet's stink, a boil on my thigh, the wretched mound of rotting shit that lies to fester in the sun, the diseases that heave and bubble in pustular quietness all over the city and the world. It is time then to rise all above the body and live in a making soul.

June 2nd

My love, my love. I dream I see them pointing and laughing at poor Will the creaking player. Play thou all old men, for that is most suited to thee. I dream of an old man cast off, owing a thousand pound, by a youthful prince that but played with him. Have I not great expectations, my lord? Aye, expect me to come and take thy black doxy away from thee.

June 5th

I see in the city riots the riot in mine own soul configured. I have walked by the brawlers with staves. It is but a matter of the price of merchandise and they glow in a ferment of high principle and the shaking of souls. Teeth are broken and young bones sorely belaboured.

June 13th

The prentices handle the buttersellers roughly for that they sell their butter at 2d the lb too much. The whole city grows harsh and unlovely over this business. Jack has kicked in the head of Tom and left him to lie in street-filth, I found what appeared to be bloody brains staining the stones by Billingsgate, an old woman, torn and limping, went groaning home, her butterbasket abandoned. The Knight Marshal's Men are in their element, they have run a blubbery young prentice through with their swords, five sword-thrusts for one poor boy's body. Dead are A. Orme, H. Nininger, T. Neale, C. Knickerbocker, L. Gann, R. Garlick, C. Fox, C. Cousland, Ed. Crabb, G. Brace, Will Biggs, J. Seymour, M. Sewell, N. Wishart, Martin Winsett and others. Torched prentices street-marching by night, cracking glass, crying for the blood now of Jew tailors, equivocators, Dansker beershopmen, Flemish weavers, for aught I know W. Shakespeare. Ah yes, and in Clerkenwell they have beaten the negro trulls, stripping one and scrubbing her to clean off her black before using her foully. She at least, she she will be safe in Holborn or wherever he has removed her for his secret pleasure. There will be martial law soon. They have arrested five prentices and there is talk of hanging and quartering them on the scene where riot first started. All this is for 2d a lb on butter. Well, what was the agitation in the city of mine own soul but that? A finger-dip into butter-smooth pleasure and the armies and rioters trample through my veins, crying Kill kill.

Buttered blood, the town is spread with it. And now the

price has risen to 7d a lb, which is 4d above what is usual. Eggs will not be thrown now, as they are 1d.

June 26th

It was to be expected, though there have been few enough brawling prentices at the Theatre. The playhouses are today closed by the Council's order. The term is two months, which brings us to plague weather, the gentry and nobility out of town, the mobled Queen (she is aware, for all her mirrors dim or painted with the reflection of a face twenty years gone, of her broken teeth) on progress. Shall I go home or not?

I can hardly move, sick not in my body but only in my soul, centre of my sinful earth. I lie on my unmade bed listening to time's ruin, threats of Antichrist, new galleons on the sea, the Queen's grand climacteric, portents in the heavens, a horse eating its foal, ghosts gliding as on a buttered pavement. Were I some great prince I could lie thus for ever, my body washed for me, a little sustenance brought, cut off from the need to act. But there are plays to be written, images of order and beauty to be coaxed out of wrack, filth, sin, chaos. I take my pen, sighing, and sit to my work. But work I cannot.

VII

(Preached, ladies and gentlemen – softe let me drinke before I go anie further – in the dark church of SS Somnus and Oneiros any night before his most despicable Lowness.)

THAT LUST AND FILTHY FORNICATION and sodomy and buggery roam this realm, beating their lewd wings and raising a coughing and stinking and blinding dust to lead reason astray, you may be well assured, aware too of God's wrath in the dread portents of the times. Is not a new Antichrist Armada bristling about our shores? Yet will men not see their fault. Is there not fresh dissension between the French and the English? Yet will men not see their fault. Is not the Queen's Majesty entered a good way into the climacterical year of her age, seven by nine which is sixty-three and the grand climacteric when, as my lord Bishop of St David's saith, the senses begin to fail, the strength to diminish, yea, all the powers of the body daily to decay? Yet will men not see how little time there is to repent of their fault.

You may take one man's sinfulness to be the type and pattern of all. There he lieth, tossing in the guilt of his lewdness, the primal lecher, neglectful of his duties to a fair wife but all too ready to plunge his sizzling steel into the slaking black mud of a base Indian. Well, he hath lost her now; there is leisure left for penitence, but penitence may be all too late, for if the occasion of that sin were to return would he shun it? He would not. There are examples enough of other poets and players who sought, when their powers failed for the enactment of sin, to whine to Almighty God of their deep and profound repentance. Yet call time back and they would be staggering anew in their drunkenness and grunting in beastly thrusting at their ragg'd and spotted drabs. There was dirty Greene and Godless Merlin or Marlin (no matter what his name; it is burnt with his atheistical writings and consumed in eternal fiery nothingness). I have news for thee, snorer. There is one, a God-fearing true Christian named F. Lawson Gent., who has been vouchsafed, by God's holy grace, a vision of these poets screaming in hell, the which he has set down in a treatise called *A Watchword against Wickedness and the Lewd Trumperies of Poetified Sneerers*, wherein he recounteth the horror of their deathless punishment in hellfire (as seen by him in his vision), a burning stinking brewis of venomed maggots and toothed worms that do gnaw to the very pia mater. Thou dost well to stir and sweat in thine unwholesome sleep.

God is almighty and all-just. Yet, in his all-mercifulness, he will oft chastise and castigate and chasten the sinner in this life as a warning of what is to come if he leave not off. This poor play thou writest of King John – it is no more than a quincunx of botched nonsense, creaking stuff. Account that to thy sin. Are not the personages therein still-born, ditch-delivered by a drab of a whining muse, even the Bastard a roaring emptiness of meaningless rant? Are not thy best lines, such as they are, filched from pamphleteers that write on the present troubles? 'Naught shall make us rue, if England to itself do rest but true.' Has not Master Covell written: 'England cannot perish but by Englishmen'? Did not C.G. of Cambridge say: 'If we be true within ourselves, we need not care or fear the enemy'? A manner of thieving. From one sin many may come.

Thou didst flaunt thy pride in the possession of a noble patron and companion. 'To me, fair friend, you never can be old, For as you were when first your eye I eyed' (oh, vile!) 'Such seems your beauty still.' What response to that? None. He is gone to Dover with my lord Essex that they may take Calais, though Her Majesty will send him flea-eared court-ward again. But, in any event, he says thou art as he formerly thought, namely an upstart, vulgar and over-familiar. Thou covetest thine old place as His Own Poet, but there be others now who are in his affections. Thou enviest Master Chapman his special new nearness to his lordship, as also his *Blind Beggar of Alexandria* at the Rose, taking the town by storm, this being accounted by many to be far better than aught WS can do. (Never fear, thou wilt steal for Dick Burbage what Ned Alleyn doth so well.) Anger comes. Good, tear thy bedsheets, throw thy water-jug out the window, rail at the little boy who brings thy penny dinner and halfpenny bread from the ordinary. And then slop into it, eating fast and beastly, sending out for more, fancying goose-breast richly sauced baked in a fat coffin of brown and flaky paste, herrings pickled in spicy eisel, a cheesy flawn with cloves and borage, nut-and-honey cake topped with cinnamon cream. Ugh, glutton. Then to thy bed, belching in sloth, to lie there, paper unwritten on save by random sprawling greasy greedy fingers, ale-drop jottings, dust settling on the pile. Aye, lie, conjuring images of lost Her, in postures of abandon before thee, moaning in nasty lust.

Let England die. Let the Spaniards come to ravish our wives and daughters, egged on thereto by the traitorous French (Papists all). Thou hast done thine own poor duty in a dull pro-patria play. Let Master Doleman write his book about the next Succession to the Crown of England, dedicating it foolishly to my lord of Essex, loosing rumbling grumblings and privy fears. Thou dost snore. The men are pressed to march coastward against the threat of invasion. Thou dost snore. Calais is feared lost and the levies are dismissed. Thou dost snore. The bells clang in a glorious Easter Day, the churches are locked on the communicants that they may be pressed once more for Doverward shogging. Thou didst and dost snore. Wretch, cause of a country's decay. 'The imminent decay of wrested pomp' (stolen from Chapman).

Wake to a great shaking.

So was it. WS blinked back to the painful world on a hot morning, openmouthed at the strong mid-morning sunray infested with motes, wondering who this shaker could be. His

mouth was sour, his head ached. On the table by his bed lay
the greasy remains of his supper. He wished to retch. First,
though, this shaker must be identified. He recognised the
hand, stubby, ingrained with ink, a dyer's hand, a printer's
hand. It was Dick Field's face that looked down on him,
gravely urgent. But Dick Field was in Stratford, entrusted
with money for Anne, a letter, presents for—

'Yes,' said WS. 'Yes yes.' He smelt, he knew, rancid, sitting
up now in a dirty shirt, rubbing his creased face awake.

'Can you understand me? I am come back early at their
request, at your wife's request I would say. It is the boy. There
is a letter.' WS took the folded note, opened it unhandily,
squinted against the mote-loaded shaft of sun, reading:

'. . . He has been given what are called apozemes and
electuaries but naught seems to shift it. He vomits all up that
he takes and grows very thin. In his sleep sometimes he
screams of devils. He talks of his father that he has not seen for
so long . . .'

'Yes yes, I see,' said WS stupidly, sitting up in bed, reading
and re-reading the trembling letter. It was, in its coldness and
sheer fact, like the letter of some very distant relative. 'It has
not been possible to go. I have sent money home. I thank you
for taking the money. You saw the boy?'

'He cannot eat. They say it is a fever out of Spain.'

'I will be too late, will I not? He will be dead, will he?'

Field, in his rider's cloak and boots, looked sweating and
awkward standing there. But suddenly he cried out: 'It is your
own son, man. Your own flesh and blood.'

'Aye,' said WS, still in bed, scratching his baldness,
examining the furfur in his fingernails. 'You have always said
that a man should live with his wife and family. I had my plan
of retiring to Stratford, a justice of the peace, a fair house, a
competence.'

'You seem not to understand,' said Field, sweating more.
'This is your son Hamnet. Dying.'

'Hamnet.' It was the name that cut suddenly through the

163

drug of sleep and indolence. 'My son.' The building for the future, the making of a gentleman that should come into his estates, range his deer-park, be dubbed knight. 'Sir Hamnet Shakespeare,' said WS. 'A proud name. He will talk of his father, who had built his fortune for him in the playhouse. Well, it is no more ignoble than the printer's trade. Would you not say so?'

'Where,' said Field, 'are your riding boots? You must take horse at once. The roads are full of soldiers. The expedition from Cadiz is coming back.'

'Cadiz. In Spain. And you say it is called a Spanish fever?' Then the news thrust properly in, burst the membrana, and flooded its meaning through him. 'Oh, God,' he said. And he was out of bed, clumsily searching his chamber for clean linen, moaning in double pain.

'It is not for me to say,' said Field primly. 'I have often thought that— It is full of distractions, London.'

'I thank you, I thank you. A man should be with his family, you have said so already.' He saw himself in the small mirror, ill, old, dirty. He splashed himself in stale cold water, towelling himself till he was covered with bee-stings. It might be good for him, he thought, a swift ride through country summer.

'I mean no harm,' said Field. 'For people of our kind there are things that can do little good. We are, so to say, in the suburbs of that world, we can never go into the centre. They have but newly read your Venus poem in Stratford, at least your father has. I was constrained to agree with him that it is—'

'That it is not the poem that a Stratford glover should write. Nor a Stratford printer print. It is altogether too pagan, it is not a dirge of Brownist godliness.' WS was fumbling himself into his jerkin. 'So a good Stratford tradesman is corrupted by wicked London and his son starts to die.'

'Oh, your father is no longer inclined that way,' said Field. 'He talks now of saints and candles. As for your mother, she will not look at your poems, nor will your wife. They are become great readers of tracts.' WS stared at him. 'Very ill-printed. But it is not perhaps stuff that good printers would wish to print.'

WS grinned wearily. 'Poor Dick Field. We are all caught, are we not, between two worlds? Our sin and our sickness is not to choose one and turn our backs on the other but to hanker after both. Well, I am ready.'

'I hope that a miracle may have happened by the time you arrive. They are praying every hour.'

'Some to a God of tracts, others to a God of candles. And I cannot pray to either.'

It was difficult riding out of London, what with discharged soldiers drinking in the streets, their doxies clinging to them, all, in their victory revelry, unwilling that any should pass through on his own business. The slobbering and shouting heroes, unbuttoned for the intense heat, invited gentlemen to dismount and quaff from this spilling tankard, see, come, let us drink to the Queen and to the final ruination of King Pip and all his saints and candles. They clawed at flanks and harness; some fell in their drunkenness and were near trampled; some were whipped out of the way. The captains were little more decorous than the men, swaggering and singing, stroking their great Essex beards. Well, it was news worth celebrating: Cadiz surrendered; the Spanish fleet burnt, save for two galleons brought home; a heavy ransom taken. The impending death of a boy in Stratford meant nothing, his cries were muffled by the clanging of the Te Deum bells.

As he rode north-west he remembered that former accession of insight (that time he had been riding back, not to) into the meaning and horror of fatherhood, the responsibility too great for any to bear. Eleven years old, that boy was dying now. Into what was he dying? Either into fire (for it was certain that God, if God existed, was unjust) or nothingness, and the road to both a road of pain. Better not to have been born, better not to bring to birth. Out of the gush of water came fire that could not be tamed to humble, sufficient processes; a thrust of opal drops in animal ecstasy unleashed a universe – stars, sun, gods, hell and all. It was unjust, and yet a man was condemned to the injustice.

But what he had somehow dimly previsioned in his son was the poem he himself could not make with words. He saw a young man, handsome, rich-suited, languid on horseback, falcon on fist, living out his own life surrounded by parkland. He would not marry, knowing that no woman could be trusted; he had once given his heart, though in the full knowledge that it would be belted into the rough like an old tennis-ball; he had recovered in gentle melancholy, his speech was full of sharp sad wit against the sex. He drank his wine in moderation, both pale hands (a single great opal on the left) about the dull-glowing goblet, talking with dim-faced friends, none of whom he trusted, about philosophy, half-lying and half-sitting in his throne-chair, loosely graceful. In him was fulfilled the true human aim of stoic awareness. Caught between the past and the future, he had no faith in either. He could not act, but he had no need to act: no violent assumption of commitment could ever come to disturb his sad calm. He read Montaigne after feeding his peafowls; he read Seneca in his bedchamber of an autumn night with the owls mousing; the intrigues of Machiavel or pseudo-Machiavel belonged to a world transmuted by art to a pearled emblem of all he rejected. This was a son who himself would be no father. But what of the name and its transmission to the far future?

He then saw that he was willing into this image his own desire for a sort of sterility. The son *was* the father. What, in a sense, he had also been willing was that son-father's annihilation. This death was something that he, not fever, was encompassing. As for the perpetuation of a name, it seemed to lie elsewhere. Nor was it really the name that was important; it was the blood, it was the spirit. But he did not yet fully understand. By Maidenhead it burst out of him, the fabulous agonised cry of all bereaved fathers. But he could not pray that his son be spared; he could only pray that whatever hellfire, awarded by an unjust God, awaited that boy after death, he himself should embrace it on his son's behalf. If he could not die for his son, let him at least be doubly damned for him. He rode on hopelessly. At Oxford he went down for two days with a fever of his own. The hostess of the Crown in the Cornmarket nursed him well. By the time he reached Stratford the other fever had been resolved.

HE sat with his father in the garden behind the house on Henley Street. It was glorious August weather. The pot of small ale in his hands were mantled with sun-warmed yeast-flowers. That sun that mantled the body in a pleasant light sweat, cooling deliciously as a breeze whispered, had played like a consort of jolly brass as the small coffin had gone under. The summer world had sung about the coldness of the church, the dull drone about ashes to ashes, the weeping family. It was a family to which he seemed not admitted, from which his own dry eyes alienated him. He had stood on the outer ring at the graveside, a cold London man in a fine cloak. The elder of the gravediggers had whistled between his teeth distractedly, then remembered himself, then darted an embarrassed smirk and a droll roll of eyes at the cloaked gentleman. And so earth took that poor boy. What could earth not take? He had shown, at the age of eleven, little promise of special distinction – neither a lust for books nor a precise knowledge of birds and herbs, no mad quickness of thought expressed in boy's mean and ragged language; a tall boy tending to thinness, in face not unlike his uncle Gilbert. He had liked to spend his after-school time with his uncle Gilbert, hearing simple scriptural tales while the patient glover's hands worked away. He had seemed not to like his uncle Richard. His sisters had sometimes petted him, more often scolded, in the manner of girls.

'They are two good girls,' said John Shakespeare, nodding. 'A help to their mother and grandmother. They will be good wives.' Good girls, thought WS, good wives. I have begotten good stodgy children. Yet Susanna was fair enough at thirteen, a young country beauty. Soon, his heart sank to think it, she would be enticed to cornfields to beguile the dullness of a country spring. Yet what could a father do, especially a father away? 'It is a comfort to have daughters,' said John Shakespeare.

'Can you say that?' grinned WS. 'I always felt that you saw your children as somewhat of a burden.'

'Oh, when a man is young,' said his father vaguely. 'I grow old now. It is good to have them all about me. You will be of the same mind when the time comes for you to settle.' He waited for his son to say something. 'Have you thought,' he asked at length, 'of settling?'

'Of making a beginning,' said WS. 'I have spoken with Rogers about my buying New Place.'

'New Place!' The old man's apple cheeks rushed, in a flash, through a whole autumn's ripening. New Place – the hub and core and flag and very emblem of Stratford gentility.

'A house for my wife and children.' WS thought an instant. 'Wife and daughters,' he emended. 'They have crowded you here a long time. For myself, it may yet be a long time before I can leave the stage.'

'Leave it as soon as you can,' said his father with gentle force. 'I do not think it can do a man much good. And now Ned talks of joining the players. He is more like you than any of them, though he cannot write sonnets and poems about naked goddesses. He says he will act, and I say one actor is enough in the family.'

'An actor who thinks of buying New Place,' said WS. 'Edmund could do worse.'

'Aye, I see about the New Place. A house of women, though; a strange house. Of course,' said John Shakespeare, 'it is not too late to beget another son. Anne is not old. Edmund himself was born very late. I have been lucky with sons, myself, but my sons seem loath to give me grandsons. Gilbert will never marry.' He shook his head in some sadness. 'There have been people saying he has a devil in him because of the falling sickness. You can see that women will hardly look at him, poor boy. And Dickon is strange, he does strange things. I have begotten a strange set of sons.'

'What strange things does Dickon do?'

'Oh, he goes away for whole days, sometimes two or three, once a full week, and comes back with money. He will never say how he got the money, only that it was fairly earned. But he was seen one day in Worcester.'

'Doing what?'

'He was with some old tottering woman, walking through the rain. It was not clear what he was doing. One thing is certain, and it is that he cares naught for marrying. He is a well set-up boy, save for this one leg somewhat shorter than the other, and there are a many wenches that would be glad of such a husband. But he will have none of them. Nor will he aught of the trade here. He is strange, going his own way. But his heart can be very soft, for those last days of poor Hamnet's sickness he was a comfort to your Anne.'

'Yes?'

'Oh, he was ever ready to weep with her and comfort with kind words. And she was much withdrawn in spirit and would speak to none. But Dickon wept with her in her sadness.'

'And I suppose,' said WS slowly, 'he said it was a great misfortune for her that her husband should be away.'

'Oh, he knows how husbands must be away to earn money. But she is glad to have you here now. Her lord and master is home, and that is a woman's best comfort.'

GLAD? Comfort? They lay together in that old bed from Shottery, the hot summer nights recalling others. It was always said, he remembered, that with the death of a son a light goes out between wife and husband. They lay on their backs, sweating, thinking their thoughts, so silent that each might well think the other asleep. At length he said, this night, 'What is it best we do? Will you come to London and bring the girls and we will set up house there?' He saw it, saying it:

169

Master Shakespeare the citizen, with Mistress Shakespeare and two daughters, renting some decent house in Shoreditch or Finsbury; no more friendship with noble lords, no more furious writing midnights, no more freedom, no more— He pulled a shutter down swiftly. He would relapse into a dull fat tradesman of botched plays. What would the gentlemen of the Inns say? Ah, hast seen his Juliet? His Adriana thou wouldst say, his Katherina. 'Will you stay here? By next year we shall have New Place.'

'You wish it so. You have your own life there. Master Field spoke to your brother—'

'Dickon.'

'Aye, Richard.'

'And what has he told you?'

'What all talk of, he says, in London. I would not live there to be laughed at.'

'So you believe all some prentice printer tells you?' He tried to gulp that back. 'Whatever it is, for I know not what. Belike what is always said by the vicious about poets and players, ever since Robin Greene died and Kit Marlowe was killed.'

'I know not those names.'

'Oh, according to the scandal-tattlers we are all atheists and drunkards and wenchers and we throw our money away on evil living. I ask you, would such an one be able to send home what I send and to talk now of buying New Place?'

'I know not what money you earn. I know that you are seen smiling in silk with your fine friends. And I know that – ah, 'tis no matter. Let me sleep. God knows I have had little enough sleep lately.'

'What is it that you know?'

'Oh.' She turned away from him with a deep sigh. 'There are poems you have written. They were brought to Master Field for his printing.'

'That is old stuff, my poems. I brought home *Lucrece*, though none here would read it. Field himself told me that my father read *Venus* but you said it was filthy or some such thing.'

'I said not that. But it is about naked goddesses.'

'Aye, a naked goddess tumbling a boy in a field.'

She did not see that. She said: 'There are little poems, and some are to men and some are of a black woman.' She snivelled. 'Thou didst never write such to me—'

'Sonnets? Is it sonnets? What is this about Field being given my sonnets?'

'I know nothing of it.' WS was already out of bed, moonlit in his shirt. 'Get back to bed,' she ordered. 'You make it clear that all they have said is true.'

'It is not that. It is that poems I have written for friends have been thumbed by dirty hands—'

'Perhaps the dirty hands of friends. Get back into bed or not, as you please. Leave the house if you wish. But let me sleep.'

'I would speak to Dickon of that. I would know more. There are thieves, traitors—'

'Richard is away, as you well know. This is unseemly, all this raving. Your son not cold in his grave.' She began to snivel again. Then she said: 'I have seen one of these sonnets, as you call them. I *have* one of these sonnets.'

'That is not possible. Where is it? Who gave it to you?' He went to the bed in moonlight, he took her moon-silvered neck between his fingers. She broke his weak hold with her own strong hands, saying:

'So, I am to blame for all this. Fool. What have I to do with it?'

He saw his unreasonableness. 'Where is this sonnet?'

'Oh, it must wait until morning.'

'I would see it now.' He took the tinder-box and worked at it, moonlight leading him to the candle in the sconce that had been there since his boyhood. 'And I would know who gave it to you.'

'Richard—'

'Aye, Dickon again.'

'It was another Richard that gave it to him, if you must know. Your friend Master Quiney.'

'Dick?' He was puzzled, he just could not— 'Dick Quiney?'

'It is in my book there.' She pointed, her fine full arm now red-warm in candlelight. 'It is between the leaves.'

WS, frowning, puzzled, took up the poor little bound volume of devotional chatter, weak warnings of the Spanish Antichrist and the End of the World. He found a folded piece of good parchment and, even before unfolding, at once remembered the May night, his own trembling fingers (were they then now different fingers?) pulling from his breast what had been defiled, turned sour and rancid, by the laughing defection of a black-haired girl and the jeers of her new lover. How many years ago had that been?

> My love being black, her beauty may not shine
> And light so foiled to heat alone may turn.
> Heat is my heart, my hearth, all earth is mine;
> Heaven do I scorn when in such hell I burn.

'Well,' he said. 'After so much time. This I wrote as a boy. Before I even knew that you— Yes, I had finished it that very day.' He peered at it. 'It is very poor stuff, but I was only young.' And then, in something like awe and fear, he perceived whose name was embedded in it. 'God,' he said, 'must we be pursued all the time?'

'Come back to bed,' she told him, 'now you are satisfied.'

HE wished to travel back to London the following morning. But his father said:

'I hoped you would have stayed longer. There was one piece of good news I wished to keep till it was in black and white, no going back on it. I had thought I would have had it by now. I wanted you, with all this sorrow, to carry back something to cheer you.'

'Well, we could all do with some private happiness to match the public.'

'Public? Oh, these French alliances and so forth and the Queen passing out of her whatever-it-is—'

'Grand climacteric.'

'Heathen superstition. These mean little to us here, out of the great world. Small things please us best. Though I would doubt this was a small thing.'

'Let us have it then.'

They were in the shop and workroom. Gilbert, older and graver than his years, was examining with serious closeness a piece of calfskin whereon he had pencilled fingers. He said, looking up from this seriously:

'Aye, such as 'tis. All are to be made gentlefolk, aye. But that cannot make little difference, as in God's eye it is all one.'

'What is all this about?' smiled WS.

'Oh, Gilbert fumbles things, as ever.' His father cleared his throat in something like embarrassment. 'I applied for arms, and it is to be granted. It is but a matter now of awaiting the ceremonious parchment from Garter King of Arms.'

'So.' WS sat down on a rough workstool. He slowly began to see what this meant. 'Arms? A coat of arms?'

'A falcon shaking a spear and a silver spear on what they call a bend.'

'And the motto?'

'I cannot pronounce it aright, it is Norman French.' He took Gilbert's pencil and traced the letters large on a scrap of paper: NON SANZ DROICT.

' "Not Without Right," ' translated WS. 'Good,' he said after a little time. 'That is very good.'

'We have always been gentlemen,' said his father, holding himself straight with a dignity that was somewhat pathetic. 'There were very hard times but, thank God, they are over. It is thanks to you. And the sooner you are out of this way of making money and back here to live like the gentleman you are—'

'We English are like that,' sighed WS. 'We like to forget how money is made. Only land is truly gentlemanly, land and property. Well, I shall do my best to buy land. And I am glad we are now acknowledged to be gentlemen.'

'Soon you may have your arms on your liveries and seals,' said his father, bubbling it out like a child. 'Rings and banners and all. It is a fine smack at the Ardens,' he grinned with child's impishness. And then, with mature seriousness, he said: 'It is strange how things be all reversed in time. Your mother forgets all about how her family stood for the Old Faith. I think it is your Anne that has brought her to this plain religion and sniffing at bishops. And I, in mine old age, take up the position she once held, though privily, very privily. At least, I see that there is more truth there than I formerly thought, and that men have been cruelly burnt for nothing. I see, I mean, in what belief I may die. They say men end as wine and women as vinegar.'

'Whatever else may come,' said WS, 'we will all end as gentlemen.'

'And think what it would have been for your son,' said his father softly, regretfully.

'Oh, well, that is all over.'

Gilbert, like a clock, whirred before striking. 'We know what we are,' he said, 'but know not what we may be.'

AND so he rode back in more scorn than bitterness. That a lord should behave so to a friend. There is one here would speak with you, my lord. He is, he says, a gentleman. It would be best to have a seal made and to twang off his scorn on fine vellum, then down with it, a spear-shaking falcon in hot wax. *Non Sanz Droict.* You have exposed my heart, my lord, to the grinning world. You have made manifest so your own unworthiness. This admired fine flower is stricken with a hidden canker. Believe me, they that understand will mark that more than mine own shame; they will know where to attribute that shame, my lord. And then and then and then. Was it not perhaps dirty Chapman (there is a vulgar name, a Cheapside name) who had, putting his own poems in that spice-smelling

174

box, stolen in spite and jealousy and run in glee to Field, thinking Field to be a ready filching printer who would pay out his few slivers of silver – drink-money, boy; for the poet naught; for me much? But was Field that manner of man? He might well be; he was not of need better for being a Stratford's son; he had said not one word that day WS had called on him with money for the family nor that other day when he had brought his crapula-quelling news. Or was it shame that kept him silent before shame's own begetter?

Still, the true enemy to be boarded was that fine and graceful lordship, silver-masted, silk-caparisoned, cloth-of-gold sails lifted proudly to any breeze of perfidy or wind of court policy, faithless, as incapable of love as of loyalty – And then a great wave of weariness washed over his own poor barque as he saw once more the boy's coffin drop into the grave, and he wondered whether, with death always lurking in alleyways, tainted meat, sour ale, death a very contending twin of life, those great cries about honour and rank and treachery were more than the bawlings of a fretful child in a cradle. Honour is a mere scutcheon. Who hath it? He that died o' Wednesday.

A mere scutcheon? A *mere* scutcheon?

VIII

Scutcheon. Escutcheon. Shields, targets, escutcheons, coats of arms, pennons, guidons, seals, rings, edifices, buildings, utensils, liveries, tombs or monuments . . .

'I noted,' said Florio, 'with pleasure—'

The seal had been cut hurriedly by a man in Fetter Lane. To bear and make demonstration of the same blazon or achievement upon their shields, targets, escutcheons . . .

'In this strange country,' said Florio, 'a gentleman may be a poet. Indeed, gentility has been taken as the primal qualification for making poetry. It is rarer to see that a poet may be a gentleman.'

'But the letter itself,' said WS, 'apart from the seal—'

'He has not seen the letter,' said Florio. 'And I think it better that he do not. He is not well, he is not solely sick of his body but also most profoundly melancholic—'

'Following the fashion.'

'Alas, no. He caught some pestilential thing in France. Alone in bed in the dark a man has no audience. As for what you say in your letter, I perceive its justice. Shall we say that my lord was careless and that my lord's friend the Earl of T desired copies of these most exquisite and mellifluous etcetera etcetera and that these then fell into the hands of Sir John F and then descended rung by rung to—'

'To some impoverished master of arts or other.' Dick Field may have talked of them in Stratford but he had not desired to print them. Some small anonymous fellow had brought them, saying he had been sent by a gentleman whose name he had been forbidden to disclose. Not Master Chapman, said Dick Field. Indeed, Master Chapman was not impoverished; his new plays of humours were doing well at the Rose.

176

'As you say,' said Florio. Florio looked fatter: something to do with the content of love, with Rosa, a poet's daughter. 'And you may also say, if you think about it, that if my lord showed your sonnets to any of his friends it would in no wise be out of malice; rather out of pride. I think you may understand that.'

'Well—' WS felt, in a kind of despair, the whole matter of bitterness and high feeling begin to slide off; he was always an actor quitting old parts for new. 'We have been somewhat estranged of late. I sent sonnets, as you will know, and the sonnets bounced rudely back.'

'I was instructed to return them,' said Florio. 'Nor was it in mine office to add aught that might explain his rejection of them. But, to speak plainly now, he was in one of these states of his – states that belong more to his rank than to the man that holds that rank. He is naturally, as you well know, free and honest. Sometimes, though, he must remember what he is, especially when great lords are going forth to wage war against the Queen's enemies. Her Majesty would not let him follow my lord Essex to Cadiz, and that rankled. He would not have it then that he was sick. And he has been much importuned by small poets and smaller players. Then there was some question of a woman, not a lady. He has had her hidden away somewhere. There has been, in fine, a fit of revulsion against what he termed the lowness of his life.' Florio gave an Italianate shrug. 'Guilt is a word you might use. The English are given to guilt. It is something to do,' he said vaguely, 'with the English being a sort of twofold people.'

'Tell me more of this lady – woman, I would say.'

'I know little. Some very dark creature, I am told. He had her taken into the country. But he has been railing against drabs, poet's drabs, as he calls them. There are times when he has a very low opinion of poets.'

'And what of this poet?'

Florio sat back comfortably in his great leather chair, black legs crossed. Behind him was a table littered with the materials for the dictionary he was making; his shelves were full of fat books. It had been a good life for him, a watching life. Symbol of his philosophical content, a fat black cat slept by the spitting pearwood fire. Autumn was cold this year. He said:

'Yourself? It is time, I would say, for you to be his friend again. The ranks close.' He grinned at that. 'Your respective ranks grow nearer, I mean. I think you have, looking back on it all, done him more good than harm.' Florio did not know everything, that was quite certain. 'You lacked authority to enforce your precepts, no more. I will send word that you have been. Do you send words, a sonnet or so. This time they will not be rejected, that I can promise.'

. . . And for his crest or cognizance a falcon his wings displayed argent standing on a wreath of his colours; supporting a spear gold steeled as aforesaid set upon a helmet with mantels and tassels as hath been accustomed. . . . WS, gentleman, went back to Bishopsgate, his head buzzing with images. 'Not mine own fears, nor the prophetic soul of the wide world dreaming on things to come—' It was a matter of looking back to that most balmy time, the mortal moon having endured her eclipse, peace proclaiming olives of endless age, but a month gone. Symbols of established order drawn from the great and public world to figure his own exaltation, to refigure what was, after all, an abiding love. As for olives of endless age, there was no such thing: fruit grew black and wizened; trees died. The lease of the Theatre was, in a year's time, due to fall in; old Burbage was negotiating to buy that fencing-master's hall in the Blackfriars, his aim being to create an indoor playhouse. Nothing stayed still. A man changed his lodging, his place of work, his mistress; between man and wife love could die, a man's art and skill grew or languished or merely changed, and all beyond his control. Only between man and man was there hope of maintaining – beyond pure animal need that misted the eyes with blood – a love nourished by will and brain and a conscious art of forbearance. And so, his comedy of the Jew of Venice put by

178

for a day or two, to sonnets of love's renewal, his own past pain, the fresh pride of a poet who was also a gentleman:

And thou in this shalt find thy monument,
When tyrants' crests and tombs of brass are spent.

In a fever of creation he wrote twenty sonnets. They were sent in a wrapper whereon he himself had carefully drawn and coloured the blazon of his arms and motto. As Florio had foretold, there was this time no rude tennis-ball smacking back of the proffer; instead there ensued a reading silence.

Then give me welcome, next my heaven the best,
Even to thy pure and most most loving breast.

A somewhat timid, a sick man's, note, of humble rather than gracious welcome came to him. WS rode, almost jump on its receipt, to Holborn. This time there was added, to the usual phalanx of flunkeys and butlers and stewards and chained staffed bearlike major-domo, a deep-bearded trio of physicians. Stay not with him over-long; he is soon made weary. I mark you. The great bedchamber was dark and musty, air excluded with shut casements, daylight with heavy curtains. A dim lamp, a votary's lamp, burned by Harry's bed. Harry himself lay thin-faced, languid, with WS's bold black-inked sheets strewn over the silk coverlet. He grinned shamefacedly through the gloom.
'So,' said WS. 'What is all this?'
'They tell me I am not well. You too perhaps have been sick?' He picked up one of the sonnets and read out: ' "Whilst, like a willing patient, I will drink—" '
'Oh, that.'
'—"Potions of eisel 'gainst my strong infection." '
'Sick with not seeing you, if you like.'
'I *do* like. I would you had not had the sickness.'
'Well, I am better already. It is the honey of being with you that cures. The absence was all eisel.'

'There is nobody quite like my Will. I think you will soon make me better. It has been some French pox or other. Sores and swellings and a fever. They have bled me and stuck foul poultices on.'

'And you must be in the dark?'

'Ah, let us have some light, for God's sake. *Fiat lux.*'

WS strode over to the casements and drew back the fine heavy curtains. November sunlight poured in, a sudden crushed cask of light wine. 'Air too?' he asked.

'It costs no more than the light.' WS opened the window a fraction, enough for a November gust to send two or three of the sonnets swirling and sailing. Harry himself, with a sort of comic feebleness, blew out his lamp. The sickroom mustiness and foul sweetness of suppurations and electuaries was blown out also. WS picked up two sonnets from the floor ('. . . Even that your pity is enough to cure me.' '. . . A god in love, to whom I am confin'd.') and stacked the whole batch together, saying:

'I hope these were some little help.'

'Oh, excellent physic. I think I could get up now.'

'It is I your doctors will blame if you do.'

'Keep away from physicians. It is all probing and guessing and pretending with them. They leave it to Nature to cure in her own time, but they take the credit. As well as very fat fees.'

'You must have been very sick, then?'

'Most inconveniently so. There is much going on at court these days and I am out of it. And I am fed on possets and broths and can have no wine. Nor women. It is strange, is it not, that a German monk first put that trio into words? Martin Luther. *Wein, Weib, und Gesang.* The Emperor's language is a very uncouth one. But it triumphs here, I think.'

'So women are out of your life?' He had to know, but he would not ask directly.

'An abeyance or intermission or some such thing.' He was very languid. 'Oh yes, there was the question of your own dark little doxy.' A great lord, he could speak carelessly. 'Hetero-doxy. It was an experience, I will say that, and an experience we shared. That seemed very strange. I seemed closer to you than to her.'

'Where is she now?'

'She wished to be a fine lady. She had, would you believe it, ambitions to marry into the English nobility, that black creature. And she comes crying to me that she is with child.'

'With child? *Your* child?'

'Who knows whose child? Mine. Yours. Anybody's. It might well be yours from the time of her having it, if my calculating is correct. Though there are untimely births. But let's talk of other things, not drabs and their brats.'

'I must know this,' said WS. 'What happened?'

Harry yawned. 'That wind blowing in makes me sleepy.' WS did not get up from the chair where he was sitting to close the window. 'Oh well, I see you are concerned. That I did not expect. I have heard all sorts of tales about her since, chiefly that her house and coach and servants were all paid for in Spanish gold and that her aim was to reach me through you—'

'I did all the wooing there.'

'Wait. And to reach Robin Devereux through myself and slay him. And even to slay other great ministers of state and then, when apprehended, plead her belly.'

'Oh, that is all nonsense.'

'There is a lot of nonsense talked these days, all, I would say, put about by the Spanish themselves – spies and equivocators, sent hither to cause confusion. She was really a harmless enough little drab, though black. She was in debt for her rent and for the payment of her servants.' He grinned ruefully. 'That, you would say, will perhaps teach me a lesson for the stealing of a friend's mistress. You can understand that I felt very bitter towards you.'

'You still have not said—'

'I sent her to Cowdray to have her bastard. Oh, I am not all unkindness. I have been known to be generous.'

'I know, I know. And then?'

Harry shrugged. 'Well, there were other things. There was the triviality of a war with the Spaniards and His Eminence in Calais, for example. She has just passed out of everybody's life. I sometimes ask myself whether I dreamt it all. And then I remember that smooth brown body very well and the rising hillock that rose yet higher day by day. Oh, let us call her part of our sickness. Let us also call for some wine. I swear I am cured now.'

But there was no wine. The trio of physicians, grave antithesis to *Wein, Weib* and *Gesang*, came to the ringing of Harry's bedside bell. WS might come in a day or two again, but he must not excite the patient as he seemed to have done this time. And, see, he had let in light and air. 'I know,' said WS, watching servants scurry in to restore fug and gloom. 'Light and air are great enemies.'

WITH the sharpening of the air and the coming of the festivals of light there was the restoration, through the sweet languor of convalescence, of the old friendship. Yet could it ever be truly recaptured, the former primaveral joy? Here was no longer a boy's body, but the weak one of a man who had ailed with a man's sickness; the free boy's spirit had changed to the crafty, seeking, politic soul, tending to meanness and spite, that Essex was teaching men at court to endue. WS felt himself ageing, dissatisfied, life nagging like broken teeth, the gaps in his life presented to a probing tongue. Sweet-tongued, honey-tongued Master Shakespeare. Well, that final act in Belmont moonlight (a real moon pressed as an involuntary actor, though unable to disguise the wintriness of its shining down on the doomed Theatre) deserved the praise and commendation it got, though no laudator's eloquence could touch the eloquence it lauded. They thought this out-topped all, but what could they know? Only he himself knew what might be done if the words and craft could descend in a sort of pentecostal dispensation of grace. He saw dimly, a vision lay coyly

182

beyond the tail of his eye. This stuff was play. There was a reality somewhere to be encompassed and, with God's grimmest irony, it might only be grasped through playing at play, thus catching reality off its guard.

The reality of life was dark; of that he was growing slowly convinced. It had more to do with evil and suffering and loss than poetry, born out of Hybla, would yet admit. A sort of masque of evil was being played out at court, but the mere fact of great seals and jostling for place, gold chains of office, the farce of worshipping as a sort of Titania a queen pock-marked, unwashed, posturing like a nymph before painted mirrors, reduced the quick scurrying nastiness to unhandily played mirthless comedy. There was this unpleasant business of Essex wishing to keep the ransoms taken at Cadiz, the Queen demanding them for her own purse, the screaming greedy old woman confronting the pouting shouting boy before ladies-in-waiting who must feign deafness. This lust for a few bits of Spanish gold grew into a faceless rage, quarrels for their own sake, the setting-up of factions. When Candlemas came round again the death of old James Burbage was much in the foreground of WS's concern, but he heard indirectly of Essex and Harry ranged, with their hangers-on, against the Cecils and the Queen herself, of the Earl of Northumberland tremblingly challenging Harry to fight matters out with steel (but what matters? What was to be gained or lost? Would there be a mouthful of bread or a spoonful of wine the less or more for anyone whatever the issue?). What made the nagging and biting the more shameful was the fact of irresolution: threats and grasping of daggers but no blood spilled in animal honesty.

The syrup of recorders and viols, the candle like a good deed in a naughty world – they seemed out of place in this cob-webbed cellar. WS sighed to think he would always be, in some manner, unable to provide the right biting word, the shaming image, for the little evils of his own time. He stood, with Dick Burbage and his brother Cuthbert (new owners of the Blackfriars and the Theatre respectively since their father's death), to take in a sour pennyworth of Chapman's new play at the Rose. They scorned to pay good silver to a rival; they folded their arms under their cloaks and stayed near the gate, in the groundlings' place but aloof from the groundlings, to taste an act or so of *A Humorous Day's Mirth* – Count Labervele and Countess Moren, both jealous of their younger spouses; Dowsecer the melancholic in his black hat. It was the times, it was London people.

'But,' said WS afterwards as they sat over cheese and ale in the Dog, 'they are not true people. They are not built out of warring elements, they are a sort of potion. Do you follow me? Human souls are not smooth mixtures like that, fixed for ever in choler or melancholy or amorousness. These creatures of Chapman's are flat, like very crude drawings. They cannot surprise either themselves or others by becoming other than what they are. Do you follow me?'

Dick Burbage happily shook his head. 'This is the new way,' he said, 'and it is rooted, so they tell me, in the teachings of the ancients. It is humours. Now I could do one of these melancholic humours very well—'

'You could do any of the humours very well, as we know. But that is just singing one air over and over and then turning to another. But a human soul is not just one repeated air, it is many. Now even Shylock has many sides – sometimes to be pitied, sometimes laughed at, hated at other times—'

'Shylock is a dirty Jew.'

WS sighed very deeply. 'That is what the people wish to believe, they wish him to be a kind of Lopez. That is the way of satire, setting up a dirty Jew or an old cuckold or a young lecher or a fantasticated gallant. But satire is a very small part of poesy.'

'It is in the mode,' said Burbage, 'whatever you may think of it. It is a kind of comedy we must give them somehow.'

'Not my kind.'

'If Chapman can do it so can you.'

184

'I can make satire of their satire, no more. No less, should I say? The times change quickly. A play should be bigger than the times.'

'That is like scorning yesterday's hunger. But yesterday's hunger cannot be stilled with tomorrow's food.'

'Oh, highly epigrammatical,' smiled WS.

'Give us this day our daily bread,' prayed Burbage. 'And money to buy houses withal. Settle this matter of your house, Will, and sit down seriously with your tongue in your cheek to out-Chapman Chapman.'

'It is settled,' said WS. 'New Place is mine, the conveyance signed and all. Could Chapman buy the best house in his own native town, wherever it is? Chapman,' he added loftily, 'is very silent on his provenance.'

'His—?'

'Provenance.'

'No gentleman,' said Dick Burbage vaguely, 'though he knows much Greek.'

'Freehold?' Cuthbert Burbage asked suddenly. He had not spoken up till now. He had been gloomily tracing geometrical tropes in spilt ale on the table-top.

'New Place? Oh aye, freehold.' WS knew what was in Cuthbert's mind. He liked Cuthbert, a prim man some two years younger than himself, precise, thin of lip, steady of eye, lately much worried – as they all, indeed, were – over this question of a lease.

'You talk of what plays to write and to act in,' said Cuthbert accusingly to his brother. 'You neglect the question of *where*. We need our own New Place.'

'Oh, Alleyn may renew the lease,' said Dick carelessly. 'He talks of doing so.'

'Not to me.'

'We shall have the Blackfriars, a warmer place than any of our old playhouses. The dwellers there cannot prevail with the Privy Council. Why, my lord himself has told me—'

The noble residents about the new theatre had complained

of the loss of amenity, the possible noise and undesirables milling to chew sausages at blood-bladders and tiring-house thunder. Dick was too sanguine; that was his humour.

'We shall have two playhouses bubbling away,' said Dick, 'you may see else.'

'And humours in both,' said WS.

'Talking of humours,' said Dick, 'Pembroke's Men have this bricklayer writing something. I saw him doing a very loud Hieronimo. He is mad about humours, he has the whole theoric of humours pat, they tell me.'

'A bricklayer?' WS frowned.

'Aye,' said Dick Burbage straight-faced, 'another poet that is no gentleman but knows Greek. He was shouting great drunken cartloads of it at the Dane's beershop, but none would listen. Anacreon, Xenophon, everything. Then he vomited on the floor.'

'A bricklayer that knows Greek?'

'Oh, he was at Westminster School. He has been soldiering and says he took his spoils off the man he killed before both camps. In the Low Countries that was. Very Greek. His father or stepfather or somebody was a bricklayer and taught him the craft. I should think a bricklayer might build very strong plays.'

'Stronger playhouses,' said Cuthbert.

'Every man to his humour,' said WS. 'Trade, I mean.' Then he remembered what his own trade was. 'What has he written?'

'Well, Tom Nashe started this thing for Pembroke's but will not finish it. It is satire again, humours and so forth. Two acts only he did, then he would do no more out of fear. Then this burly Ben man comes in and says he will write the other three, where is paper and a pen?'

'What name?' asked WS.

'He is called Ben. Ben Jonson.'

'A good bricklayer's name.'

'Very strong humours. Nashe bites his nails in fright that it goes too far in satire. But this Ben says he fears no Greek nor anybody.'

'Who is the satire against?'

'Oh, everyone,' said Dick Burbage vaguely. 'City and Court and Council and everyone.'

A SMALL THING, another man's play. Who could have thought that it might ease open a door best kept locked? An empty summer of work loomed, Harry off to harry the Spaniards with Essex. 'A secret,' he told WS. 'But I will bring thee back some little gift of Spanish gold or a black Spanish beard roughly wrenched out or a *donna* or *señorita* or whatever they be called.'

'Speaking of black women—'

'They are not all black. Some are red-haired, so I hear.' He drank off his Canary, belched like the hulking bulky warrior he was not, then said: 'Ah, it is the sea that is calling. Tonight I ride to Plymouth.'

'Beware of the fair maids of the West. To revert to that one of the East that is not fair and not a maid—'

'I know nothing. She is not heard of. But she is much in thy mind still.'

Well, yes, so she was. So many paths of sensation led back to her body, as he wrote, as he lay in bed unsleeping because of the heat, as he wandered the City, marking types, faces, words, humours. And then the crass motions of public life, against which he could not encastle and moat himself, drove her out. What was this, who were these, fellowships and families of the ragged and near-naked tramping and limping on flat horny feet out of town? The beggars were leaving town. Why they were leaving town he did not know. He asked his barber.

'Ha' you not heard?' said this onion-smelling man, snipping at WS's crown, greying auburn. A little boy in the corner sniffed up snot between the phrases of his song; his father nudged him in irritation with the elbow of the hand that plucked tinny accompanying chords on his lute. 'It is the

Council that saith how all the old sojers and beggars and such are to be sent out to fight in Piccadilly—'

'Picardy?' frowned WS. The lutenist accompanied that with a final *tierce*.

'Picardy is what I mean. I was thinking of somewhat else. And the Lord Mayor likes not these orders for he will not be ordered so by the Council, and he has let it be known what was ordered to be done and so all the poor folk and beggars have time to shog out of London. But there will be trouble yet, you may see.' And he cut a lock viciously, like some small vital organ.

Trouble yet. What happened now bumped itself at the Chamberlain's Men like a coalheaver's sack; it did not have to be filtered through barber-shop talk. Dick Burbage came in shaking with news of what the Council was to do, and this in a plague-free time of good business. All the playhouses were to be shut down.

'Shut down?' squealed Laurence Fletcher. They were rehearsing *The Merchant*. Some small readjustments of casting. A line or two to be expanded. Things were going well.

'This bricklayer has dropped his bricks on everyone's toes,' shouted Burbage. 'I said that *The Isle of Dogs* was enough in its very title to have the Council growling.' This was the satire on everyone he had spoken so mildly and vaguely about, full of strong humours. 'Now they go mad and bite us all.'

'It was the Mayor that asked the Council,' said Augustine Phillips. 'You may blame the Mayor as much as the Council, and they were at loggerheads over the pressing of the beggars.'

'Trust none,' said Burbage. 'They are all the same. This fool of a bricklayer deserves not the name of player or poet or anything except clumsy ape.'

'Come,' said WS. 'It is not just he, surely. He but completed the play, and Pembroke's had their tongues hanging out to put it on.'

'You have not heard all yet,' said grim Burbage. 'It is not just a matter of closing down till we are good boys again. There

188

is talk of bringing in the breakers to demolish the playhouses altogether. The Justices are given their orders, so I hear.'

'Over our dead bodies,' said Heminges.

'Oh aye,' snarled Burbage, 'over our dead bodies. They will smash playhouses and players together and hug themselves at the godly thing they have done.'

'So much,' said WS very quietly, 'for your new mode of satire.'

'What was that? What did you say? What did you say then?'

'And what has happened with Pembroke's?' asked Harry Condell.

'Nashe knew all this would happen,' said Burbage. 'He was wise and has gone to Yarmouth. But they have put this Jonson and Shaw or Shaa or whatever his name is and Gab Spencer into the Marshalsea. They could not find any of the others. And this Jonson lumbers over to the Rose before they seize him and joins the Admiral's and begs four pound in advance out of Henslowe.' Burbage suddenly let out a shout of bitter laughter. 'Four pounds out of Henslowe, and no hope of aught in return.'

'O rare bricklayer,' murmured Fletcher.

'This is the sort of man you have coming in now,' said Burbage, back to his snarling. 'Rude and loud and knowing no discretion. There was a time when we were all gentlemen's sons. There was a time when things went well for us all.' WS could not, to be honest with himself, remember such a time; there had always been something.

'Well,' said Cuthbert Burbage, 'it is but a matter of ante-dating. We are losing the Theatre sooner rather than later.'

'It will blow over,' said Kemp. 'It always blows over.'

'But what do we do now?' said Phillips.

Ride home, pay Stratford a surprise visit. New Place and a coat of arms: those were solid enough, those would endure.

'Go home,' said WS.

AND SO HE WENT HOME, and it would have been better, ladies

189

and gentlemen, if he had not gone home. Days of gorgeous sunlight on the August roads, and a welcome from the mistress of the Crown in the Cornmarket at Oxford. And at last, his heart beating beneath his fine doublet with gentleman's pride, to Stratford. Prepare, ye spirits of dead great Stratfordians, to do blue-lipped homage to a new son that hath made good. Bow down, town, about him. But first, entering by Shipston Road, there is the Clopton Bridge to be crossed. The spurgeoning of the back-eddy. Back to the strait that sent him on so fast. He smiles, thinking of Tarquin. He sees again the great white slack body, the misshapen southern king go to it. His smile is nervous; a cloud goes over the sun. Then the cloud unclamps the god of day and it is Clopton's own thrown cloak he passes over. His chestnut glories in his rider. Bridge Foot, left to Waterside. Give you good den, your honour. God bless you and keep you, sir, credit to your town and country. Sheep Street, in fleecy sunlight, Chapel Street belled in summer heat, and there—

There it was, the peak and crown of endeavour. New Place, Clopton's own house. It was the first time his fast-beating eyeballs had gazed on it as his own, the conveyancing having been done remotely, himself busy in London. His wife and two daughters had, he knew, moved in; he had sent them money for furnishings. The great door gleamed in the Shakespeare-honouring sun. Must he knock? No, he would not ask, not even with his fist, to enter his own house. The front door was locked; he passed, honeyed stone on his left hand, through the little wicket that led to the garden. It was overgrown, there was work to be done here. Underhill, its former owner, had neglected it. Hollyhocks, lupins, larkspurs, a shaped yew hedge; WS foresaw a neat pleasance. And in the centre of that lawn there a mulberry tree.

The kitchen door yielded to his unlatching. It was a fine cool kitchen, gleaming with copper pans, but no bare arms were at work, scouring, skimming. He passed through to the living-rooms. Plain furniture well-polished, a betrothal chest, simple hard chairs. He shivered a little, for it somehow seemed not to be a house for the living. Where was Judith? Where Susanna? Where was Anne? It was as though he had bought the house literally for himself. He walked softly to the stairs, as though his own corpse lay unhonoured in one of the bed-chambers above. He mounted the stairs.

On the landing he surveyed, irresolute, the five closed doors. For some reason the name of John Harington came into his mind. Ajax. A jakes. A water-closet. Why there should not be in this house? It was a cleanly idea. He had a sudden unbidden image of Dick Burbage, in melancholy hat, dis-closed seated upon one. He said softly, 'Anne? Anne?' At once there seemed to be an explosion of soft panic, whispering and rustling, behind one of those doors. Puzzled, he went to unlatch. He opened. He saw.

White slack nakedness gathering itself, in shock, together. 'It was, she was, that is to say,' twitched Richard, in his unbuttoned shirt, grinning, ingratiatingly smirking, trying to hide his, though it was fast sinking in its own bestial shame, instrument of. WS stood there, beginning to glow and shiver with the cuckold's unspeakable satisfaction, the satisfaction of confirmation, the great rage which justifies murder and the firing of cities and makes a man rise into his whimpering strong citadel of self-pitying aloneness. He marked the bed, her bed from Shottery, nodding. She wrapped her ageing treacherous bareness, bold as brass, into a night-gown. 'She was sick,' went Richard on, 'and lying thus for the heat and I came in now and—' Suddenly, limping a pace, buttoned soundly, he changed his tune. 'It was she,' he said. 'It was she that made me.' He began to whine. 'I did not want to, but she—' He even pointed a trembling finger at her, standing, arms folded, bold as brass by the second-best bed of New Place.

'Aye, aye,' said WS, almost comfortingly, 'it was the woman.'

IX

I<small>T WAS THE WOMAN</small>, it was the woman, it was the woman. He did not expect it, but he rode back to London in terrible calm. I thank you both for that cornuted manumission, there is naught like cuckoldry for the promotion of a man's health and vigour, it is a kind of gift of money to spend on one's own sins (*nota:* guilt, gilt, gild, geld, Danegeld). As for the abandon of rage and striking (even with that gentleman's hanger that swung at his side, sheathed), did it not smack too much of the stage? I am paid to act, I act not gratis. That is why I bowed out, my dear wife, I will be back for supper and to have a word with my daughters, if they be mine. For you, my little brother, practise your trade of comforting elderly female flesh else-where, nuzzling worm, worming into abandoned holes.

Oh God, God, God.

Despite all, he was numb, only half-there. The business of London autumn impinged only in dream-voices.

A<small>NDREW</small> W<small>ISE</small>
Touching the publication of this play,
Richard the Second, I the stationer
Wise, wise in my station, do propose
Prudently the prudent lopping-off
Of that tendentious scene which does present
The king's deposing. There be Privy eyes
Glinting for hinted treason in these times
When e'en the whisper of the word 'succession'
(What is 'succession' but a whispering word?)
Can, in a wink, swell to an autumn gust
To blow down heads like apples—

RICHARD BURBAGE
They have relented: we may play again.
Gain, though – what gain? Only the Rose hath gained
With three new petals that to us be thorns.
Spencer and Shaa and pestilential Ben
Have navigated the rough Maishal's sea
And are three masts now for the Admiral.

ANDREW WISE
It doth well, marry, aye. In Paul's Churchyard
At the Sign o' th' Angel they with silver clamour
To buy this tragedy of Richard's death
And Bolingbroke's – but that's a dirty word.

RICHARD BURBAGE
'Tis gone, our Theatre's gone, with lease expired
Vile Giles, the villain Alleyn, has prevailed,
Our art is homeless—

CUTHBERT BURBAGE
                    Yet there's Curtain Close,
Its eponym the Curtain that our father
Did buy ten years back with that brainless, gross
Grocer John Brayne. Let's welcome winter in,
Like to heap gold, like autumn, in our laps,
For plague's in exile, Parliament is called,
The City will be crammed.

O God, God, God.

RICHARD BURBAGE
Not so, for newly come to Court is one
That says the Spanish fleet is on the sea,
A laggard captive searched, her papers read,
Wherein it doth appear a great Armada
By Falmouth hovers off. For Parliament,
It is adjourned, the City empties fast.

CUTHBERT BURBAGE

Fast is the Don dispersed, the rumour goes,
God striking, as in 'eighty-eight, our foes
With vengeful thunder: fifty ships are gone
Full fifty fathom down, the rest as one
Vile whining ragged pack turn tail for home.

ANDREW WISE

Oh, it sells well, since that my lord of Essex
Is back at Court, brawling his wrongs. See how
So many feign to see his lineaments
In Bolingbroke's.

Oh God, God, God, God, God.

They do not even descry their own folly, not the folly of
wrong but of poor art. For adultery, aye incestuous adultery,
calls for craft in its enactment; to be caught is poor craft. But
we expected not— No, and yet our plays are full of the husband
returning unexpected, from Corinth or Syracuse or Stoke
Newington, it is the very stuff of comedy. I can hardly forgive
the ignorance, the rank folly, the want of craft.

If only I had not known, not seen.

And so, best release, into his own craft and the big buffeting
wind of history and public events, wrapping his own wincing
and withdrawing soul in a mountain of blubber, a jouncing
armour against grief of every kind, save perhaps later for the
treachery of a noble defecting patron.

'YOU ARE BECOME altogether too moral,' said Harry, one leg
over the arm of the best chair in his friend's chamber. 'First
you have Robin as Bolingbroke triumphant, then he must
grow old and relent, and then you must have this Hotspur,
which is Robin again, and he must die and be picked up by
a fat coward and so dishonoured.'

'I had not my lord Essex in mind for either. It was merely
that *Richard* sold well and I thought I would be carried further
by that wind. And,' mumbled WS, 'I was asked for humours.'

'They are all saying that it is Robin,' said Harry, pouring some of the Canary he had himself brought. WS would not have any. 'And we all said, when we saw your *Richard* on the stalls, that we had found a poet for our cause.'

'What cause? What do you mean?'

Harry drank, somewhat gloomily. Then he said: 'This cannot go on. The Queen fleering and jeering of the Lord Admirable, as he thinks himself to be since his new earldom. Robin played the hero at Fayal, and fat thanks he has had for it.'

'I heard that it was Sir Walter that took Fayal.'

'Whose side are you on? Robin has been treated very harshly, and there are some who will soon pay for it.'

'I,' said WS gently, 'am on nobody's side. I mind my own business, a humble and disregarded poet.'

'And no longer my friend?'

'Oh, Harry – My lord – I have nothing to say about these big storms, being only in their suburbs, so to speak, and feeling mere little breezes. What have I to gain or to lose by speaking allegiance to this cause of yours, as you call it? And what, for that matter, have any to gain or lose by my speaking?'

'There was a Roman poet,' said Harry, turning his goblet between his fingers and using a rather mincing accent, 'you may have heard of him, his name was Publius Vergilius Maro. He sang the glories of the Emperor Augustus—'

'So my lord Essex is to be the Emperor Augustus, is he?'

'You have no doubt, I see,' grinned Harry, 'that you are a sort of metamorphosis of Vergil.'

'I would rather be Ovid.'

'Aye, exiled among the Goths. Look, I would speak seriously on all this. The Queen grows into her dotage. These mad rages at Robin, the slights, the injustices, even – the other day – a blow; did you know that? – a blow on the face, and all for nothing, all these show her waywardness, the turning of her mind. Abroad we cannot hold what we have: look at the quality of the generals she would send to Ireland. Aught that Robin suggests is flouted. She is past rule.'

'Treason, my lord, my dear dear lord.'

'Treason in a poetling's chamber, aye. And was that of Bolingbroke's treason?'

'Kings and queens are not to be deposed.'

'Oh, hark to our grave-bearded preacher of divine right. None shall harm the Lord's anointed. So Henry the Fourth was an usurper and it was right that Hotspur should rise – is that not so?'

'Henry the Fourth was an anointed king.'

'I will anoint that singing beggar out there in the street,' said Harry. 'I will have myself anointed as Harry the Ninth. This must be very precious ointment.'

'Those old days are gone,' said WS. 'I have been reading of them in Holinshed to make plays out of them, the days when right belonged to the grasper. Those days ended on Bosworth Field.'

'Aye, aye, I saw the play—'

'We do not want them to come again, barons growling at each other for a gold hat that will not even keep off the rain.'

'That is so the ointment may be washed away,' said Harry. 'You shudder at usurpers and rebels but your plays make them very eloquent and persuasive.'

'There's a devil in all of us,' said WS. 'We are full of self-contradiction. It is best to purge this devil on the stage.'

'You may purge yourself, forgetting that you inflame others. They are at least logical that say to castigate folly you must first exhibit folly as a castigable thing, and in showing folly you thus cause more folly. Well, you may commit your own share of treason in a play about England's history. As for treason and folly,' said Harry, 'they are but words.'

'You sound like the Duke of Guise himself. That, you will remember, was when we first met, when you were with this Emperor of yours at the Rose. Machiavel,' said WS. 'I doubt it was poor Kit Marlowe or any other of us poor poets corrupted you.'

196

'I am not corrupt,' said Harry calmly. 'I spy corruption in the State. The State is crumbling and collapsing with corruption. The young men must cleanse it.'

'Harry,' sighed WS, 'I am ten years older than you— No, I will not say that, I take that back, there is no virtue of itself in age. Let me ask rather if you would live to my age.'

'Life,' said Harry carelessly. 'If there is no virtue in age of itself, then to live to be older is nothing. I would do things. If I die doing them, well then – I die. I might have died on this Islands voyage.'

'You acquitted yourself well, I know. You were made a knight. Sir WH.'

'Oh, there are a many Essex knighthoods.'

'But death then would have been honourable. Would death be honourable if it were like the death of that poor Jew, a comic death with the crowd roaring, your flesh pulled aside like a curtain to discover guts for the pulling-out? I mean a traitor's death. For, mark my words, I see that for you. Nobody will drag this queen off her throne. She will live out her days, and there cannot be many of them left.'

'She will grow older and older and pull the country into more ruin,' said Harry. 'She mumbles over the farthings in her purse, eating bone-soup three dinners running. And we must lean to her stinking breath, her teeth are all rotted, and prate of her eternal beauty. She cackles, she confounds her French and Italian and Latin, she peers at little stories of love in her bedchamber, drooling and slavering over them.'

'The French Ambassador was full of praise for her wisdom,' said WS uneasily. 'At least, I have heard so.'

'Aye, you have heard this and seen that, but you know nothing. The Queen is a rotting heap of old filth. I know, I am at Court. What we want from you, Ovidian metamorphosis, is something, play or poem, which shall show what is wrong and what is wanted. Something that shall encourage the young and point the way. A play about some old mad champing tyrant that is deposed.'

'When,' said WS slowly, 'I have written poems in the past, I have written them for your pleasure. I ceased writing them when it seemed that you took no more pleasure in poems, even in sonnets. I am not hurt by that – your time was come for taking your place in the world, with little leisure for poetry—'

'Aye, aye, come to your point.'

'My point is that I will write to give pleasure to you still, if you wish it, but only lawful pleasure—'

'Ah, Jesus, our moralist speaks again.'

'I will not write anything inflammatory. I will not make my pen a servant to treason. Oh, Harry,' he said, pleadingly, 'do not mingle yourself with these madmen at Court.'

'Am I to go on scraping to a madwoman? And I will not have you continually using this word "treason". Who are you, what are you, to be warning me against *treason*?'

'A friend, a lover. I thought a friend had certain rights—'

'In that you say you are a friend and lover,' said Harry with a kind of prim grimness, 'you may rightly talk of your rights. First, though, you must prove yourself both by showing duty.'

'Duty,' repeated WS with some bitterness. 'Ever since I was a tiny boy I have been told gravely of my duty – to my family, church, country, wife. I am old enough now to know that the only self-evident duty is to that image of order we all carry in our brains. That the keeping of chaos under with stern occasional kicks or permanent tough floorboards is man's duty, and that all the rest is solemn hypocrite's words to justify self-interest. To emboss a stamp of order on time's flux is an impossibility I must try to make possible through my art, such as it is. For the rest, I fear the waking of dragons.' He saw the slack development of that metaphor ready to form on Harry's lips. 'And,' said WS, 'do not start talking of dragon-slayers, for out of dragon's blood are formed new dragons. Let them sleep, all of them.'

'It is much,' said Harry, 'the view of life of the small greasy citizen. Well, I ought to have expected it from you, old age creaking on. Rheum and plum-tree gum and all the rest. You will lend no words to leadership, for you are afraid. What you will churn out now is what the citizenry wants as its own badge and image. London Bridge built on woolsacks. Where is your furry gown and aldermanic belly and, oh yes, your young wife to be courted slyly by young men with flesh in their codpieces? There you break the pattern, true.'

WS smiled very sourly. 'Oh, if you want your true toothless citizen's picture you may have it. I can outdo all in patriot's fustian and panting over gold-counting and even in cuckoldry. Behold one cuckolded by his own younger brother.'

'Cuckolded—! By—'

'You heard me. I saw it. I saw the nakedness and the leaping out and the shame and the shamelessness. The woman, you know, is never ashamed. That is a sentence to put down in your tablets.'

'Tell me all, I must know all.'

'I went back to Stratford when *The Isle of Dogs* shut the playhouses for us. Unannounced, unexpected. My brother and wife were busy with sacramental ceremonies, ensuring that New Place be a true house of love.'

'Tell me all, everything, everything that you saw.'

'I have told you enough.' WS saw the seething of his friend's laughter ready to raise the lid. 'Too much.'

'Too much!' Harry's mirth broke hugely. WS had never liked his laugh – high-pitched and maniacal; he had never liked the way the smooth face collapsed with laughter into an ugliness the more frightening because of the miracle of beauty it displaced: it was as if that beauty was nothing to do with either truth or goodness. 'Ah, no!' screamed Harry. WS saw the decay in a bared dog-tooth; the tongue was caked and yellow. 'Too much, too too too much!' The laughter tumbled out, an icy burn with the sun on it, then met sudden rocks of coughing. The thin body shook and throbbed under its finery. 'Oh, God.' He was weak, he lay back limp. 'As you say.' His arms trembled as he sought wine from the writing-table. 'Much too much.'

'The cuckold is always comic,' said WS, sickened by the transport he had seen, a transport as obscene and shameless as the image that had been its first cause. He remembered Gilbert's words, some odd country sentence twisted and transformed by Gilbert's peculiar genius. 'We know what we are,' he said, 'but know not what we may be.'

'Oh, sweet Jesus, I ache all over.'

'The goat and the giant codpiece,' mused WS. 'That act contains all. But why then cannot the cuckold be tragic?'

Harry choked on a mouthful of wine. Laughter buffeted it out, a bubbling spray. WS felt the wetness prick his face; a splash took the corner of his mouth and he tasted the sour sweetness like the end of friendship. He took a spotted handkerchief from the table and wiped and wiped and wiped. 'I pray to God that you too will learn,' he said. 'The bitterness of life may make you a man.'

'I have broke a rib.' Harry groaned in the pain of laughter's recovery.

'You will learn about order in time. Marriage is order. One suffers but cannot break it. Learn from that. One suffers that order may be maintained.'

'Well—' Harry rudely grasped his friend's handkerchief from the hand that still wiped; he mopped at his eyes, blinking away water.

'The ambiguousness of tears,' said the ready word-man.

'– Order or no order, you have made me suffer.' Panting, he felt his sore ribs.

'One thing, then – you will today ask me for no more poems or plays on this theme of foul tyranny and the duty of usurpation. You will leave here bearing instead the picture of a cuckold.'

'Cuck—' That word was ready to flint fresh laughter. Harry set his lips primly and brushed down the breast of his doublet as though laughter had been a rich pasty shedding crumbs. 'Aye, well, you have diverted me from state matters. It is the brother, I think, that is the cream of it.' Cream. His face moved once more towards disintegrating; he cracked the laughter to quiescence: down, wantons, down.

WS began to see that the final weariness was approaching, soft-footed down a long corridor. This boy, this great lord, had, in boy's or great lord's carelessness, bared a friend's viscera like a hangman: see you, this sonnet here; herein he saith – Now here was a sweet story for the telling, God knew. It is the brother that is the cream of it. WS said coldly:

'If you want all for your retailing, the brother's name is Richard and he is full ten years my junior.' It would not be carelessness next time, not that innocent manner of carelessness. 'And now, my lord, you may go.'

Harry stared an instant. Then, amused, he said, 'Oh, I may go, may I?'

'It may be that a common player's horns will be too lowly a joke for your great friends at court. It will serve, then, for your tavern acquaintances. Whatever it may be, you are heartily welcome to it. And now leave me.'

Harry got to his feet, laughing again, though not in the rich creamy ecstasy appropriate to the tale of a friend's cuckoldry. 'That is one thing I cannot do,' he said at length. 'I can never leave you. You have too august an impudence and pertness for me ever to take offence at aught you say. It is a kind of Tarquin superbity.'

'Let's not shut our eyes to the truth,' said WS. 'The long spring is over.'

'Well, I see I must go,' smiled Harry, 'and come back when you are in a more loving temper. Do not say now that I am not yet grown up.'

'Oh,' cried WS, 'can you not yet foresee what you will feel when you are truly grown up? You will understand the disappointments then. You will see where metaphors go wrong, that the door is most tight-shut when it seems most open, that we are condemned to dying more than to death. Let me tell you the manner of our dying away from each other, which is not yet a death. I must age and put off fancies and abstractions, you must feed a greater and greater appetite for power. There is no going back for you, as I see it. You will follow Lord Essex to the very block, for, by a paradox, the path up is always the path down. That is why it seems so delightful and easy. You will justify every treachery, every lust and minor ambition, by reference to some noble sentence, such as "It is for the good of the commonweal". You will even conceive of an image of self-sacrifice when you are encompassing only self-indulgence, self-fulfilment, that self being not the self you think of, for your mirror will be as distorting as any of the Queen's.'

'If it is for this I must stay, you were right to bid me go.' Harry wrapped his cloak about him, its encircling breeze driving a scrawled sheet from the work-table.

'I cannot make myself clear on all this.' WS picked up the sheet, groaning an old man's groan, returning to the vertical in dizziness. Vertical, vertigo. Words. He felt a whinging nostalgia for words. 'I feel only that if I cannot save your soul I must at least try to save mine.'

'Back, as always, to cheesy Banbury cant,' sneered Harry. 'How you make me vomit, you new Puritan gentlemen, with your bit of wealth in candles and corn and dimity and plays. Go to it, then. Save your paltry little Puritan's soul. I prefer my hell, if it is to be a hell. Save your mean little cuckold's soul.' He tossed his head, hatted Frenchwise, making the great black feather in it nod. 'Beautified,' he sneered, re-membering an old jibe. 'You cannot disguise the truth of a man's nature. Capon,' he added. 'Not Without Mustard.' He crowed a last laugh. 'How they all mock you. You are more comic than all your comedies.' Then he left, laughing not at all as he clumped like a departing coalman down the uncarpeted stairs.

WELL, then, let it be so, for he welcomed pain. It passed over his head, the gushing of Francis Meres (Plautus and Seneca accounted best for comedy and tragedy among the Latins, so

Shakespeare among the English most excellent in both kinds for the stage), the printing pirates after his work, the 'Sweet Master S' fame. We know what we are but know not what we may be. But he thought he knew what he might be could he but draw down on himself the right pain, achieve the right releasing agony. The goddess, he was convinced, abode in the air, an atomy, ready to rush into a wound, were but that wound deep enough. What did young Master Meres know about it? As for the world's madness, his pain in it was diminished by the inoculation of foreknowledge; it seemed, as he packed his 'humours' about Falstaff, that there might well be an exact art of prediction of human folly – the Queen striking Essex over this matter of who should be sent to flay the wild Irish to submission; the paralysis of rule and the two thousand sent to their death in the foul bogs, ambushed by bog-dwellers. And Harry Wriothesly's decent to folly and impending self-ruin was most predictable of all.

Yet was it not in a measure a folly rubbed off himself, as though poet had infected patron in the manner of his being ensnared? WS watched, with becoming show of sorrow, the slow-treading funeral cortège wind through the summer London streets. Burghley dead, the old times and virtues gone; Ireland near-lost. The flies buzzed. In pathetic optimism the kites wheeled far above that well-lapped corpse. But among the great mourners no sign of one who should be chief in his weeping. Ha' you not heard? He is run off to France with a woman. Defunctive music brayed in the heat. Nay, he hath got a woman here with child, and one of high quality. Soft feet marching slow over the cobbles. But life always to balance death. (Mistress Vernon is from the Court and lies in Essex House. Some say she hath taken a *venue* under the girdle and swells upon it; yet she complains not of foul play but says the Earl will justify it.) A Royal Maid of Honour a maid no longer, not this year nor more. Seven months, is it? He had best be hurrying back. Maids of Dishonour. They say he is back secretly these four days and secretly hath—

WS hardly heard the bitter words of Cuthbert Burbage as they sat gloomily in the enclosed tavern heat, they two and Richard and Heminges and Phillips, Pope, Kemp. He was thinking of the calm gay words of Florio (black-suited but not for Burghley): 'My lord is in the Fleet.' A rehearsal for the eventual Tower; WS saw it all so clearly: two steps from the ultimate block. 'Slow lechery and hasty marriage. Gloriana is not mocked. Her wrath, I hear, was terrible. One of her Glories, but think, and she kept unaware. But my lord played the man and is in the Fleet as his reward.'

'The Fleet,' said WS aloud. His fellow-players stared; Kemp giggled. Cuthbert said:

'Had I my way I would have him in the Fleet, but his crime is against nature more than law.' WS frowned, puzzled; then he recollected. Giles Alleyn. The lease. 'I had feared it, I must say,' went on Cuthbert. 'Never trust an Alleyn. By making of these half-promises of renewal—'

'It must be taken more slowly,' grinned Kemp, 'for our gentleman here.' Keep away from the great world, WS was thinking. The new Countess too in prison. ('She will get over all this, never fear,' Florio had said. 'The Queen's Majesty, I mean. My lord is not to lie wasting in the Fleet while there are kerns jumping and howling in Ireland.' But the next step the Tower, and after the Tower— Words were safe, words, safer than reality.)

'Half-promises of renewal,' said Cuthbert patiently. 'The lease of '76 said the timber should be ours still if removed before expiry. Now he knows I will not accept of his new terms, that he knows. It was drawn up, this new lease, in that fore-knowledge. So now he will break up the Theatre and call the timber his own.' Richard Burbage growled.

'The Curtain will not do for ever,' said Heminges, chewing a little nut.

'Kill Alleyn,' suggested Pope. 'These nights are without moon.'

'Leases live on like souls,' said Cuthbert sententiously. 'It is more to the purpose to consider of where we shall find a new home. Dick here and I have walked this garden in Maiden Lane, a fair enough garden but we do not wish it for flowers. It is not far from the Rose, if we are talking of flowers.'

'A new playhouse, then,' said Phillips.

'We two,' said Richard Burbage, jerking a sort of imperial thumb at his brother, 'are to meet half. You five the other half, if you will agree.'

'Wake up, Will,' said Cuthbert Burbage.

'The expense of building,' said Heminges, chewing the bit of beard that curled up under his underlip. (It is right that I go visit him in the Fleet, WS was thinking. One does not dissolve friendships so easily. And what if he prove haughty and will not receive me? It is a terrible thing for one so high to be brought so low. He will squeal at the rats, he had ever a fear of rats.)

'It must be met,' Cuthbert was saying. 'It can be met. We are talking,' he cried to WS, 'of a new playhouse and the building of it south of the river.'

'There is no such thing,' said WS, wondering at the confidence with which he spoke, 'as the death of anything. There is no making new, there is only renewal. Can love really die?'

'Oh, sweet Jesus,' prayed Kemp, rolling his eyes to heaven.

'The earth turns and there is no new day, only a renewal of the old. In tomorrow's bread there will be a piece of today's dough. You can only build your new playhouse out of the old one.' They stared at him. 'Pull it down, set your timber on carts, send it over the river. Why should the niggling and nasty forces prevail? Alleyn rubs his hands. Cheat him.'

'He is right,' said Heminges. 'By God, he is right.'

WS felt a sort of promise of the renewal of youth's energy.

'Yes,' said Cuthbert Burbage, 'he is right. That is what we will do. We will wait till Alleyn is out of town—'

'What is the name of that builder?'

'Street. A *master* builder. Peter Street.'

Love took new forms, that was all. Forms like compassion.

X

COMPASSION? Did that then seem the proper balm wherewith to anoint his soul's bruises? They struck, my wife, my brother, but knew not what they did. I will feel no anger, I will resent nothing. I stand above, blessing, forgiving, with lips untwisted in bitterness, brow all alabaster-smooth, a statue. He saw, in a shock that was the shock of involuntary blasphemy, whose that statue was. Compassion, pity: are they not much the same? What right have I to bestow pity? At the very gates of the Fleet, hearing the carousing noises of the better sort within ('Farewell farewell, my blessing; too dear thou art for any man's possessing'), the lute and treble voice of mockery among the busy-whiskered rats and the immemorial stench of urine and hopelessness, he knew he would be rejected of his lord. His lord was entering at last into his realm, grotesque bridegroom and father but a man at last, ready for the final treasonous gesture. He rejects his old friend, professes not to know him, his gay but harmless youth was a dream.

WS stood, pitying among the many cheering, on Cheapside towards the end of March. It was a brisk but sunny day, the smell of new green and the maaaaaing of lambs borne in from the near countryside. All was forgiven by that capricious Queen: Essex was bound for Ireland, his commission signed a fortnight back. Thirteen hundred horse and sixteen thousand foot were under his command. He rode out of London with the cream of his officers, gracious, bowing, sun-king heading a riot of liveries, silken banners mad in the wind, the horses prancing, stumbling, recovering on the cobbles. The crowd roared and waved, children were lifted on to shoulders, caps were thrown in the air. WS stood silent. There was that lord

206

whom he had once called friend, aloof on his chestnut, the shame of his imprisonment quite forgotten, a great captain bound for the quelling of the kerns. Steed after steed after steed, richly caparisoned, the harness jingling, an ancient dream of chivalric riding between the mean and bowing rows of shops. WS broke his silence to call: 'God bless you, God save you', but it was a feeble cry among the hoarse loud benisons of the London mob. 'God help you,' his heart murmured. A victorious general would return to claim his due – not bays, not laurels. Those nearest to him in loyalty would then be in most need of God's help. The cavalcade went by in jaunty magnificence; a ragged party of well-wishers joined on behind the wagging cruppers of the rear. Ahead the cheers were still raised under the March sun.

Compassion, compassion. He roamed the streets, alone with his compassion. He dined in an ordinary and walked back to his lodgings, now in Silver Street. He sat at his table to work. Ironic, this play of the warlike Harry assuming the port of Mars. In the late afternoon there came an unexpected darkness, black clouds rolling over the March blue. Then lightning attacked, the punctual unison of kettledrummers grumbled all round the heavens, and balls of hail tinkled and crackled on the pavement. God help us all. He went to his window to look out. After so fair a day's start. He saw a bedraggled march, wet faces, mouth wide in curses unheard under the downpour, cloaks and liveries drenched, the golden hair of his former lord and friend all rats's tails. His pity welled up as he peopled the naked street with this image. But it was the pity one feels for the failed grand gesture, an unworthy pity. His quibbling brain meanwhile juggled with keywords – a March day's march marred, Mars netted, howling like a child.

And now the reward for his compassion. She is coming again, my heart, coming to these very lodgings. But not in rain; let her not arrive begging for his all too easy pity. It was fine spring weather once more, that great ominous gesture of the heavens trundled off. There was a timid knock. He opened.

'You?' In a plain cloak, unattended, she stood, her eyes lowered. 'It cannot be, how could you know, where did you, who told you where?' They stood, paralysed WS and she demure, unsure of her welcome.

'I did see dis man, I have forgot his name, he is de cloon in your—'

'Kemp, you mean? Our clown, you would say?' Then he shuffled out of his staring trance. 'Enter, enter, you are heartily, come in, it is something untidy in here, see, I will clear these papers from this—' She undid the strings of her cloak, the hood fell from her black curls. An intense agony thrust into his heart as he saw again that delicate brown of her skin, the flat nose, the thick lips whose every fold and contour his remembered kisses knew. It was the agony of knowing that it was departed, all, the insanity of former love (had, having, and in quest to have), leaving behind this deadly godlike sobriety of pity. But why pity? 'You will have,' he said, 'a cup of wine, you have travelled far perhaps, how did you come?'

She sat in the straighter-backed of the two chairs. 'From Clerkenwell only. Dis Kemp was in Clerkenwell yesternight. He was looking for black women, he said. He is a merry laughing man dat is full of jokes.'

'You are not— What are you doing in Clerkenwell?'

'What can I do?' She moved her delicate shoulders. Giving her wine, WS noted dispassionately the shaking of his hand. 'I have no money. Our *tuan* is gone to de wars. He will dream at night only of his wife and his child. For dose he did love he has no more any time.'

Our *tuan*. It was a word of her language. 'So,' said WS slowly, 'he gave you money. You were a paid paramour.'

'I know not dat word. But, yes, he did give me money. I was living in dis place where he was born, Cowdray it is called. Den I did have my child. Den— Oh, I will not talk of dese tings.'

'Tell me of the child,' said WS, his heart thudding. 'Tell me who is the father of the child.'

She looked at him very steadily before replying. 'De child, I tink, has two faders.'

'Oh, that is not possible, that cannot be, that is all against the rule of nature—'

'If it is not one it is de oder. I remember of de time well. I was not to be blamed. It is you or it is he.'

'And,' insisted WS, 'where is—' Then, 'No. There is another question. Is the child a girl or a boy?'

'A son,' she said with some pride. 'I had a son. A heavy son dat cried much. I said to him dat he must not cry, for he did have two faders.'

'And what name did you give him?'

She shook her head many times. 'Dat I will not say. I did give him my own fader's name. And den I tought dat he must be *bin* someting, for dat is our custom. He must be *bin* and den his fader's name, for *bin* does mean "de son of". But it is you dat have de noble name, not he, our *tuan* dat is gone to de war.'

'I? I am not noble. I am a gentleman, true, but not noble.'

'You are a *sheikh*,' she said simply. He stared at her. Then he asked:

'Where is he – my son?'

'He is wid good people, kind people. Dey are in Bristol, people dat are rich from slaves and are now sorry for dat. And when he is older he will go back, back to my country.'

WS's head span. It was inconceivable. So his blood would, after all, flow to the East. It was his blood, it must be his blood. Suddenly she began to weep, soundlessly. Crystal tears flowed. Crystal. Angrily he shook away the formal image. This was the mother of his son, a woman, not a sonneteer's ideal wraith. He gave her his spotted handkerchief, the one that had wiped away the tears of Harry's laughter. 'Why are you crying?' he asked.

209

'I cannot go back. I can never go back. But my son must go back to my country.'

WS nodded. He saw that. 'You must be with me now,' he said. 'We must be together. You were mine before you were ever his. You broke your bed-vow, but that is all over and forgiven.'

She wiped her eyes, sniffling. 'And so it must go,' she said. 'An I were in my own country I would be de wife of a *raja*. But here I must be a mistress. And I grow old and am not wanted. In Clerkenwell I will not be wanted, not when you trow me away as he did trow me away. And yet cannot I go back, for de ships go not to my country. Some day dey will go, and den my son will go wid dem. But now—' She wept again.

'I have a wife,' said WS unhappily. 'A wife and daughters. It is not in Christian countries as in the paynim ones. I cannot put my wife away, even though she has committed adultery. Here there is no divorce. All I may do is—' What was all he might do? He could give her money, pay the rent of her lodging, but, as for installing her here— He caught for an instant an image of Green and his pocked mistress, sister of Cutting Ball, the shrieking bastard Fortunatus, crammed into the filthy room where, belching on Rhenish, cursing loudly for quiet, the poet had hurried at *Friar Bacon and Friar Bungay*. No, the days when that might have been possible for WS were gone: a gentleman, keeping a black mistress in his lodgings, that would not do. 'I will find some place for you,' he said, 'some quiet and decent place. And give you money.'

She nodded, sniffing away the last of her tears. Weeping had made her seem ugly, more in need of his compassion or pity, whatever it was. 'Do dat. Give me money. Much money.'

'As much as I can,' said WS carefully. His palm itched, the cloven hoof of the business-man filled his shoe. 'And,' he added, 'there is little I would ask in return. I am not the man I was.' She stared at him.

IT WAS, indeed, a phase that was come on him again. A man's

natural desires, the voluptuous image after meat or before sleep or on dawn waking – all, all scared away on very conception by the memory of that afternoon in New Place: the girls packed carefully off to their grandmother that the act of adultery might deliberately and brazenly be performed. Or else the laugh of his late lord, friend, patron rang out all down the corridors of his brain, chilling the starting flesh into subsidence. His substitute for tumescence was there on Maiden Lane, south of the swanned river. It had been a bold Christmas venture, that march over the snow and glassy frost, under the tingling sky, trundling carts laden with the hacked limbs of the body of the old Theatre. The *fait accompli*, as the French called it (the Huguenot family had helped him with his French; he had needed a whole scene in French, delicately bawdy, for *Henry V*), and Giles Alleyn, back from the country after Christmas, unable to do anything but rage in impotence. Through the spring and early summer the timbers of the old were transformed into the new, the best playhouse ever: it was a raised fist at the times which Essex, even in absence, haunted with threats of order lost, the string untuned to discord. The censors were at work burning books, gagging the news from Ireland, forbidding whispered rumours of all going badly there, of the Queen's declining health and her successor still unnamed. It was a time of ragged nerves and great and small dissensions.

'Go then, go! Threaten no longer but go!' That, to his surprise, was WS himself, crying at Kemp. 'We are sick of your jigs and botched extemporisings. I have been sick these seven years. An you will not do what is set down for you to do then you may go and well rid?'

Kemp's fat jigged in his anger. 'Upstart,' he panted, unconsciously borrowing from an earlier and different vilification. 'It is I that they come to see. Words, words, all words with you, you are naught but a word-boy.' Richard Burbage stroked his beard, saying nothing. 'I warn thee, I will not be told what I will do, your crazy honorificibillibus or whatever it be. It was I,' cried Kemp, glaring around the rehearsing assembly, 'that taught ye all. Now it is all his words that we must bow down to.'

'It is the new way, Willy,' said Heminges, speaking quietly. 'We cannot perpetuate the past, however the ground-lings love you.'

'There,' cried Kemp, 'thou hast the infection from this word-boy here. Perpetuabilitatibus.' Even in his wrath he must needs clown, popping the plosives with puffed cheeks. One or two of the prentices laughed.

'We all have had to learn,' said WS loudly. 'We have to move, to make better. I cannot have my play made bottom-heavy with his leering bawdry.'

'I will take you at your word,' shook shouting Kemp. 'It will be an ill day for you all, I promise. Such as Cavaliero Kemp are not ten a penny.' Robert Armin was standing modestly apart, trimming his nails with his teeth. 'It is this one that is the trouble,' Kemp cried, pointing at WS with a pudgy trembling finger. 'I made him, this fine gentleman. Not Without Mustard. He came whimpering to me and poor dead Tarleton for work. Now he is a fine man with a black doxy.'

'That is not to the point.' WS blushed. Who had perpetrated that sneer at his family motto? 'The point is that if I am to make plays—'

'I think,' said Dick Burbage to Kemp, 'that the time is come. You may sell your shares to myself or to my brother.' Kemp stared at him aghast, a comic Caesar. 'You have done well, you have had longer than any in the game.' Kemp visibly shrank. 'We must part, and there's an end on it, but we ought not to part enemies.'

There were tears in Kemp's eyes, soon his voice was a whine; he had never had the gift of control. 'It is dying,' he cried, 'the good old way. It is being killed by upstarts. You,' and he came up to WS, his blubber cheeks wet, 'you.' He raised a feeble arm to strike. WS stepped back; he said:

'Believe me, all this is not a question of friendship. It is a question rather of what is right for the stage.'

'Puppy, do you not prate of what is right for the stage. I was on the stage before you were—' He stood there, dropping his arms to his sides. 'Ah, it is no matter.'

'Let it be a good exit, Willy,' said Heminges. 'An exit, and then we can drink together and laugh.'

'An exit, yes,' said Kemp. Then he recovered his loudness. 'Aye, an exit for good and all. A sort of desperate ingrates. I shall be glad to leave. God curse you,' he gibbered at WS, 'traitor.' He began to march off.

'Forget not your trill-lillies,' said Armin softly. Kemp did not hear. 'For oh, for oh,' sang Armin in his sweet tenor, 'the hobby-horse is forgot.'

TRAITOR, traitor. 'My head aches,' said WS. Her lodgings were in a little house on Swan Lane, within smell of the river and hearing of the watermen's cries.

'Lie down,' she commanded. 'I will soak dis handkercher in cold water.' She busied herself at the ewer, a tiny brown housewife, while he watched her, feigning shut eyes, from her bed. The room had a spicy smell, sun-warmed, a pocket Indies. 'Now,' she said, and she laid the damp cool poultice on his brows. 'Make room,' she ordered, and she was there beside him.

'A comfort,' he said. 'There is this world of men, and sometimes it smells heavily of the sweat of men's contention. It is good to be here.'

'Lie quiet and say naught.' His doublet was off, his shirt open for the summer warmth; she smoothed his thin chest with her small hand, down, down to the belly then back again.

'I would not ever have thought,' he said, feeling the aches of the day recede, 'that I could lie thus quietly. There was a time when I would seize you in my greed like a boy who can never have enough sweetmeats. I would want to cram you in my mouth.'

'And now not.' His eyes shut, he could still tell that she was smiling. 'Well, I must make you as you were.'

'I like well of this friendly calm, the two of us lying together content like this.'

'I like well too of de oder way.' She bared her breast and laid his head there, still stroking. 'It is what man and woman is for.' Idly his tongue caressed her nipple. She shuddered. 'You must not play like dat if you do not mean—' And then she showed him what, failing of the power of the other, final act, he might do to give her pleasure and release. About his unwilling hand she climbed her ladder to its topmost rung then leaped to her death through air that was all silken cushions. She lay panting for a time. He said:

'You will think little of me. I will learn again soon, fear not. There are things that the soul will do to the body.' Sweat lay on her forehead; he wiped it gently off with the handkerchief that had fallen from his own brow to the pillow. Soon she opened her eyes and smiled.

'Aye,' she said, 'dou wilt learn again soon.'

But it was not till high summer that he learned again. On a July day he stood with the Burbages, Heminges and the rest on Maiden Lane. Street the master builder made a secret masonic sign; the workers folded their aprons. *Consummatum est.* For some reason WS could not get those words out of his head. He thought of them not as Christ's words but as Faustus's – the signing of the bill with blood. He foresaw that here his best blood must flow. 'It is,' said Fletcher, 'a brave erection.'

'They have promised our flag by noon tomorrow,' said Dick Burbage. 'Hercules and his globe.' A brave name for a brave erection. The Globe. *Totus mundus agit histrionem.* And a brave motto. The whole world, no, all the world acts a play, is a stage . . . He must work something out. And now—

'Now we must drink,' said Dick Burbage. The prentices, grinning, uncovered their baskets. Cups, flagons. 'We will drink at every entrance, at every point and corner. We will make it smell of wine, not paint and size and wood-shavings. We will baptise it.'

'*Ego te baptizo*,' said John Wilson, '*in nomine Kyddi et Marlovii et Shakespearii*.' WS blushed.

'Amen amen to that fair prayer say I.' Dick, followed by his brother, led them to the entrance. Before going in they downed a dedicatory cup of harsh ferrous wine, sun-warm. It was like drinking blood. Then they swigged another as they looked about them – the tiered galleries, the jutting apron, the canopy, the study not yet curtained, the tarrass. They mounted the stage, posturing, strutting, waving their spilling cups. They remembered old lines, ancient business, missed cues. They remembered Kemp and, for a moment, were abashed. Armin tried to shin up one of the stage-posts. Chanting a growling war-song they marched from the left stage-door to the right, ran like mad down the steps, across the gloomy echoing cellarage unseen, up the steps that led to the left entrance, then resumed the stately tramping on-stage, an endless belt of an army, each man altering his shape and stance to make himself a new soldier at each entrance, but none ever letting go of his cup. Condell moaned like a ghost deep below the stage. Dick Burbage squeaked Juliet, swaying on the balustraded tarrass. They tested the strength of the boards with thudding high la voltas, they performed a mincing but stork-legged pavane. Watermen and beggars looked in, mouths open at the free show, drawn by the song, laughter, shouting. Overhead the clouds lumbered over the July blue and there was a brief afternoon shower, but, under their canopy, the Lord Chamberlain's Men did not feel it. When the sun came out again the flagons were empty and the playhouse had been well-anointed with bloody iron-smelling wine, either straight from the flagon or, in more intimate libations, from the body's wine-vessels. They began to totter home, those that could, arms round each other in players' brotherliness. Two bodies lay, dead out, on the apron. Armin,

sober, thinking his own thoughts, sat on the stage, swinging
his legs over its edge, and sang a melancholy song:

> Farewell, farewell, my blessing;
> Too dear thou art
> For any man's possessing.
> And so we part.

But WS by that time, high-flown but yet capable, was on his
way to Swan Lane.

'DRUNKEN,' she said. 'Dou hast drunken much wine.' She
twitched her splayed nose at him, her arms folded. WS had
near-fallen into her chamber and now lay, booted, on her bed.
He groaned.

'Little for most,' he said. 'Much for me. I have no stomach
for it.' He closed his eyes. 'Uggggh.'

'Dou had best sleep awhile den.'

'Today it is finished. Our new playhouse. Cause for vinous
joy. All were drunk but I less than most.' He giggled sillily.
'A brave erection.'

'I have somewhat here dat you must drink,' she said, and she
began ladling a brown silvershot gravy from a pipkin into a
horn cup. 'You may drink it, it is not more wine.'

'Nay, I cannot – I will—'

'You may drink it and den sleep. It will give you a better
stomach.' She brought it over to him, holding his shoulders
while he drank. It had a taste of somewhat fetid sweetness.
'Dere,' she said.

He dived shortly after from a high tarrass into sleep. The
dreams he had were enacted at some very deep level of his
brain. There were not unhappy dreams, but their ingredients
were unpleasant. He saw great crowds bearing down on him,
familiar faces that he knew he had never seen before, mostly
faces of the low, sweaty on the cheeks and jowls, bad-toothed,
stinking of old garments that stank of rancid mutton stew and

old brown earwax. The black pegged mouths roared at him, whether in anger or laughter or love he could not tell. But his own answering roar was a mirthful one, delivered from a high pillar to which he clung with lusty embracing arms and legs. He shouted words of occult meaning which he knew were also nonsense. At the same time, by some contorting miracle, he threw off various of his garments, of which he seemed to have many (a whole playhouse wardrobe), and hurled them at the crowd. In mid-air they changed to cuts of red flesh, inner organs, ribs, three necks (he smiled in his dream at the absurdity of it), and they were seized without thanks by filthy hands with ragged nails and then devoured with juicy munching.

The scene changed to a great park in sad summer evening light, well-laid with young trees. An eternal silence covered all; he was aware of the roundness of the horizon, as though all this green were the green of the sea. The silence was, as it were, pinned to the tender heavens by the call of a solitary chaffinch. There sprouted from the ground at the tail of his darting eye statue after statue, each melting away as he looked full upon it; these were of ancients who, he swore in his dream, could never have existed: Totimandus, Efevrius, Blano, Follion, Dacles. A young boy in the costume of an earlier Tudor reign played hide-and-seek behind these statues; he did not move from statue to statue but, looking out brightly at WS, he was behind each one at the tail of the eye, vanishing with it at the dreamer's full gaze. And now, trotting between the trees in a silver light that seemed his own emanation, a young man in a feathered hat sat his chestnut proudly, his sad eyes ever before him. The dreamer wept.

And then it was the Tower and the block and a head rolling. A head, WS noted, could not roll like a ball because of the ears. The masked executioner laughed at the hogshead measure of blood that spurted from the severance while the rich-robed witnesses smiled gravely in their beards. But the head too smiled from the dirty flags, even while a file of blood-eating insects marched towards it. 'Fall to,' a voice said, and WS picked up the head with one hand. It was feather-light and spongy and its taste was of delicate honey-cake. WS, to the assembly's murmured approval, was fain to gobble it all up.

Then he was faced with the philosophical paradox of a globe being also a tower, but he saw in his dream the meaning of the riddle. From his own groin the new building steadily arose, a playhouse from a tangled garden, and he laughed in triumph. 'But this is not Maiden Lane,' he cried, and that seemed to be the best joke in all the world. So he climbed steadily out of sleep with easy breathing though a pounding heart to find himself cool in the July evening, washed by another shower as the drops on the window-pane attested, and that tall playhouse stood before him and everything was solved.

She lay beside him stark naked, slim and straight, a wonder of gold. He was unlaced and unbuttoned but he must have this full nakedness too. He threw off his clothes like emblems of guilt and then, full of strength and readiness, clasped her in his arms. It was the best of plays, act melting into act and ending in death that promised resurrection. His seed spurted, it seemed, straight into her own cry of attainment. Tightly clasped, they billowed down together through miles of aromatic air to come to rest on swansdown. And the glory and, as it were, grace were proclaimed in the ease of renewal, so that the night was a counterpart triumph to the day.

His youth, sought afresh with her before but pushed out by guilt, now knew its flower; his dream of plunging into the Indies was fulfilled, his appetites for strange fruits fed without disgust or guilt or the gnaw of responsibility. There were no bounds set to pleasure: every tiniest vein on wrist or breast or ankle, each finger-joint, each several black filament of her eyebrow, even a shed lash marooned on her cheek could rouse fire. His hard strength was incarnated in a familiar that yapped like a dog tugging then snapping his chain, he was else all trembling jelly. Treading the pavement, he could feel the earth beneath it; he would start and whinny at a fly. He entered her like some fabulous sphinx that, raging into a royal city, was suddenly awed by the gold surrounding it, made aware thus of the spark of divinity that begot it, then was driven to the expression of this godhead by a sort of quintessential beastliness.

London, the defiled city, became a sweet bower for their lover's wandering, even in the August heat. The kites that hovered or, perched, picked at the flesh of traitors' skulls became good cleansing birds, bright of eye and feather, part of the bestiary of the myth that enthralled them as they made it. The torn and screaming bears and dogs and apes in the pits of Paris Garden were martyrs who rose at once into gold heraldic zoomorphs to support the scutcheon of their static and sempiternal love. The wretches that lolled in chains on the lapping edges of the Thames, third tide washed over, noseless, lipless, eye-eaten, joined the swinging hanged at Tyburn and the rotting in the jails to be made heroes of a classical hell that, turned into music by Vergil, was sweet and pretty schoolday innocence. But it was she who shook her head often in sadness, smiling beneath her diaphanous veil as they took the evening air in passion's convalescence, saying that autumn would soon be on them, that love's fire burned flesh and then itself – out, gone for ever.

'Dou must go on, dou wilt sail past mine island, dou hast work to do.'

'This is my work and this *our* island.'

And indeed they were, twined and knotted into each other, all insulated from the panic news of the Spaniards landing on the Isle of Wight, the women screaming through the streets that clanked with heavy chains, the city gates shut. The trained bands paraded, citizens in armour, free from their wives for a space, made free of the taverns. She kept indoors after one trembling encounter. 'She is an Hispaniola. See her black skin.' She had run, had sniffed at one of her bottles (dis is for a beating heart) and bloomed faintly in a transitory blue tinge about the lips. She locked both herself and him in her lodgings, both in her bedchamber. The Spaniards, it was said, were at Southampton. Scotland harried the border with forty thousand foot and two hundred screaming pipers; Ireland darted her head from the bogs, yelped and bit rabid; the friends of Spain stiffened her armies; France sneered and waited. But, on that narrow bed, right history was enacted and true reality revealed: it was holy, a sort of nobleness. The struggles and invasions were toward the setting up an honest short peace, not a cynical eternal one; the engaging armies carried the same banner.

And then the alarms of the City proved without base: the thirty thousand tramped home from Mile End, the gates were opened up. But there had been a demonstration of the easy gathering together of an army, that at least. But in defence of Spain only? Ireland, for its lack of news, seemed blanketed in summer snow, no campaigning weather. But who knew when he might not return, insolent in victory to claim what he believed his due? There would, however, be an unpaid rabble behind him, beguiled with talk of pillage, feet rotting from the eternal Irish damp, pox-stricken.

WS was aware of a qualifying of the euphoria of that spring that had so speedily caught up with summer. It could not, he thought, be expected to go on for ever. He had belike over-taxed his powers, he was no longer a young man, he had drunk overmuch (without wine Venus takes cold) to prick the renewal of appetite. He stood naked one morning in his own chambers and curiously surveyed his body. It was, on one level of viewing, as ever – thin, white, with a gentleman's lack of muscle; on another level it was a temple glorified by her. Standing thus, surveying, he felt a response appropriate, through this last month's associations, to his nakedness. He desired her then so much that he would willingly have thrown off the easy lust as a thing of no great value, unworthy of her, as one might rinse a cup clean with the first wine from the bottle: he would have projected her image on to his chamber wall and fought out the night's gathering of seed against one of her garments (he had begged a piece of her underlinen, a stocking, a shoe). And then he noticed a minute spot, drab red, of the size of a small coin, matted into a manner of a plaque, sharply defined on the tight-stretched skin. He had, a day or so before, seen but a lentil-sized mark there, pink. Puzzled but not alarmed, he gently drew back the hood from the bishop-head and found that the sore (and yet it was not a sore; there was no pain) flicked over like a coin with the movement. Well, this was strain, no doubt, or her passionate nails, or his own importunate harsh frotting. The body smiled on love's misuse of it; what complaints it ever made were gentle good-humoured murmurs. But he would not, even with so paltry a blemish, dare to approach that golden tabernacle in any finality of hunger . . .

'I am,' he said to her, 'a little unwell. I am not,' he smiled, 'so young as I have been.'

She was all cool soothing solicitude. 'It is a pain? Where is de pain? See, I have dis – dis *ubat* here.' *Ubat* was 'medicine' in her language. 'I can make better most every pain.'

'No pain,' he told her. 'I am something tired, no more.'

'An dou art tired come now to bed.'

'I cannot stay long. There is the new play. I am expected for rehearsal.' She pouted at that. And then he was aware of the promise of a strange slight heaviness in the glands of his groin. He frowned and she saw him frown as she lay, half-naked for expected love, on the bed. She also saw his hand move incontinently to the site of this small hidden drama and she became solicitous again. She came over to him, saying:

'Let me see.'

'It is nothing. I had best be going now. I but called— We shall meet tomorrow.'

'I will see,' she insisted. And she probed at him, unresisting, and she saw. What he saw first was the shocked widening of her eyes and then, in this context of her presence and desirability, that the embossed red coin was more than something to be given and quickly spent in love's trafficking. It came back to him – the time of his writing *Romeo and Juliet* and his smirk at the irony of Girolamo Fracastoro's being a physician of Verona. What had been the name of that shepherd in Fracastoro's poem? A Greek name, he thought, meaning 'swine-lover' or some such thing. But the subtitle: '. . . *sive Morbus Gallicus*'.

They looked at each other. Instinctively she drew round her the loose night-gown that had lain open; her tawny nakedness was packed away, like everything else of summer at summer's close. He had a confused accession of images – sacked and burned cities, a roaring rabble of soldiers, a mob swarming across the Thames to hack down the Globe. And then, with almost the bright tones of actuality, he saw himself as a happy child in Stratford ('76? '77?) reading a book from his father's scant shelf: *A Breviarie of Health*, by Andrew Boorde. 'In English *Morbus Gallicus* is call'd the French pocks, and when that I was young they were named the Spanish pocks.' He had asked his father: 'What then are these pocks?' His father had replied: 'Oh, it is some ailment that they have and their bodies are all eaten and they go mad with it.'

They looked at each other still, and then she backed away to the farthest corner of the chamber as though what had been drawn there was not a flaccid two ounces of sad flesh but a sword. He had the sensation of being pulled on, as from this late August day, to the slow unravelling of his last instalment of destiny. He waited for rage to well up in his throat as he looked at her brownness, the colour of a dirty river, but he knew only this compassion, itself perhaps a disease.

'I will go now,' he said. 'There is work to do.'

'Yes, yes, go den.'

'If you need money—'

'I have dat.'

'I will be back,' he said, 'in a day or two. When I am feeling less unwell.'

'Yes, yes.'

As he made his way to the Globe in sunlight he had the somehow joyous sensation of his having become, in mad contrariety, filled with seed, though not by her: she was but an agent of the unseen and unknown. What he must, in the fullness of gestation, give birth to could hardly be human or mortal. He saw with a kind of terrible clarity that gods and goddesses did not, after all, descend; they were immanent but rarely willing to emerge, they made themselves blind that they might not find a door too easily. But when they did find a door they might burn up the globe.

The flag slept, furled. It would break in the sun with trumpets that afternoon – Hercules with the globe on his shoulders. WS felt his own shoulders ache in anticipation of a burden not so easily limned though, he was sure, no lighter. As he approached the playhouse entrance he had to stand aside an instant to let a bowing smiling wraith come out – sweet Master Shakespeare.

Epilogue

(i)

I AM near the end of the wine, sweet lords and lovely ladies, but out there the big wine is being poured – thin, slow, grey. Never more shall I taste the oncoming of this particular darkness. But I shall not be sorry to go. I am not seduced to this life by the dainty lusts, clothed in cold green and clean linen, of an English spring. If you plunge into that dark there you will emerge at length into a raging sun and all the fabled islands of my East. And that is what I shall be doing tonight, off like a bird. I see you have your pennies ready, ladies. Twitch not, hop not about nor writhe so: I shall not be long now.

Let's swell a space on the irony of a poet's desperately wringing out the last of his sweetness while the corrosives closed in. It was she, though, the goddess, unseen as yet but stirring and kicking like a foetus, that dictated the titles, for this was indeed much ado and that what they willed and the other as they liked it. Meanwhile that bud I carried opened like a pomegranate, the roseate macules and papules blossomed and later grew to a tint of delectable copper – coins over my body, the hint of a leopard's (not a tiger's) hide. When it left, it left a stain as of dirty eaters. All my parts must be hoarse parts (thou wilt make a ghost yet, see if thou wilt not, that is a very graveyard voice). Had I had the clown's gift I could have ambled about the stage to great laughter, drawing out teeth with little pain, blinking from gummy eyes, breaking off bits of finger-nail.

– Here, look you, is demonstrated the frangibility of the body.

– Bless thee, thou art by no manner of means immaculate. I'll tan thy pelt to Dalmatian leather to make outlandish shoes withal.

– We will have astrologians pore over thee like a very map of the heavens.

– Scratch, sirrah, scratch.

And the fever, the delirium. It was like wandering through mist, wondering whence came that music, all thin piping and lutes, the distant voices of buried ancestors (Do you not know us? Do you not remember?), the dream-poems which contained time's secret and dissolved on my waking to fix them on my tablets. Rhythms cranked through, of remote but terrible meaning:

> And odds affriculous their fancies break
> But to give ear to none. Soft then, thy might,
> Lest Titan burst the tenor of his eyes
> And grant the owl for waxing . . .

It was at nightfall the fevers were most intense; then kings came down on ropes and Gilbert had many faces, all of which frothed, and the heroes creaked by, all mounted on the periphery of a fiery wheel, each crying 'Ooooooooh' from the square lips of a Grecian mask as he touched my pillow and revealed himself made of candlewax.

All this could be borne by myself, but I wept at the injustice done to my poor body. A hundred ulcers pitched their tents on my skin during the night and were, in the winter morning, a neat and well-ordered camp. Oh oh oh, I cried and tried to kneel to my body to beg forgiveness, though I must first beg forgiveness for making my body kneel with me. In sleep I could step out and look down on it and drip my compassion. If I had done wrong my body had not, and yet my body must bear the punishment. I saw my paper as the body I once had, I longed towards it. I was fearful, though, of disfiguring it with blots and scratches; I must limn always on this smooth whiteness words of fair and even shape. Take breath, I told myself each morning, and then create your improbable Edens all remote from this after-fall state of a dishonoured body crusted and oozing and swimming in a fever that is like fingers of mist. Undress these creatures of Arden and you will find them sans holes sans rods sans even the most minuscule pimple. They are pure and know nothing of the Seven Deadly Sins.

And still, with my flesh all caked and swollen tender bladders at my groin and in my oxters, I could not myself see sin. Some say that the very act of love, when not sanctified, is a way into hell, but, for all my guilt, I could not see it as more than wrong. Right and wrong were the mild engines that drove the pretty poems and plays of Sweet Master S; evil was yet to be born. I could best see love unsanctified as mere clownishness when the burden of seed was dropped. Ben, I remember, Englished Petronius:

> Doing a filthy pleasure is, and short;
> And, done, we soon repent us of the sport.

Well, there was mountainous belching Ben, a great hod of bricks falling on some poor croshabell, growling and grunting in his ponderous frotting, what time she cried, 'Oo, th'art a ton weight, ow, hast knocked all wind out on me.' And yet Ben's destiny was far removed from my own, blessed as he has been to be able to take the world skin-deep – humours and manners – and to know that the world takes itself skin-deep, though not with Ben's laws and systems. To some it falls to suffer the fateful lesion and to have that seed enter which fertilises the egg which will hatch the truth about the world.

I rode to Bath for the waters when the apothecaries and herbalists afforded no help. Riding, I thought of her, trying to pump up bitterness. What she had given me she had to be herself first given. There was no one to blame; we all choose what we will have, but it is unfair that the choice must so often be made in the dark. God is a sort of roaring clown full of bone-cracking japes. It is as though Will Kemp had been monopolist of the Globe.

226

What properties those Bath waters had I cannot say, but I was purged to wraith's thinness. More, my eyes cleared and I could see the world in very sharp colours: its paint seemed hardly dry. More, it was as if length and breadth and height had been but newly created. I wondered what these creatures were that laughed and plotted and chambered. I savoured the word 'man' over and over as it were the name of some new animal brought back by sea-adventurers. I was creating man afresh, planting him in a garden with clean white body and the innocent eyes of a deer. But he would not stay there: he must needs leap out to his plotting and blood-letting and sniggering nastiness. Will was knotted within him but it was will towards something that I, as God, could not have made. Therefore there was an opposite to God. This I could see but I still could not feel it. The time was not yet.

For the present it was enough to ride back to London and castigate the filthy world which I had rendered more filthy. Limping about Bread Street and Milk Street, inhaling Fleet Ditch, I was drawn to searching out my fellows in disease, gloating on a nose-sore like a raspberry, a lip glistening soft, wet, huge, coal-shiny, a naked arm that was yellow streaks and rose pustules, a stone eye mined by worms. Then I reeled with my discovery of what I should have long known – that the fistulas and imposthumes, bent bones, swellings, corrupt sores, fetor were of no different order from the venality and treachery and injustice and cold laughing murder of the Court. And yet none of these leprous and stinking wretches had willed their rottenness. The foul wrong lay then beyond a man's own purposing; there was somewhere, outside time's very beginning, an infinite well of putridity from which body and mind alike were driven, by some force unseen and uncontrollable, to drink.

Was there not somewhere a clean world? Theocritan shepherds piped – Damon, Lycidas, Syphilus (that was the name; that was from Fracastor) – but I saw them too eaten, their sheep with foot-rot, the southern torrents crunching their

227

mean shelters like apples. I turned to the tales of Greek and Trojan and expected to find again what I had known as a boy – war all smiling postures of the dance, a game of buffeting with reed spears. But, of course, they were like ourselves. They were braggarts, cowards, traducers, whores. So I started a play on Troilus and Cressida in disgust that man should be born in baseness and nastiness and my sickness found me a new language for its expression – jerking harsh words, a delirium of coinages and grotesque fusions. I made Ariadne and Arachne one, a fair heroine become a spider by virtue or vice of her labyrinthine weaving. Ariachne. Some cold man some day, reading, will cure that name.

Here, then, was the end of all sweetness. But I wept to see the end of the honey days, winced to turn Cressida into a whore of the Court. Dust hath closed Helen's eye. But disease had closed it long before – a swollen ring of corruption. Die in dust but live in filth. Well, if we are to live with it we must somehow ennoble it.

(ii)

WORMS feed on Hector brave. And on proud sulking Achilles. An atomy dreaming of the subversion of order he erupted – Essex, Felix, Bolingbroke – and was a sore on the white body of the commonwealth. There he was with his mob, advancing on the Capitol. You are all there with your bills and cudgels – Prindable, Lillington, Liddell, Alabaster, Anguish, Edgecumbe, Gildersleeves, Lympe, Pogue, Shackles. Briefly to this end: we are all diseased; and with our surfeiting and wanton hours have brought ourselves into a burning fever. So then the horror was immanent; Essex (Chapman's own Achilles in the dedication to his Homer) but broke the skin to let it gush in foulness. In my delirium the City was mine own body – fighting broke out in ulcers on left thigh, both armpits, in the spongy and corrupt groin. And then came the end of Essex – a fair head rolling, an heroic head – and near the end of Harry. But Harry was but sent to the Tower.

My most utter shame that year was to stand at my father's graveside shaking with my disease, eyes curiously on my head-patches naked of hair and the ulcer on my mouth. He is truly a great gentleman now; he hath, see, the aristocrat of diseases. All I could see in Anne was the memory of old orgies and that particular orgy I had interrupted that day of my sudden homecoming. Let me keep away; I will lodge this night not in my own house but at the inn. Tell my daughters it is nothing, but a slight distemper, no more.

I could tell the time was coming when I should know the great revelation. Meantime I could only cling to my image of order, the smooth white body of a hardly imaginable Eternal City. I dreamed of myself as Caesar, old and with Gilbert's falling sickness, and Brutus was, for some reason, Ben, chider, mocker, an opposing spirit. The image of the falling city, prefigured in the prodigies of a night, was drawn from my own body – the bloody holes, the burning hand. The fall of the commonwealth is so terrible because it is the fall of the body. It is no sweeping away of things abstract but the tearing of sensible nerve and the wrenching of tissue to draw blood.

(iii)

I AWOKE in the middle of the night – the bellman calling that it was four and fine – to find her there at last, the goddess. It was without formality, unannounced by trumpets or prodigious harbingers. She was in the likeness of F, gold-skinned, naked. I could meet the terror of her eyes with calm. In her hands she held a small vial wrought of some stone like porphyry. This she placed by my bed and then, without smiling or utterance of any word of love, bore down on me, caressing my scabby and pocked flesh. I was her unwilling succubus. The moment of total possession was marked in me

229

by a sense of something breaking, the rupturing of a hymen unknown to anatomists. She, at this moment, unstoppered her porphyry vial and released—

She released unbelievable effluvia. It seemed not possible. The hopelessness of man's condition was revealed in odours that came direct, in a kind of innocent Eden freshness, from that prime and original well. The rest of my life, such as it might be, must be spent in making those effluvia real to all. For the first time it was made clear to me that language was no vehicle of soothing prettiness to warm cold castles that waited for spring, no ornament for ladies or great lords, chiming, beguiling, but a potency of sharp knives and brutal hammers. I understood what she herself was – no angel of evil but an uncovenanted power. But, so desperate was the enemy, she had been drawn by an irresistible force to become, if not herself evil, yet contracted to be the articulatrix of evil.

She did not so much leave my chamber as disintegrate into particles which settled themselves, as in a permanent home, into the orifices of my body – disturbing the hairs in my nostrils, the labyrinth of my ears, the sore lower entrances. What was now most palpable was what, before, might have seemed only a transitory vision of the nature of the world, a sick man's fancy. But of the primacy of what there was no single word to describe (save the word *no*, perhaps) I was aware as of something physical.

Oh, the cruelty of the joke and the shameful weakness of the forces of good. Why had no poet seen it before? No poet had seen it before because only these times were reserved for the first seeing of it. My disease was a modern disease; it was the same disease as that which cracked order in State and Church and the institutions of both. We have had the best of our time.

(iv)

THERE he is, John Hall, the quality's own physician, my son-in-law. He surveys me frowning, pursing his lips, stroking his

230

beard. Little time to go now, he thinks; perhaps in tomorrow's early hours. He will record nothing of his father-in-law's disease in his notebooks. He is one for purging and letting, most of his patients – Sir This, Lady That, my lord Such-and-such – suffering from surfeits of pigeon-flesh and cream. His father-in-law's disease was one only to be whispered about: he saw what the world was and he wrote it down to the dictation of a goddess.

– Plays? He wrote plays?

– Aye, plays. His plays were first all flowers and love and sweet laughter or else the stirring true record of England's progress towards order. Then he brooded on what he called evil, aye.

– Evil? Wrongs, that is?

– Nay, not wrongs, for wrongs, he said, were man-made and might be redressed. But he thought that the great white body of the world was set upon by an illness from beyond, gratuitous and incurable. And that even the name Love was, far from being the best invocation against it, often the very conjuration that summoned the mining and ulcerating hordes. We are, he seemed to say, poisoned at source.

– How showed he it?

– Oh, he created these great men powerless against evil. There were good men drawn into its web or weak men who beat their fists vainly at it. Or there were men who themselves embodied the disease, the breakers and corrupters of the State. Though it was not always the State; sometimes it was marriage.

– He has been happily married?

– My mother-in-law has been, I believe, a good wife to him. She has been faithful throughout. He himself, though, has been guilty of bed-breach.

– Let us hearken. He mumbles something.

– Aye. It will not now be long. He will come very soon now to his final utterance.

– Was he a great man? Shall we take the utterance down?

Daughter can overcome power of evil. Son not. Nor Hamlet nor Othello, both my sons. That poor Kate Hamlet was drowned for love. Water and a virgin girl. They are our only cleansers.

– The last word is usually nonsense.

(v)

My summary, physician.

I thought, that day, that what happened to me was manner of a contagion from my brother Gilbert. It was on-stage. It was *Hamlet*. I was the Ghost, croaking my objurgations. Then (they told me this, shocked, thereafter) I let forth a great shriek, fell, foamed, kicked, rolled. The audience accounted it fine acting.

What followed was of little use to the playhouse. I forgot lines, my brains were constantly tired, I neglected my affairs, I raged, I hated then loved, loved then hated. One day I shocked myself by pissing openly near Whitehall. I woke three nights with so extreme a desire for ale that I went out, near-naked, to knock up the landlord of the Triple Tun. I took to brothel-going. And there it was, in Clerkenwell, that I—

She looked not diseased, only her golden flesh seemed changed to an iron-colour. Her breasts sagged, her belly pouted, her hair was a tangle of wires, here and there a tooth was gone. We looked at one another, and I saw myself in her eyes – hair vanished in tufts, fat stolid face, doublet unbuttoned for the greater ease of my flesh. I nodded and nodded in a sort of satisfaction that we both exemplified the rottenness of the world. And then I said what had long been on my mind: –

– A gift from him, was it not?

She hung her head, saying nothing. We might all then, the three of us, be drawn into the one corruption. But the work of those two was done. *Consummatum est, erat.* I could no longer lie with her. Yet, leaving, I could have wept, had there been in me any longer the capability of tears, for all the Beauty that the Enemy took away. I must eternise that tawny queenliness, cursing.

Not lie with her, but with others. Joan, Kate, Meg, Susan, Margery, Tooth, Samson, the Yellow One. The cock crowed to bursting. Meantime I spent my money, often without premeditation – on the house in Blackfriars, the red Hungarian cloak, a job of malt, a share in a company that did not exist, a pipe of Canary, horses (one an Arab), a doublet studded with glass cut like jewels. Back here in Stratford I roared my greatness out. That night with Ben and Drayton in the inn I shouted that I was God. But the goddess was firm within me: she had opened up these terrible Indies but remained as my navigatrix. The lands, Hoby, you told me of, the strange birds, the talking fruit, the three-legged men – they all exist; you were no liar.

(vi)

QUESTIONS? You wish to know how ventriloquial all this is, who is really speaking? This is no impersonation, ladies and gentlemen. When the Poisoner comes he comes to break, and walls are among the things he breaks. I am sick and tired and long for my East. Take off at. Your faces are very dim about me.

What is your great crime, then?

Love, love, and it is always love. Not wisely but too. Fatimah. I will distribute copies of that sonnet after the lecture. You can never win, for love is both an image of eternal order and at the same time the rebel and destructive spirochaete. Let us have no nonsensical talk about merging and melting souls, though, binary suns, two spheres in a single orbit. There is the flesh and the flesh makes all. Literature is an epiphenomenon of the action of the flesh.

233

How about blood?

The West is eveningland, the East morningland. He sent his blood out there. I am of his blood. The male line died in the West. It was right it should continue in the East. Summon no one. I shall be all right. One short sleep past.

Subject-matter?

Oaklings, footsticks, cinques, moxibustion, the Maccabees, the Lydian mode (soft, effeminate), the snow-goose or whitebrant, rose-windows, government, the conflagration of citadel and senate-house, Bucephalus, the Antilegomena, Simnel Sunday, the torrid zone, Wapping, my lord's top-boots, the shoeflower, prostitute boys, dittany, face-ague, cosmic cinefaction, the Antipodes, the Gate of Bab, Fidessa, Rattlin the Reefer, Taliesin, the dead head in alchemy, the bar, dungeons, skylarks, the wind, Thaumast, the dark eyes of London, the fellowship of the frog, *Gesta Regum Anglorum*, Myrddhin, faithful dealing, A Girle worth Gold, viticulture, the Queen that's dead (bee, meadow, chess, Bench, regnant), imposts of arches, pollards, sea-fox and sea-hog and sea-heath, the sigmoid curve, cardinals, touchability.

What would you have now?

No more. No no no more. Never again.

One last word. One last last last last word.

My Lord.